"Mr. MacLaren—" Maude began.

"Do you think you might call me Jonas?" he dared to ask. "At least when 'tis just us?"

Her eyes bore a guarded glint now. "I'll call you Jonas if you wish," she said, in that delicious Texas drawl that made everything she said land pleasantly on his ears—even what she said afterward. "But, Jonas, what do I know about you, really? You're a man of secrets—you keep more than you give up. How am I to trust you?"

He saw it as she must see it—he was asking her to trust him without any basis in truth, without any transparency on his part.

"Trust doesn't come easily for a MacLaren," he said. "Not after what we've been through."

"Without trust there can be no honest caring," she told him then. "If you don't trust me enough to show me your true self, how can I know who I'm caring for in return?"

The idea that some part of her, at least, *wanted* to care in return gladdened his heart, if only for a moment. *But how could he bare his soul to her, knowing that if she knew everything, she'd whirl away from him in horror and disgust?*

Laurie Kingery is a Texas-transplant-to-Ohio who writes romance set in post–Civil War Texas. She was nominated for a Carol Award for her second Love Inspired Historical novel, *The Outlaw's Lady*, and is currently writing a series about mail-order grooms in a small town in the Texas Hill Country.

Books by Laurie Kingery

Love Inspired Historical

Hill Country Christmas
The Outlaw's Lady

Bridegroom Brothers Series

The Preacher's Bride Claim

Brides of Simpson Creek Series

Mail Order Cowboy
The Doctor Takes a Wife
The Sheriff's Sweetheart
The Rancher's Courtship
The Preacher's Bride
Hill Country Cattleman
A Hero in the Making
Hill Country Courtship

Visit the Author Profile page at Harlequin.com.

Hill Country Courtship

LAURIE KINGERY

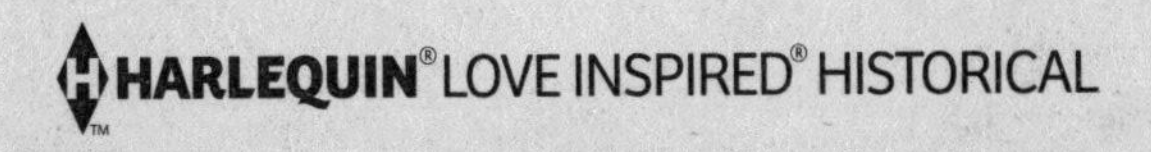

Recycling programs for this product may not exist in your area.

™ LOVE INSPIRED BOOKS

ISBN-13: 978-0-373-28303-3

Hill Country Courtship

This edition published by arrangement with Love Inspired Books.

www.Harlequin.com

Printed in U.S.A.

This is the Lord's doing; it is marvelous in our eyes.

—*Psalms* 118:23

To Danielle, my daughter, who as a doula
is dedicated to helping women achieve a good birth,
and as always, to Tom, my real-life hero

Chapter One

Simpson Creek, Texas, November 1869
Gilmore House

At the ripe old age of twenty-five, Maude Harkey had begun to resign herself to being an old maid. So it didn't bother her, that November afternoon at the Spinsters' Club Fall Barbecue and Social, that none of the male guests particularly singled her out for attention.

As president of the Spinsters' Club, all that mattered to her was that plenty of eligible bachelors had come from the ranches outside Simpson Creek and from nearby counties to meet the others in the club. No one was misbehaving—either from having stopped at the town saloon before arriving at the party or becoming overfamiliar with any of her ladies. Everyone appeared to be enjoying themselves.

Her friend Ella Justiss, who was due to be married next Saturday, was having a particularly good time, radiant with the joy of new love. Nate Bohannan, the devoted groom-to-be, couldn't have been more attentive, fetching her punch and barbecued chicken, seemingly unwilling to be anywhere but by her side. By the time one of them decided it was time to have a party again, Ella would be happily serving refreshments at the party, as the Spinster "graduates" usually did, and possibly already expecting their first child.

Maude was happy for them. It wouldn't have occurred to her to be jealous of her friend's good fortune. And, indeed, with all the challenges that Ella had faced in her life, she richly deserved the happiness she was blessed with now. Though Maude had to wonder from time to time why she, the daughter of the late town doctor, was still unwed while so many others in the club had found their matches. And she *did* wonder how she was going to be able to stand continuing to live at Mrs. Meyer's boardinghouse without her good friend Ella.

After Maude's father's death, it had been difficult to leave her house behind and move into a rented room. The home she'd shared with her father had been quiet and peaceful, with Maude fully in control of all household matters. The boardinghouse was noisy and chaotic, and she'd struggled to settle in. Losing the comfort of her routines and the security of her position as mistress in her home had been heavy blows to a heart already burdened by the loss of her dear father.

But Ella had made it much easier to bear with her friendship and support. Maude had come to count on Ella to keep her company and chuckle with her over the quirks of some of the boardinghouse's other residents. Now she would be the only female occupant of the boardinghouse, not counting old Mrs. Meyer, the proprietress.

Mrs. Meyer had hinted only yesterday that she intended to pass along ownership of the boardinghouse to Maude when she died. Was *that* to be her fate, then? Running the town's only boardinghouse, with its eight rooms and mostly male occupants, with three meals a day to cook, and forever having to listen to grousing from the tenants that the beef was too tough, the chicken drumsticks too few, or that one of the traveling drummers took more than his fair share of the apple dumplings?

Her father had certainly expected a brighter future for her than that. He'd once told her he pictured her with a houseful of children with hair as red as her own and a husband whose greatest pleasure was satisfying his wife's slightest whim. Maude felt she was easy to please, so she didn't need an overindulgent husband, but the thought of living her whole life without *any* husband or children made her sad. She enjoyed caring for others, had cherished her role as nurse in her father's medical practice. She'd always hoped that one day she'd have a family of her own to whom she could devote her time and loving attention. But apparently that wasn't meant to be.

Pull yourself together, Maude Harkey, she told herself sternly. *No one needs to see a melancholy face at a party. And if the Lord wants you to remain single, then there's a reason, no doubt.*

"Who's that?"

She hadn't noticed Violet Masterson and Caroline Collier, two of the other ex-Spinsters, coming to stand beside her, but now she followed the former's discreetly pointed finger.

A man stood at the edge of the throng, hat in hand as was polite in the presence of ladies, but there was nothing humble about his bearing. Rather, he reminded her of a golden eagle perched high above a flock of sheep, looking for the tastiest lamb to pluck from the herd. The red-gold hair that he raked back from his forehead just then only served to further the image.

"I don't know, but goodness, he's a late arriver," Maude said, glancing over her shoulder at the long table that had been heaped with food before the party. "I hope there's enough barbecued chicken and potato salad left to feed him." The male guests had gone through the food like a plague of locusts, and it would be a wonder if there was a sufficient amount to fill even one more plate.

"Oh, that's Jonas MacLaren," Caroline Collier said, following her friends' gazes. "He's the man who bought Five Mile Hill Ranch, out past Collier's Roost. I heard he bargained hard with Mr. Avery at the bank and ended up getting it for next to nothing."

"Since he's here at our social, are we to assume there's no *Mrs.* MacLaren?" Violet asked with a sidelong glance at Maude.

Maude did her best to hide her wince. She ought to come right out and tell her friends she'd decided to stop looking for a husband in hopes that they would stop looking for one for her. She knew her friends only wanted her to be happy—as happy as they were with their husbands—but she'd grown weary of the endless attempts to match her with men who clearly had no interest. Perhaps if she resigned the presidency of the Spinsters' Club, it would make the message clear that she no longer considered herself in the market for a husband. Besides, if she *was* still looking, she wouldn't look in Jonas MacLaren's direction. The man looked positively *fierce*.

"There *is* a Mrs. MacLaren," Caroline informed them, and Violet gave a disappointed sniff.

"What's he doing here, then?" Violet said, indignation sparking in her well-bred English voice. "Doesn't he know this is a party for eligible *bachelors* to meet the ladies of the Spinsters' Club?"

Caroline chuckled. "Ah, but the Mrs. MacLaren in question isn't his wife, she's his mother," she said with the triumphant smile of one who has withheld vital information until just the right moment. "She's from Scotland, I hear, and quite a Tartar."

Maude stared at Caroline, confused. "A what?"

"A Tartar," Caroline repeated, then explained. "A person of irritable or violent temper." Caroline had been a schoolteacher before she'd married Jack Collier. Her time spent running the schoolhouse and finding answers for the children's endless questions had left her with a wealth of unusual facts at her disposal—along with an extensive vocabulary.

"I see," Maude said, giving a little shiver. "Have you met her?"

Caroline shook her head. "No one has. She doesn't leave the ranch house, I've heard. Very few have met her son, for that matter," she added, nodding toward MacLaren, who was still studying the attendees. "I wouldn't know it was him, but he came to Collier's Roost to ask Jack something about the area. When Jack invited him inside for coffee, he declined, saying he had to get back to his ranch."

"Perhaps she's an invalid," Violet suggested.

"Well," Maude said, squaring her shoulders, "I suppose I should go and introduce myself and try to make sure he gets refreshments."

It was a scary prospect. Something in the man's gaze told her he might devour maiden ladies for breakfast.

A Harkey does not shirk her duty, Maude told herself, and forced her steps in Jonas MacLaren's direction.

She saw the moment that he noticed her approaching, the way his tall frame stilled, though his eyes—hazel eyes shot through with gold, she noted, which further enhanced his golden eagle-like appearance—remained vigilant and guarded.

"Welcome to our party, Mr. MacLaren," she called out as she drew near. "I'm Maude Harkey, current president of the Spinsters' Club. Won't you come have something to eat and drink?"

He studied her from head to toe as if sizing her up. "Pleased to meet you, Miss Harkey." The Scottish burr of his voice was pleasant to the ear, though it took a little careful listening for her to figure out what he'd said. "I will," he continued, "but I can't stay long."

Maude blinked in surprise. "But there are several young ladies here who'd love to make your acquaintance," she said, forcing her lips into an appealing smile. She wasn't the only Spinster who hadn't yet made a match. Of the original group, Jane Jeffries was also still single, as were Louisa Wheeler, Daisy Henderson and a handful of newer ladies. "Why don't I show you to the refreshment table, then invite a few of them over to meet you?" With any luck, he'd be so charmed that he'd stay long enough for the dancing to begin inside Gilmore House, the home of the mayor. The mayor was a strong supporter of their club, for he was the father of Prissy, the sheriff's wife and former Spinster Club member. If Mr. MacLaren stayed through that, he might develop a fondness for one lucky girl. "I think you'd enjoy talking to Louisa, for example, or Jane—both ladies happen to be standing right over there, under the grape arbor."

She gestured in their direction, but Jonah MacLaren's gaze didn't leave hers. "Why don't *you* sit down with me, Miss Harkey, and I can explain why I'm here."

He was direct, she'd give him that. Was it possible that he had decided at first glance that *she* was the one for him? The idea gave her a pleasant little tingle. The man was attractive, though a little intimidating, and it was always nice to feel wanted. But she didn't believe in lightning-fast attraction. He'd have to prove to her that he was worthy of her consideration, after all, if he was going to ask to court her.

"All right," she murmured, and ushered him toward the food table.

To her relief, there was still a respectable amount of barbecued chicken, green beans, buttered rice and pecan pie left, as well as cold tea and lemonade, and within moments she was sitting down with him at a long table under one of Gilmore House's venerable live oaks. They were alone at the table, since most of the guests had arrived earlier and already eaten their fill before becoming part of standing conversational groups.

She took a sip of the cold tea he'd poured for her. "I understand you bought Five Mile Hill Ranch, Mr. MacLaren," she said, silently blessing Caroline for furnishing her with an opening. She wondered for a moment if he knew that his ranch had been owned by the infamous Drew Allbright, who'd been jailed for the attempted murder of Raleigh Masterson, Violet's husband. It seemed wisest not to bring it up.

He finished chewing the chicken he'd just gnawed from the drumstick. "That's right," he said, but didn't elaborate.

"Where are you from?" she inquired, hoping her question sounded as if she was merely interested rather than prying, so he might open up a little when he answered it. His replies weren't long or drawled, the way she was used to from Texas-raised men, but maybe that was due to his Scottish heritage. "I mean, it's obvious you're Scottish, but did you come directly to Texas from Scotland?"

"My mother and I last lived in Missouri, but only for a time. Before that it was New York. That was where we first arrived when we came to this country."

Missouri had been a border state in the War Between the States. It made her wonder which side he had fought for, if he had fought for either. The war had been over only four years ago, so it was still a consideration in whether a man was respectable or not. Doctor Nolan Walker, her friend Sarah's husband, was the only Yankee who had successfully joined the Simpson Creek community. And even for Nolan, acceptance—particularly from Sarah herself—had taken time and persistence. But if Mr. MacLaren had been in the country for less than four years, then perhaps he had missed the war entirely.

"Then may I welcome you to San Saba County? We're glad you've decided to settle here."

He lifted a brow, and she suddenly felt her remark had been pretentious. She had no right to speak for everyone, especially when she didn't know yet if his coming was a good thing or not—or how much a part of the community he'd be. Especially if, as Caroline said, he preferred to keep to himself. With the location of his ranch somewhat distant from town, he would need to be determined to socialize in order to truly become part of the community.

"Thank you," he said, after a long moment.

His direct gaze left her flustered. "How did you hear of the party, if I may ask? Did Mr. Collier invite you?" Oh, dear, did it sound as if she was prying again? Glory, it was hard to talk to such a closemouthed man. She tried to recall every suggestion she'd ever learned about conversational gambits, but she was drawing a blank.

He finished chewing, then said, "My *segundo*, Hector Gonsalvo, heard of it from one of Collier's hands."

Segundo, she knew, was a Spanish term Texans sometimes used for foreman, or second-in-command, especially when the foreman was a Tejano, a Texan of Hispanic heritage. She wondered if the Spanish term sounded as strange to Mr. Gonsalvo in a Scottish accent as it did to her.

"He thought it might be the answer to my needs," MacLaren went on, then maddeningly left it at that.

The answer to his needs? She could only assume

the man referred to his need for a wife. Goodness, the man was too plainspoken! She felt a flush rising above the neck of her royal blue dress.

Stalling to gather her wits, she sipped her tea. Land sakes, she might as well be as frank as he was. "So you've decided it's time to settle down and raise a family, and you're looking to find a wife. Well, a Spinsters' Club party is certainly the right place to begin, Mr. MacLaren."

He drew back, and his intent gaze was now shuttered. "The last thing I'm looking for is a wife, Miss Harkey."

He saw the exact moment when she misinterpreted what he'd said and came to a scandalous conclusion. Her indignation at the suggestion sparked a temper as hot as her hair was red.

Maude Harkey rose to her feet, some five feet eight inches of spitting-mad female. "Mr. MacLaren, I'm afraid you've formed the wrong idea about our little group. The Spinsters' Club was founded by ladies seeking *marriage*, not a…a dishonorable alliance! If that's what you came here looking for, I suggest you seek it down at the saloon—one of the girls who serves whiskey might be able to accommodate you," she said, her voice as icy as her temper was blazing.

He rose, too. "Miss Harkey, simmer down. I wasn't suggesting anything remotely like what you're thinking. My intentions are entirely honorable. I'm simply not looking for a wife—romantic claptrap has never appealed to me, you see—"

"'Romantic claptrap?'" she echoed, a dangerous

chill remaining in her voice. "Is that what you call our efforts to make matches here?"

He shrugged. "Courtship and that other nonsense is all very well if that's all a man or a woman is looking for," he said with a dismissive gesture. "But it seems to me most of these single young women would be much better advised to be seeking employment, not matrimony. And it's employment that I have come to offer—with nothing scandalous or unseemly to it at all. What I'm looking for is a companion—for my mother, that is."

She sank back to her seat, her face fiery red. The flush rather became her, he noted—though he'd thought she looked even more striking moments before, with that fierce fire burning in her eyes. "I…I see. I beg your pardon, Mr. MacLaren. Your mother is in need of a companion?" she asked, her voice now scarcely stronger than a whisper.

He sat down again, too, and felt a moment of compassion for her embarrassment. "Yes, she's got rheumatism and a host of other ailments that keep her from moving around easily, and it's made her a mite… crotchety, shall we say?" Not that her medical condition was solely to blame for her behavior. Ill humor was as much a part of his mother as her piercing eyes and the strident voice that never failed to find fault and clamor it to the skies. "The ranch keeps me busy from can-see to can't-see, and I thought if she had another female to keep her company, it might make it easier for her."

And a lot easier for me. He'd taken the brunt of his mother's ill temper for far too long, and each time he hired a companion for her and the unlucky female quit after being subjected to Coira MacLaren's tirades, her irritability toward her son grew worse.

"So you wish to hire a companion for her," Maude Harkey said carefully.

"That's about the size of it," he agreed with a nod. "I'd pay the lady well, of course, and she'd have a room of her own."

"I'm afraid it's out of the question, Mr. MacLaren," Miss Harkey told him, her tone warming from icy to crisp. "Pardon my plain speaking, if you would, but I don't believe there's a single one of my friends in the Spinsters' Club who would be willing to risk her reputation living out on a ranch with no one but an invalid to chaperone her."

"She wouldn't be alone," he informed her. "Senora Morales is my housekeeper and cook. She lives in the ranch house and is always present. Are you quite certain no one would consider it? What about *you*, Miss Harkey? You look like a capable female. Do you have any encumbrances that would prevent you from taking the job?" He found he rather relished the idea of his mother's temper meeting its match in Maude Harkey's. Perhaps each flame would douse the other. Sen ora Morales would stop threatening to quit on a daily basis, and he'd have a peaceful household for a change.

"No, thank you," Maude Harkey said, getting to her feet again. "Feel free to speak to Jane Jeffries about it, but be aware she has two lively boys who would not do well, I think, in a house with an invalid. You might ask Louisa Wheeler, but she is devoted to her job as schoolmarm, or Daisy Henderson—but she's got a son, too, and what the hotel would do without her as cook, I have no idea. There are other newer young ladies in the Spinsters' Club with fewer ties to bind them to Simpson Creek, but I'll leave it to you to discover who they are." She gestured vaguely in the direction of the clumps of ladies and male guests clustered around the punch table and chatting in pairs at various points around the spacious lawn in front of Gilmore House.

"Failing that, you might consider putting an advertisement in the *Simpson Creek Intelligencer* or in the Lampasas newspaper. I'm afraid I must go now and fulfill my duties as hostess by mingling with the other guests. I wish you all the best in your search, but I'm afraid I can be of no further help to you. Good day to you, Mr. MacLaren," she said, and sailed off in the direction of the veranda.

Regretfully, he watched her go, noting absently how gracefully she moved, even while perfectly conveying her wrathful state. There had been a moment there when, after realizing how much she had misunderstood his meaning, he'd thought he had a chance of getting her to consider the matter, if only to make up for thinking he'd been up to no good.

He stared around him at the other females of her so-called Spinsters' Club who seemed to be unattached, but none of them appealed to him. Every one of them looked too young, too giggly or too meek of manner to survive his mother's temper. He wasn't sure which one Jane Jeffries was, but the very last thing Coira MacLaren would stand for was the presence of two noisy, ill-mannered boys in her home, though enough room to accommodate everyone in the vast, mostly empty ranch house certainly wasn't a problem.

No, he wanted Maude Harkey for the position, he realized, and suddenly no one else would do. He didn't want to examine his reasons too closely. The woman didn't have to suit him, just his mother, after all. He wasn't seeking a bride, as he had told her. Romance held no interest for him—not anymore. Whatever companion he hired would see as little of him as possible. One MacLaren would be more than enough for her to have to deal with.

Of course, if he was truly seeking someone only to suit his mother, then one of the meeker, more pliable young ladies might please her just fine. She'd have someone new to chew on, which she might enjoy for a time—until she'd worn the poor girl out entirely.

But he would hire Maude Harkey or no one. At least, no one here.

After taking a last look around, he retraced his steps past the wrought-iron gates of Gilmore House, found his horse where he'd left him tied at the saloon and headed for Five Mile Hill Ranch.

Chapter Two

"The *nerve* of the man!" Maude seethed to Caroline, finding her on the veranda. "To imagine that this was an event where he could hire a—*a nursemaid*!" She stared back out over the green expanse of lawn, but she didn't see him. Perhaps he stood speaking to one of the ladies out of sight, or perhaps he had taken his silly offer and left. Either way, she cared very little, except to hope that he had not spoiled the party for anyone other than her.

"As he put it, the *last thing* he was looking for was a wife—as if anyone would have him as her husband with an attitude like that! Can you imagine, he called the idea of finding someone to love and build a life with nothing more than 'romantic claptrap'!"

"A companion," Caroline corrected her. "Not a nursemaid. At least, that's what you said he called the position. It's honest work."

"I don't see the difference," Maude snapped, then was instantly contrite. "I'm sorry, Caroline dear, but there was something so high-handed about him that irritated me right down to the bone. I didn't mean to take it out on you."

"No offense taken," Caroline said cheerfully. "But perhaps you ought to consider his offer, Maude. Wouldn't living out on a ranch be better than the boardinghouse? From the sound of it, you'd have only one cranky old person to live with, rather than all those complaining boarders with all their tobacco spitting and biscuit hogging. And perhaps Mr. MacLaren would be so grateful for your help with his mother that he might lose some of that high-handedness and realize what a treasure he has in you. He might be quite a pleasant man underneath that initial curtness."

Maude stared at her friend. Of all the things Caroline Collier might have said, she hadn't expected her to hint that MacLaren might decide to take a shine to *her*, after all.

"I don't think Jonas MacLaren seemed like anything but a confirmed bachelor and dedicated misogynist—how's *that* for a word?" she asked the former schoolmarm with a chuckle.

"Very good, Maude. You must have been reading the dictionary again," Caroline teased. "If you're that fixed against the man and his offer, then so be it. I can see that you won't change your mind. But perhaps he'll convince one of our newer members to take the job and whisk her off to his lair at Five Mile Hill Ranch, never to be seen again," she said with a droll imitation of an evil cackle.

"And you must have been reading fairy tales," Maude shot back. "In any case, I am *not* desiring to exchange my room at the boardinghouse for what might well be a worse existence. If Mr. MacLaren's rude and dismissive manner wasn't reason enough, the isolation of living out there would be. It's so far away from everything I'm used to. I've only ever lived in town, you know. And out on the ranch, I'd never get to see any of you, or come to church..."

"Pshaw, you make it sound like it's the end of the earth," Caroline said.

"It's ten miles if it's an inch from here," Maude argued. "Maybe farther. There's no use arguing, Caroline, my mind's made up."

Caroline sighed. "All right, then. Forget I suggested it. Perhaps we should tell the fiddlers to start tuning up so our single Spinsters can invite the men inside. Too bad Mr. MacLaren left—there'd be another man to partner the ladies."

Why did Caroline have to mention him again? Now Maude would be tormented with the image of Jonas MacLaren, his arm around her waist, gazing down at her through those intense hazel eyes as he swept her around the floor in a waltz...

But no, she refused to clutter her mind with such nonsense! She had no interest whatsoever in dancing with the man. And even if she did, he likely had no interest in "romantic claptrap" like dancing, either. Indeed, the rest of the evening—and, as far as she was concerned, the foreseeable future—would be far more pleasant without Jonas MacLaren.

Maude was startled out of her sleep later that evening by the pounding on the front door of the boardinghouse. *Gracious, it's got to be the middle of the night,* she thought, as the remnants of her dream faded like smoke in a breeze. *Didn't the sign on the porch plainly state that new boarders must arrive by no later than eight at night?*

But Mrs. Meyer was no stickler for rules when she had a vacancy. The boardinghouse provided her livelihood.

Still drowsy, Maude huddled under the quilt and heard rain drumming on the tin roof overhead. Then she heard Mrs. Meyer's footsteps below and her sleepy voice calling out, "All right, I'm coming, I'm coming! Stop pounding or you'll wake everyone in the place!"

Mr. Renz, the drummer from Kansas, had left just this morning, so there was an empty room, Maude knew—the one right next to hers. In a few minutes there'd be footsteps on the stairs, and she'd hear Mrs. Meyer's muffled voice informing the new arrival of the house rules before she turned over the key and let them all get back to sleep.

But, instead of that, the next sound she heard was Mrs. Meyer's running feet, followed by a pounding on her own door.

"Maude, Maude, get up, I need your help! There's a woman here, and I think she's about to *give birth*!"

Hoping she was still dreaming and there would be no one there when she got downstairs, Maude threw her wrapper on and trudged to the door, rubbing her eyes with her knuckles.

It was no dream. Mrs. Meyer stood there, wearing a threadbare, patched wrapper, her iron-gray hair in a thick braid down her back. Trembling, she clutched a candle in a tin holder. Her shakiness left a dancing shadow on the wall.

"Where is she?" Maude asked, for Mrs. Meyer was alone in the hall.

"Downstairs at the entrance," the boardinghouse proprietress said in a hushed voice, jerking her head toward the stairs behind her. "She's drenched—and bleeding, too, I think. She didn't look strong enough to make it up the stairs, even with me to help her."

Down the hall, a couple of the other inhabitants' doors creaked opened and curious faces peeked out to see what all the fuss was about.

Mrs. Meyer seized on the closest one. "Delbert, come with me. There's a girl downstairs about to have a baby. I need you to assist Maude to get the poor girl upstairs to the vacant room, then I want you to run for Doc Walker. I'll get the bed ready. Hurry, now—she's about ready to drop—"

Whether "drop" meant to deliver the baby or Mrs. Meyer thought the woman might collapse, Maude didn't linger to clarify. Darting a glance at Delbert Perry, who looked thunderstruck at the older lady's words, Maude dashed for the stairs.

The girl huddled in the circle of lamplight cast by the kerosene lamp Mrs. Meyer had left burning by the door, clutching an abdomen that looked impossibly large in such a small frame. In the flickering light she was waxy pale, slight in stature and possessed of a matted wild mane of a nondescript color. An irregular splotch of blood stained the floorboards beneath her battered short boots. Mrs. Meyer's statement seemed correct in both interpretations. The baby was clearly coming—and soon—and the pregnant girl herself looked as if she might swoon from exhaustion at any moment.

"What's your name? Is it your time? Is the baby coming?" Maude demanded as she skipped the last two steps and landed with a thud next to the girl.

"April Mae Horvath, and yeah, it's comin'. I bin havin' pains since early mornin'," the skinny girl told Maude, then drew back her lips to let loose a scream as another pain seized her. The small pool of blood on the floor widened. "Is Felix here? This was where he told me he stayed when he came to Simpson Creek—he *has* t'be here, t' help me..."

"Are you talking about Felix Renz, the drummer?"

The girl nodded emphatically, her eyes lit with a weary hope.

"No, he left this morning."

The girl clutched Maude's arm so tight it would undoubtedly leave a bruise, her eyes desperate. "But he *cain't* be *gone*!" she cried. "I come fifty miles here to find him!" Big tears rolled down her pallid cheeks and trickled into the rain-drenched neck of her dress.

"Is he your husband? He never said—" But she'd given her name as Horvath, hadn't she? So Renz hadn't married this slip of a girl who now claimed him as the father of her soon-to-be-born child. Inwardly, Maude consigned the drummer to the nether regions for leaving this girl to whatever fate dealt out. But she couldn't afford to spare more than a thought to him, wherever he may be. Her attention right now had to stay focused on the girl. His problem was now *their* problem, and she meant to deal with it as best she could.

Maude stopped talking and grabbed the laboring girl just as she sagged toward the floor in a faint.

"Delbert, *help*!" she yelled up to the town handyman, who still stood transfixed at the top of the stairs.

The four years since her father had been cut down on Main Street by raiding Comanches fell away as if no time had passed at all. She'd assisted her father at a score of deliveries. Admittedly, the situation had never before been quite so…fraught. But, still, she knew what needed to be done. "Get her arms," she told Delbert, "and I'll get her legs. Ella—" for her friend was awake now, too, and hanging over the railing above, watching with wide eyes "—as soon as we get past, you run down to the kitchen and set some water to boiling while Delbert goes to fetch the doctor." Even as she rattled out the instructions, she said a prayer that Nolan Walker would be able to stanch the bleeding. From the pallor of the girl's skin, she'd already lost way too much blood.

Once they'd helped April Mae into the bed whose covers Mrs. Meyer had hastily pulled down, and Delbert had dashed out into the downpour in the direction of the doctor's house, Maude and Mrs. Meyer assisted the girl out of her blood-drenched dress and into one of Maude's clean nightgowns. Every three minutes or so they had to stop what they were doing while April Mae shrieked her way through a contraction.

"April Mae, don't scream!" Maude ordered her. "*Breathe* with the pain, don't hold your breath. You're just making it harder for that baby to come. Watch me, next time it starts, and I'll show you—"

"Ain't F-Felix h-here?" April Mae panted, ignoring her, while Maude grimly shoved dry towels under her to replace the blood-soaked ones she'd just pulled out. "He said he always stays here, when he…comes to sell his wares in San Saba County… You got to find him, lady," she said to Maude, watery blue eyes pleading.

"I'm Maude," Maude told her, realizing she hadn't introduced herself during all the ruckus. "We'll find him," she promised, though she had no idea where the drummer had been heading. And when they did find him, she was going to give him two black eyes before she'd let him see his baby, she vowed. "But first we've got to help you give birth to his son or daughter. How old are you, April Mae? Where are your parents?" *And why did they give you two months as a name?*

"Fifteen last week," the girl told her with a wan attempt at a smile. "And they're back in Vic—" Her words broke off as another contraction seized her in a merciless grip. Maude tried to help her breathe through it—to demonstrate the technique that would help with the pain—but April Mae was too frightened and pain stricken to pay her much mind.

After an endless minute, the contraction passed, and April Mae continued what she'd been about to say. "Don't bother writin' them—they disowned me after they figured out I was gonna be a mother and that Felix wasn't likely to come back. I've been living on what I could beg or steal ever since I set out for Simpson Creek…"

Maude mentally consigned the parents to the same place she'd wished Felix Renz. How could parents abandon a daughter who needed help, no matter what she had done? And only just fifteen, at that. That meant she'd been nothing more than fourteen when that wretched drummer had taken advantage of her innocence. Still just a child, without the wisdom or understanding to avoid falling for the wiles of a charming man.

Just then Ella arrived with a pot of steaming water. "I boiled a knife in the water, Maude, in case you have to cut the cord. Good thing you told me about that time you helped your papa deliver those twins, or I wouldn't have known you'd need one."

"Good girl," Maude praised her friend with an appreciative look. She hoped Ella wouldn't be too frightened to get married after tonight, knowing childbearing would likely be part of her lot.

But where in the world could the doctor be? If he didn't arrive soon, he might miss the main event entirely. She'd just seen a hint of fuzzy hair while checking the laboring girl's progress during the last contraction, so delivery was imminent. She was going to have to handle the delivery herself, Maude figured.

Both women started as the door banged open below.

"I cain't get the doctor!" Delbert bellowed up the stairs. "He's away fer th' night, his wife said, at someone's deathbed out on a ranch. But she says she's comin' t'help just as soon as she can take her young'un to the preacher's wife!"

This might well turn into a deathbed, as well—a double one of both mother and baby, Maude thought grimly, as blood continued to stain the sheet crimson beneath April Mae. She'd be glad of Sarah Walker's help, if she came in time, but while Sarah had assisted her husband, just as Maude used to assist her father, there was a limit to what either of them could do. While they'd both helped deliver babies in the past, she doubted Sarah knew any better than Maude herself how to stop the bleeding that was draining away April Mae's life.

"Did you hear me, Miss Maude?" Delbert called again. "I said Doc Walker ain't comin'! You want me to ride t'San Saba for their sawbones?"

April Mae's eyes had grown even more frightened at what Delbert had yelled up the stairs, and her cheeks grew paler, if that was possible. Her breathing came in panted, ragged gasps.

"Tell Delbert we heard him, so he can stop bellowing. There's no time to fetch the Saba doctor," Maude told Mrs. Meyer, who stood at the door as if guarding it from the other inhabitants—though she doubted any of the other boardinghouse residents would try to enter. This room was the last place any normal man would wish to be.

Maude gently took hold of the girl's chin and directed it so that April Mae looked at no one but her. "Don't you worry, April Mae," she said steadily. "I'm the daughter of a doctor and I've assisted at dozens of deliveries so I know exactly what to do." It wasn't quite a lie, but it was certainly an exaggeration. "The doctor's wife is coming to help, and she, too, has assisted at births. *And* she's a mother herself," she added, praying Sarah would hurry. Sarah wouldn't be able to run, for she was just about to give birth again herself.

Lord, we could use Your help here, she prayed, and then April Mae's hand tightened around her wrist.

"It's *coming*!" she cried.

And it was. After another fierce, long contraction, April Mae's baby girl slid into the world, screaming at the indignity of it all, with a thatch of black hair as thick as her drummer father's.

By the time Sarah Walker arrived half an hour later, breathing hard and rubbing her distended abdomen, they had the squalling baby wiped off and wrapped up warmly, and she had taken her first suckle from her mother. April Mae had fallen asleep with a weary smile on her face after telling Maude the baby's name was Hannah.

Mrs. Meyer had gone downstairs to make coffee, which Maude sorely needed. April Mae well deserved the rest she was taking, but Maude had resolved to stay awake until she was assured that all was well with mother and child.

"I see you've taken care of everything," Sarah said to Maude. "See, you didn't need me after all. How is she?"

Maude motioned for Sarah to leave the room with her. "We'll be right back, Ella."

Her friend looked up from where she sat holding the sleeping baby and nodded. "We're not going anywhere."

"I'm worried about her, Sarah. She lost too much blood. Did you see how pale she was?"

Sarah nodded, her face solemn. "Did you check her abdomen?"

Maude knew she referred to whether or not the womb had firmed up again after the delivery. The difference could be felt through the skin. If it hadn't, April Mae might continue to bleed. "It's still softer than I'd like, but I kneaded it." Both women knew rubbing the area firmly could make the womb tighten up and stop the bleeding.

"You'll have to keep checking every so often. Why don't we pray, and enlist the help of the Great Physician?" Sarah suggested, holding out her hands to Maude, and together they stood in the shadowy hallway, as Sarah began, "Lord, we come to You in great need of Your healing touch for April Mae Horvath…"

"So yer trip inta town was an utter failure, Jonas?" Coira MacLaren inquired from her rocking chair near the fire. Her brogue was as thick as a stack of Scottish oatcakes, as if she'd just disembarked the ship that had carried her and Jonas from Scotland this month rather than six years ago. Though her son sat behind her, not wanting to be so close to the heat, she didn't turn to aim her disapproval. She knew quite well the power of her spiteful words. Whether she faced him or not, she could be certain they would hit the mark. They always did.

Still, Jonas was glad she couldn't see his involuntary stiffening. "I didn't find anyone looking for work whom I thought suitable to see to tend you, Mother, but I wouldn't call the trip a total waste of time," he said, keeping his tone calm. "I had a pleasant meal." *One free of your carping.* He wasn't about to tell her he'd attended the barbecue put on by the Simpson Creek Spinsters' Club or she'd be on him again about marrying and producing a bairn or two before she died.

Before he'd gone into town, he'd been vague about the details of his intended trip, only implying that he'd be in a position to speak to several females about becoming his mother's companion.

"Whatever you ate, 'twas nothing you couldn't have gotten from Senora Morales without wasting precious coin," his mother grumbled. "But I warn you, Jonas, the time will come, and soon, when that poor overworked woman will refuse to do all the cooking and cleaning *and* tending of your old mother, and then she'll quit altogether. Then where will you be? It's not as if you could do all of that extra work and still tend your ranch, could you? You didn't speak to a single lass about hiring on here?"

An image of Maude Harkey's riot of red curls and eyes the hue of spring bluebonnets swam into his head. "Aye, I did speak to one, but she didn't want the job," he said, and hoped his mother would leave it at that.

"Just one? You'd said you'd be able to speak to several," Coira MacLaren snapped.

His mother's health wasn't robust, but there was nothing wrong with her memory, unfortunately. Her mind was sharp as a dirk and her tongue just as cutting. He'd learned to cope by pretending nothing she said affected him, or sometimes, when his temper was truly frayed, by responding in kind, but it didn't make him feel better to do so.

"There were, but I thought the one I spoke to was the best candidate." He couldn't say why he thought so, other than the air of competence Maude Harkey wore like a shield—and the firmness of her resolve that made him believe she might be a match for even his mother's cantankerousness. It certainly wasn't that he was attracted to her for his own sake. No, he was done with all that.

"Did you think to be a miser and offer her less than the thirty dollars a month we agreed upon?" his mother asked, suspicion threaded through her voice like the tightest-woven wool tartan.

It was ironic that she accused him of miserliness—normally it was his mother who took Scottish frugality to the extreme.

"No." He hadn't even gotten to the subject of wages, as he recalled. As soon as Maude Harkey learned what he was asking, she'd refused to consider his proposition outright. Now he wished he had gone ahead and taken the time to meet some of the other young ladies at the barbecue. He shouldn't have let the redheaded Miss Harkey blind him to the possible suitability of the others. As he'd said, it wasn't as if he was seeking a wife.

"Well, you'd best be searching for *some* way to convince a woman to come out here," his mother continued. "I've no time for your nonsense or your dillydallying."

Jonas gritted his teeth and forced himself not to respond. After all, his mother wasn't entirely wrong. He did need to find her a companion as soon as possible. He resolved that he would make another trip into town, as soon as he could find the time to get away from the ranch.

And this time, he wouldn't leave until he'd found a woman who'd say yes.

Chapter Three

After their middle-of-the-night ordeal, Maude slept right through Sunday breakfast. When she finally awoke, she felt a pleasant sense of accomplishment. Despite April Mae's sudden and entirely unexpected appearance on their doorstep, they had helped her deliver a beautiful, healthy baby. Maude's father would have been proud.

She couldn't help grinning. There was a *baby* in the boardinghouse, a pink innocent creature all fresh and new, with that incomparable baby smell. Soon they'd have to do what they could to track down tiny Hannah's errant father and insist he do right by April Mae and their child, but for now, Maude could enjoy the presence of an infant in her dreary life for her to care for.

Excited about the prospect of holding tiny Hannah, Maude dressed, washed her hands with water from the ewer, dried them on a towel and left her room. She'd go to church, then on to Ella's café and help her friend there for awhile, but she couldn't resist taking a few minutes to cuddle the baby first and see if the new mother was resting all right.

She found Mrs. Meyer had beaten her to it. The old woman was sitting in the rocking chair in April Mae's room, humming, little Hannah in her arms. An old wooden cradle sat on the floor between the bed and the rocking chair. Mrs. Meyer must have brought it down from the attic, Maude thought. Had it been from that long-ago time when the proprietress had been a young mother? *How nice that it was getting used again.*

April Mae's eyes were closed, but she opened them at the creaking of the opening door. Her gaze darted first to the infant, then, satisfied, to Maude.

"How are you feeling?"

"Tired. Sore...but ain't she purty?" April Mae said, smiling at her child, her eyes bright with pride.

Mrs. Meyer rose and handed Maude the baby. "I'd better go start workin' on dinner—noon'll be here before we know it," she said, and left.

"She's perfect," Maude agreed, even as she took note of the purple shadows under April Mae's eyes. Her face was slightly swollen from the exertion she'd gone through the night before, but Maude told herself not to jump to conclusions that anything was amiss. All women looked like that after delivering a baby, more or less. "Is she nursing all right?"

"She's getting the hang of it," April Mae said, still smiling, but her eyelids flickered drowsily.

"It's all right to go back to sleep," Maude assured her. "You need to rest up after the wonderful job you did last night, bringing Hannah into the world. I'll just sit and hold her for a few minutes, then put her in the cradle when I have to leave. Will you be able to get her if she wakes?"

"Mmm-hmm..."

Within seconds, her soft snores told Maude the girl slept. Now she had time to think about how April Mae and the baby's coming was likely to change life here at the boardinghouse—and how that was likely to affect her.

But the image of Jonas MacLaren and his job offer, delivered in that delicious accent, kept intruding on her mind.

Reining in his horse on the knoll overlooking the flock, Jonas MacLaren doffed his wide-brimmed hat and took a moment to rub both temples with his thumb and fingers.

"What's wrong, *patrón*?" Hector asked, bringing his mount alongside Jonas's. "You got *dolor de cabeza*? A headache?"

Jonas gave his *segundo* a sideways glance. "I'm all right."

"With respect, senor, you do not look it," his Tejano foreman said in his forthright manner. "I think you are hungry. Why not go back to the big house and have something to eat? You been out with me since dawn, and I'm thinking you did not break your fast before you left the house, *sí*? The flocks will still be here when you return."

Jonas stared down at the peacefully grazing cluster of merinos that dotted the slope below like so many little clouds of creamy white, though some of the "clouds" had long, curling horns. They were but a small portion of his flock, which numbered about two thousand. Scattered among these were Angora goats, similarly colored, that produced prized mohair.

"Maybe I'll see what's in the pot in the bunkhouse," Jonas muttered. "It's not real peaceful in the big house at the moment."

Hector's dark eyes took on a gleam of understanding. "Ah. Senora MacLaren, she is on the warpath again?"

Jonas couldn't suppress a rueful smile at his mother being compared to a rampaging wild Indian. Between all the Spanish and "Texanisms" he was picking up since he'd bought the ranch and moved himself and his mother to the Hill Country of Texas, he'd added considerably to his vocabulary.

"Yes, she is. This morning she threw a dish of huevos rancheros at Senora Morales, saying respectable scrambled eggs didn't need heathenish peppers in them."

"Ay yi yi," Hector said, but his attempt to look concerned was utterly defeated by the grin he couldn't quite stop. The senora's tantrums were legendary, and on the ranch they had become a source of great amusement…to those who didn't have to experience them firsthand.

"You smile, but Senora Morales told me if I didn't find a companion for the senora within the week, she would leave and go back to her sister's in San Antonio."

"Do not worry, *patrón*. She doesn't mean it."

Jonas raked a hand through his hair. "This time, I think she just might," he insisted.

"If she left, I could ask my sister, the one who lives in Refugio to come and be your cook," Hector offered. "It would take her a while to travel so far, though."

Jonas shook his head. "You already told me how sweet-tempered she is. I'd hate to inflict my mother on someone like that. And it really is too much work, to handle the cooking and cleaning, and care for my mother on top of that. No, she needs a dedicated companion. And to fill that role, I'm starting to think what my mother needs is someone as strong willed as she is."

Unbidden, the image of Maude Harkey came to mind once again. He resolutely banished it. Miss Harkey had already said no, and that was the end of it.

Hector shrugged. "It's possible."

"Meanwhile, I'm heading for the bunkhouse. Tamales eaten in peace are better than risking my ears in the ranch house right now." Maybe he'd get an inspiration while he ate for where he could find the right lady.

He had missed his chance to speak to several ladies at once by not taking full advantage of the Spinsters' Club barbecue. It was unlikely he'd find so many potential candidates in one place again. But he wouldn't let that obstacle stop him. If he knew anything, it was that no man in the world was more tenacious than a Scotsman. He *would* find the right woman to see to his mother's needs.

But in the meantime he'd enjoy a quiet meal, and he might just grab a siesta afterward on one of the empty bunks. He would find a companion soon, but not tonight. And in the absence of someone to abate her tantrums, he knew he'd need his rest before he had to face his mother again.

"You go ahead, Maude," Ella Justiss said that evening, when the last customer had left the little café that Maude helped her run. "I'm just going to wash these few remaining dishes. Would you want Nate to walk you home? By the time he did that and came back, I'd be ready to go." She nodded toward Nate Bohannan, her fiancé, who was sitting at one of the tables, having just finished a helping of Ella's fried chicken. "I know you want to go check on little Hannah."

"I'd be happy to walk with you, Miss Maude," Nate confirmed.

"There's no need, but thank you, Nate. I'll be fine. You two have wedding plans to discuss." She had no fear at the prospect of walking back to the boardinghouse by herself. Simpson Creek was a safe little town, even at night. Untying her apron, she hung it up on a peg by the door and removed her shawl from another peg.

"I'll light a lantern for you, at least," Nate said. "Then you can be on your way."

Maude couldn't deny that she was eager to see that tiny little bundle of perfection, with her rosebud mouth and the thick thatch of downy black hair, so she walked quickly across the bridge over the creek and down darkened Main Street, taking a shortcut via the alley between the mercantile and the hotel to reach the boardinghouse on Travis Street.

She would discuss finding the baby's father with April Mae, too, Maude decided, after she'd made sure the new mother had eaten some supper. Now that the girl wasn't in labor, she should be thinking more clearly and might remember where Felix Renz had planned to go next on his circuit. The man sold pots and pans and other kitchenware from a cart, so he wouldn't be traveling all that fast. And it was high time the man was made to take responsibility for the girl he'd left in the family way—and the new baby that had come into the world as a result. Surely when he saw that precious infant, he'd want to do right by her and her mother.

Maude heard the familiar buzz of conversation as she entered the boardinghouse kitchen through the back door. But when she proceeded into the dining room, she saw Mrs. Meyer wasn't presiding over the long rectangular table, and the boarders were taking full advantage of her absence to leave their manners by the wayside, grabbing huge portions and wiping their mouths on the tablecloth. The serving platters were already empty.

Delbert Perry looked up from the biscuit he'd been buttering. "Evenin', Miss Maude. Mrs. Meyer said you was t'come upstairs soon's you got in—somethin' about the little mother havin' a fever."

Fear seized Maude's heart with fingers of ice. April Mae was so weak after the birth. If a fever set in strongly, would she have the energy to fight it? Without saying another word, she turned and dashed into the hallway then fairly few up the stairs without pausing to acknowledge what Perry called after her— "Th' doctor's been sent for."

Little Hannah slept in the cradle, a thumb firmly planted in her mouth.

Mrs. Meyer looked up from where she was bent over the bed, a cloth in her hand. "Oh, Maude, I'm so thankful you're here. Sarah Walker thought her husband might be home any minute now, but—"

If the older woman finished her sentence, Maude wasn't aware of it. Her eyes flew to April Mae's flushed cheeks, her overbright eyes and the pearls of perspiration beading her pallid forehead. Her heart sank at how fragile and exhausted the girl looked already.

"She's burnin' up with fever," Mrs. Meyer said unnecessarily. "And every so often, she starts shakin' fit to rattle the bed frame apart."

Maude didn't have to reach out a confirming hand to the new mother's forehead to believe it. "April Mae, when did you start feeling ill?" Maude asked, careful to keep her voice calm, even though her spirit quailed within her. Childbed fever—the dreaded sequel to so many births, the cause of so many deaths among new mothers. She thought back to the few preparations she had had time to do in the too-brief span of minutes from the girl's arrival to the delivery, procedures her father had always insisted were essential—washing her hands, placing clean linens under the laboring girl, boiling the knife that had cut the cord in a pot of water…

Had she done enough? Had she left out some essential step that would have protected April Mae from the fever that racked her now? She couldn't think of any precaution she'd omitted, but it *had* been a long time since she'd assisted at a delivery and her memories of those births were not as crystal clear as they had once been. The thought that she might be in some way responsible for the state that April Mae was in left her feeling sick herself.

"I started havin' chills this mornin' after you left for the café, Miss Maude," April Mae said. "Then I got so hot...an' my belly hurts..."

Maude kept her expression blank. "Then we'll just work on getting that fever down. I'm sure Dr. Walker will have something to make your belly feel better, too, when he gets here." She couldn't remember her father ever having lost a patient to childbed fever, or Dr. Walker, either, though, so she didn't know what that "something" would be. Laudanum? And what about Hannah—what did this all mean for her? Would it be safe for the baby to continue to nurse while her mother was battling this illness, especially if April Mae was given laudanum?

Telling the girl they'd be right back, she motioned for Mrs. Meyer to follow her out into the hall.

"It's bad, isn't it?" the boardinghouse proprietress said.

Maude nodded. She felt like a fool for having gone to work at the café as usual. She should have known this was a birth prone to such an infection, what with April Mae's youth and her long, hard journey to reach Simpson Creek. She should have remained at the boardinghouse and stayed vigilant.

"Mrs. Meyer, do you know of any woman around Simpson Creek who might be nursing a baby right now?"

The older woman's eyes grew wide at the implication of her question. "You think she's going to die."

Maude shook her head. "I hope not, but I don't know if it's safe for the baby to nurse if Dr. Walker gives April Mae a sedative."

Mrs. Meyer pursed her lips. "No, I can't think of anyone..."

Just then they heard the door open below. A glance over the stair railing brought the welcome sight of Dr. Nolan Walker entering the house.

Within moments he had been introduced to April Mae, washed his hands and examined her, his expression becoming more and more grave as he went on. "You're giving her willow bark tea to reduce the fever?" he asked Maude.

"I did," Mrs. Meyer said, "an hour ago."

"Good." He turned back to April Mae. "I'm going to give you a mild dose of laudanum to help you sleep."

Once he'd done that, he indicated that Maude was to follow him from the room. They descended the stairs and went into the parlor so that April Mae couldn't overhear.

"She's very seriously ill," he said. "I think you know that."

Maude nodded. She had known, but to hear Doctor Walker say so, and see his solemn expression, stole her breath. She had hoped that the doctor's knowledge and expertise would offer some easy solution that was out of her grasp—some way to make April Mae's situation less tenuous.

"As you probably know, there's not a whole lot we can do but treat the fever and try to keep the patient taking in fluids—and pray," he added. "All of which you're doing already, I know."

Walker's faith in her warmed Maude, but she had no time to take comfort in it.

"What about the baby, Dr. Walker? Is it safe for her to nurse from her mother, especially with the laudanum April Mae has taken?"

Walker rubbed his chin. "It would probably be better if she didn't, until—unless—this infection starts to get better."

"Do you know anyone who could…feed the baby?" Maude said. Men and women ordinarily didn't discuss such intimate things, but she'd grown up with a doctor as a father and she knew this was no time to be prim. The baby's well-being was at stake, and that was more important than some silly notion of propriety.

Walker looked thoughtful. "I've just returned from the deathbed of a young man, a Tejano who lived just outside Simpson Creek—that's why I wasn't able to come when Miss Horvath's baby was born. His unexpected demise sent his wife into labor just after her husband died, and unfortunately her child came too early and was stillborn."

"How awful!" Maude said, feeling a rush of sympathy for the unknown girl as she tried to imagine surviving the loss of husband and baby in the same day. "Would she… Do you think she would agree to come and feed April Mae's baby? Would she be able to—would she have milk?"

"There's one way to find out," he said. "The widow just happens to be Deputy Menendez's sister. He and their mother are at his sister's home with her right now. I could send Sheriff Bishop out to ask if she would be willing to come into town and provide for this baby. I'll go do that, and let my wife know I'll be attending Miss Horvath tonight, then I'll be back."

Silently, Maude sent up a quick but grateful prayer, thanking the Lord that Doctor Walker knew someone who might be willing to serve as a wet nurse, and also that the doctor would be helping her care for April Mae tonight. She felt the sensation of a great burden sliding off her shoulders.

Just then a thin infant wail drifted down from upstairs. Maude felt her heart go out to the baby, so new to the world and yet so alone in it, and silently promised herself that the tiny girl would not lack for care and comfort in the next few days, no matter what happened to Hannah's mother. Maude herself would see to that.

Despite all their prayers and Doctor Walker's skill, April Mae Horvath slipped into eternity two mornings later.

"God rest her soul," murmured Juana Benavides as Doctor Walker closed April Mae's eyes. Dressed in mourning, she was the young widow who had—to Maude's enormous relief—come to nurse little Hannah two nights ago.

"I'll let the undertaker and Reverend Chadwick

know on my way home," Doctor Walker said, straightening.

By tacit agreement, Mrs. Meyer saw Dr. Walker out while Maude, carrying the sleeping baby, and Juana went next door to a room vacated by Felix Renz. The other drummer boarding in the house had departed just that morning. He'd promised to keep an eye out for Felix Renz as he made his rounds. Unfortunately, they had no clear idea where to look for him, specifically. April Mae had never recovered sufficiently for Maude to be able to ask.

Maude settled herself onto the room's only chair, while Juana sat on the bed.

"Poor motherless child," Maude murmured, staring down into the sleeping, innocent face of baby Hannah. "You don't even know you've lost your mama."

"You care about this baby very much," Juana said with the quiet kindness she had exhibited since arriving at the boardinghouse, as Maude bent to kiss the little girl's downy dark head.

"Yes." Even while she had helped Doctor Walker fight for April Mae Horvath's life, she had begun to love this helpless little life with more devotion than she had ever thought possible. She had loved before in her lifetime—her family and her friends—but something about Hannah's helpless state made her feelings for the child deeper than any love she'd felt before, and it filled her with determination to guard the child from any further harm. *With God helping me, I won't let any more tragedy touch your life*, she promised the sleeping infant.

"Perhaps you could be little Hannah's new *madre*," Juana suggested.

Maude blinked at the other girl. "But…but she has a father," she stammered. "Even if we don't know where he is right now, it's not up to me to decide what is best for the child."

Juana made a dismissive gesture, as if Felix Renz were no more than a bit of dust she had dropped from the palm of her hand. "Bah! Even if that worthless hombre is found, what kind of a life can he give her, a wandering seller of pots and pans? He did not even care enough for the little *pobrecita's* mother to stay with her after he had gotten her into trouble."

Juana hadn't even met Renz, as Maude had, yet her assessment of the man was accurate enough, Maude thought. Felix Renz wasn't wicked or cruel—if he was, Mrs. Meyer would not have permitted him to stay in her boardinghouse. But he was shiftless and irresponsible. Not the sort of man who could be trusted to take proper care of a newborn, even if the child was his own.

She gazed down again at Hannah's sleeping face as Juana's words began to take hold in her heart. She had conceived a fierce, protective love of this child from the first moment she'd held her, a love that did much to fill an empty place within her she hadn't even known existed. Hannah needed a guardian and protector… while Maude needed someone to love. *Yes. She wanted to keep this baby and call her her own.*

Then she felt a pang of guilt, remembering that Juana had been the one who had been nursing this baby, despite her grief over her own lost child and husband. “But what about you?” she asked Juana. “Don’t you want to—” The infant in her arms gave a little squeak, and Maude realized her arms had tightened around her too much, in instinctive fear that the little one might be taken away from her. She relaxed them immediately, and Hannah resumed slumbering.

“I love that little dear one,” Juana said, nodding toward Hannah in Maude’s arms. “She has given me a purpose and kept me from despair after losing my Tomás and my little Tulio.” It was the first time she had mentioned her dead baby’s name, or her husband’s, since she’d arrived, though Maude often heard her weeping at night through the their common wall. “But she is an Anglo baby, *sí*? I love her, too, and I will stay with her as long as she needs me, but if I raised her as her mother, she might not be accepted in either the Anglo world or the Tejano one, do you see?”

Maude stared at her as the simple, stark truth sank in. However good relations were in Simpson Creek between the Tejanos and the Texans—or Anglos as the Tejanos called them—outside of it there was much anti-Mexican prejudice on the part of the whites, and resentment on the part of the Tejanos, who had settled this land first. A child caught between the two worlds would face the worst of both communities’ prejudices. Juana was right—it wouldn’t be fair to do that to Hannah—and it was all the more reason for Maude to keep her.

But if Maude kept Hannah and raised her—assuming Renz never returned to claim his daughter—she would need Juana’s help, and Juana couldn’t stay here at the boardinghouse indefinitely. Maude knew Mrs. Meyer well enough to know that as fond of Hannah as she was, the old woman was already fretting about the loss of rent from the room Juana was using. She'd had to turn away one customer already. And several of the men had lost no time in complaining about the noise of the baby's crying.

Maude would have shared her own room with Juana gladly, but the room was tiny and the bed too narrow for two. Her funds wouldn't stretch to the rent for two rooms. And that still wouldn't resolve the problem of Hannah's crying disturbing the other boarders. Even if Maude tried to arrange some deal with Mrs. Meyer to rent the two rooms, Maude doubted the woman would agree if having the baby on the premises drove away any of her other customers.

Juana's mother lived in town, and the girl had mentioned that she wanted her daughter to come home now that she was widowed, but if Juana took Hannah there, the child wouldn't know Maude by the time she was weaned. And Juana was young and attractive. Men might not wait long to come calling. And if Juana remarried, she might move away and Maude would lose track of Hannah forever.

She thought of the little cottage on the grounds of Gilmore House, the sumptuous mansion where the mayor and his wife lived. They would have let Maude and Juana use it for nothing, and it would have been perfect for the purpose. But Ella and her new husband would be occupying the cottage until Nate could build their house behind the café, which might not be for months unless the winter was very mild.

What to do? Please, Lord, show me the way...

Just then a knock sounded at the front entrance below. She tensed, thinking she might need to answer it, but then she heard Mrs. Meyer's steady, measured steps heading for the door. It was too soon to expect the undertaker, in all likelihood. Would Mrs. Meyer have to turn away another customer? Was there any chance it was Felix Renz? Had someone found him already?

Maude rose and pushed open the door of Juana's room about halfway, so they could hear who it was. She saw the swift look of understanding in Juana's eyes.

"Yes, sir. What may I do for you?"

"My name is Jonas MacLaren, ma'am," Maude heard the newcomer say. "I'm here to see Miss Harkey, if I may?"

Maude's felt her heartbeat lurch into a gallop. *Could the Lord be answering her prayer already, just a moment after she had prayed it?*

"You have a gentleman caller?" Juana asked, a small smile playing about her lips. "An *amante*—a sweetheart?"

"No, nothing like that," Maude said. "Juana, do you *want* to go home and live with your mother?"

Juana Benavides's reaction was quick and unmistakeable. "No, I do not. I love *mi madre*, of course, but her house is *diminuto*, tiny. And full. My *abuela*, my grandmother, lives there, and my brother Luis, and my younger sisters…I have been a *wife*, Maude. I do not want to go back and live like an unmarried daughter." Her eyes were wistful and sad.

"How would you feel about living on a ranch, at least for a while, until Hannah is weaned?"

Juana's lovely forehead furrowed with confusion. "You have a ranch? Then why do you live here?"

"No, I don't own a ranch. But I have an idea. I'll explain everything after I talk to the gentleman downstairs—if he's agreeable."

Chapter Four

Jonas watched her descend the stairs, regal as a queen, despite the fact that the dress she wore was everyday calico and the stair treads she set foot on were threadbare.

He stepped forward to greet her and she stopped on the last step, so they were at eye level. "Good morning, Mr. MacLaren. How nice of you to come calling." Her blue eyes assessed him, as if daring him to admit right now that the reason for his visit wasn't in the nature of a simple social call.

He'd take that dare, he decided. He didn't have time to dance delicately around the matter.

"Good morning, Miss Harkey..." He hesitated, as one of the male boarders loomed suddenly over the railing, staring down at him curiously. Jonas's gaze darted around the hallway. "Is there somewhere we could talk privately?"

Maude's smile was serene. "I believe the parlor is free at the moment," she said, leading the way and gesturing for him to follow her.

He chose a straight-backed, cane-bottomed chair, leaving her the more comfortable horsehair-stuffed sofa next to it.

For a moment, neither of them said anything. She just sat there waiting expectantly, while he searched for the right words, the right expression, that would ensure she gave him the answer that he wanted. He could brook no more delays in finding a companion for his mother, and he knew down to his bones that Maude Harkey was the right woman for the job. But could he make *her* see that?

He cleared his throat, which had become thick with apprehension. "Miss Harkey, when we met Saturday, you will recall that I asked you to consider a position as companion to my mother. At the time, you declined to consider it."

Out of the corner of his eye, he saw her nod.

Why was he speaking so formally? She knew as well as he did what had transpired in their conversation that day. Why did he feel he had to restate the case, as if he were some starchy-collared lawyer?

He cleared his throat again. *Should he just come right out and ask her once more if she would be willing to take the job she had seemed so opposed to before, as if he just assumed that she would have reconsidered and decided to take him up on it? As if by coming here today, he was merely sparing her the trip out to Five Mile Hill Ranch to ask him if the job was still open?*

No. It might be too easy for her to take offense if he took that approach. Better to be honest, to lay all his cards out on the table, so she would feel as if *she* was the one doing *him* the favor. Which she would be, of course. He'd make that clear, too. She deserved to know what she was in for if she accepted the position.

He turned to face her. "Miss Harkey, I beg you to reconsider. We need you—my mother needs you—very much. If I don't return with at least a promise that you will come and help us, our housekeeper will quit. I have a ranch to run, ma'am, and all I'm getting done is pacifying Senora Morales so that she will stay one more hour, one more day."

Miserably, he let his gaze drop to his hands once again. Maude Harkey was going to refuse once more, he was certain of it. He would have to retreat to his fallback position, which was pleading with her to introduce him to one of her friends who might be willing to take on the job she would not accept.

"Actually, Mr. MacLaren," Maude said, "my…um, circumstances have changed since the barbecue in such a way that I would be willing to take the position you have offered."

It was a moment before his mind caught up with the fact that she was *accepting*, not rejecting his offer. He was so surprised that a heartfelt *thank You, God* almost escaped his lips. Almost. It was bad enough he'd used the word *beg*. His pride was a bruised and battered thing now, after everything that had happened to him, but he clung to it all the same, as any Scotsman would. Stooping to begging grated on him, as necessary as it had been. It would have been disastrous if he'd actually thanked the Lord aloud, as if he'd been drowning and she'd been the one to throw him a rope.

He had to remember that he would be her employer, and as such would need to get and keep the upper hand from the first.

"Thank you." He was pleased to note that he sounded completely normal. "How soon would you—"

She held up a hand. "But I have conditions upon which my acceptance must be based, before we can be in total agreement, Mr. MacLaren."

Now who sounded like a starchy-collared lawyer? "Conditions?" he echoed, suddenly wary.

"Yes, conditions. After the barbecue, a young girl presented herself here at the boardinghouse in the middle of the night, soaked to the skin, and—forgive me for being plainspoken, Mr. MacLaren—in an advanced stage of labor. She sought the father of the baby, a traveling merchant who often stays here on his rounds, but her timing was unfortunate. He had left Simpson Creek just that morning and has not returned since. That night, she gave birth to a baby girl, and all seemed to be well."

He stared at her, trying to make sense of her story. *Why was she telling him this?*

"What does this have to do with me, Miss Harkey, and the job I have offered you?" he asked.

She turned very blue eyes on him. "Unfortunately the baby's mother died of childbed fever, Mr. MacLaren, just a little while ago—leaving baby Hannah, for all intents and purposes, an orphan. I am resolved to keep her and raise her as my own, assuming the father doesn't turn up and want to take responsibility, which I highly doubt will happen. My acceptance of the position you offer is contingent on being allowed to keep baby Hannah with me at your ranch—and to bring Juana Benavides, a young widow, with me to nurse the child. Senora Benavides's baby was stillborn the same day she lost her husband, the same night that Hannah was born—you see, so she is able to feed the child."

Now that he was beginning to grasp the enormity of what Maude Harkey was asking him, he marveled at her audacity. And it didn't help just then that said infant chose this moment to start squalling from upstairs, loud enough to wake the dead.

"You're expecting me to let you bring a wailing baby to the ranch house—*and* a Mexican woman to feed her?"

Those blue eyes narrowed. "Senora Benavides is as Texan as you are—actually more so, since as you told me you come from Scotland and her forebears lived here long before Anglo colonists came. Juana is a Tejana, Mr. MacLaren, not a Mexican."

Her attempt to shame him—or at least that was what he thought had motivated her last words—sparked irritation in him. "You can call her anything you want, Miss Harkey—"

She went on as if he had not spoken. "And it's not as if Juana would do nothing more than nurse the baby, Mr. MacLaren. She is quite willing to help your housekeeper with her duties, whenever she is not caring for little Hannah."

"Miss Harkey, I did not come here prepared to hire two servants," he informed her, determined to regain control of the situation. "Or to invite the presence of a screaming infant in my house. I'm looking for *more* peace and quiet, not less."

Above them, the baby's wailing suddenly ceased.

Maude Harkey smiled. "There, you see? She was probably just hungry. Babies' wants are simple, Mr. MacLaren, and once satisfied, they stop crying. I will pay Senora Benavides out of my wages for the first week, until you see what a good worker she is."

"It's out of the question, Miss Harkey." He could only imagine the explosion of temper from his mother if he returned with not only the promised companion for her, but a noisy infant and her wet nurse.

Maude stood, her posture as stiff as any general about to order a charge. Her blue eyes blazed icy fire at him. "Then my coming to be your mother's companion is out of the question, as well, Mr. MacLaren," she said. "Good day to you."

He recognized defeat when he saw it. Worse than his mother's wrath at the compromise he was being forced to make would be the consequences of returning to Five Mile Hill Ranch empty-handed. Not only would it enrage his mother, it would also signal the exodus of Senora Morales. He certainly couldn't stay inside and take over that woman's duties. Perhaps if he portrayed the deal as getting two servants for the price of one? The housekeeper, he knew, could use the help. She was no longer a young woman, and keeping the house clean and getting meals on the table three times a day was no small task.

"Fine," he snapped. "You may bring the infant and her w—that is, her foster mother," he said, feeling himself redden at almost saying the phrase "wet nurse" to a lady.

Apparently she didn't like "foster mother" either, judging by the way she lifted her chin.

"*I* will be little Hannah's mother," she said. "The only mother she will ever know."

Jonas thought he glimpsed a longing deep within those blue eyes, but he ignored it. He didn't want to think too much about Maude's softer qualities. Forcing an all-business tone to his voice, he said, "Very well, Miss Harkey. But being a mother to this baby must not interfere with your duties as my mother's companion."

She nodded, gracious in victory. "It won't."

"How soon can you be ready to leave?" he asked, hoping she would be that uncommon female who could pack quickly. If she was able to ready herself within the next hour, then with any luck, they might even reach Five Mile Hill Ranch before full dark, and he wouldn't have to make another trip.

"We will have to remain here in town for Hannah's mother's burial," she told him. "I haven't spoken to the undertaker yet, but the earliest that could possibly take place would be tomorrow morning. So we could possibly return with you tomorrow afternoon."

"Possibly? Miss Harkey, I think I've more than met you halfway by agreeing to accept the baby and her—Mrs. Benavides," he snapped. "My mother's need for a companion is urgent and cannot brook any delay. I fail to see why it's necessary for you to remain for the burial of a girl you barely knew rather than coming to the ranch to begin work immediately."

"Because April Mae Horvath—that's the name of the girl who died—has no one, Mr. MacLaren," she said. "That's why. Her parents disowned her when they learned she was in the family way, and her sweetheart abandoned her. Those of us who spent the past few days caring for her…we were strangers, but we were all she had. And someday, I must be able to look my daughter in the eye and tell her that her birth mother wasn't put in the ground with no one present but the preacher and the grave digger."

There was a steely resolve in her tone that brooked no argument. He rose. "Very well, Miss Harkey. I'll send a wagon and one of my men to collect you, the others and your effects tomorrow afternoon. You and Mrs. Benavides should be ready to go. Good day to you." He nodded to her, then found his way to the door, feeling her gaze on him until it closed behind him.

Maude Harkey was a troublesome, headstrong female and no mistake. He felt as if battle had just been joined and he had *not* come out the victor. At best, they had fought to a draw and then postponed further hostilities for another day. He had to admire her ethics, though. Not many women would consider it their moral duty to attend the burial of a girl they'd only known for a few days, especially one who'd been foolish enough to believe a man's empty promises and end up with child.

He considered taking a room in the hotel and waiting for her in town, but knew instinctively that spending some twenty-four hours cooling his heels in a rented room would make him restless as a caged wolf.

The thought of paying good money for a lumpy, strange bed didn't appeal to him, either, and he wasn't the sort to while away the hours drinking whiskey and gambling in a saloon.

Going back to the ranch and sending Hector with the buckboard the following day would be better. Jonas would have time to prepare his mother for the arrival of not only her new companion, but two unexpected additional people. Maybe this way Coira MacLaren would have a chance to vent the worst of her spleen before her new companion's arrival.

There was the added benefit that Jonas wouldn't have to force himself to make conversation with Maude Harkey on the long drive to Five Mile Hill Ranch. There was something about the woman that got under his skin—and that was a dangerous symptom. He had no intention of letting a woman muddle his head ever again.

Excepting, of course, his irritable, irrepressible, unignorable mother, whose endless litany of complaints echoed through his mind night and day.

Did Maude Harkey wonder why he put up with his mother's difficult behavior, or did she just assume he paid as much attention to the Fifth Commandment—to honor one's parents—as much as the others? She'd wonder more after she met the woman, that was sure.

As his mother's only child, it fell to him to care for Coira MacLaren. He was indebted to her for his existence—in more ways than one. His debt to his mother was too great to leave her to fend for herself. He was a man grown and then some, but he'd never forget he owed the woman his very survival. He'd keep her secret—*their* secret—forever.

He would not shirk his duty to ensure her well-being in return, even if the weight of the load sometimes felt like more than he could bear. He had no choice but to carry it alone. He had no siblings living to help him, and there was not—would never be—a wife to share his life, to halve his burdens and double his joys.

What had happened in the past had kept him from marriage, both before the war and since. He wouldn't subject a wife to the kind of man he was likely to become as his father's son.

Juana found Maude beating the kitchen rug, which she'd hung on the line, as if she meant to smash it into clumps of thread. Particles of dust flew from the abused rug at the ferocity of her blows.

"Maude, what are you doing? I expected you to come back upstairs and tell me what the man said. Instead I find you trying to murder a rug, no?"

Maude turned to the young widow, realizing she was out of breath and that her right shoulder ached with the exertion. Perhaps she *had* been beating the rug just a hair too vigorously. "N-no," she panted, but couldn't smother a chuckle at the thought of murdering a rug.

"Oh, Juana, h-he just makes me so angry! Not only did he expect us to drop everything and leave with him this very day, but after I explained that out of decency I needed to attend April Mae's burial first, he said he'd send a wagon to come and *collect* us tomorrow afternoon—as if we were sacks of flour! Honestly, if I didn't need to provide a home for little Hannah, I'd tell him he could take his wagon and drive right off a cliff!"

She wasn't about to tell Juana how MacLaren had bridled at the idea of taking *her* and baby Hannah, too. Juana might well refuse to go if she felt that she would not be welcomed at the ranch—and who could blame her? Then the whole plan would fall apart. A home for Hannah would do no good if there was no way to see to the child's needs at the ranch.

Juana studied her, worry furrowing her brow. "*Mi amiga*, you have the temper of a true *pelirroja*, a redhead. And you are overheated," she said, reaching out to brush a red curl that had escaped from Maude's coiffure away from her damp forehead. "Come sit down on the porch for a moment and I will fetch us some lemonade. Then you can tell me all about the man and what he said. I would like to know more about where we will be going tomorrow. Remember, you only told me we might be going to live on a ranch."

Maude felt her fury slipping away like an ebbing tide in the face of Juana's calm. She did owe her new friend an explanation. With a guilty start, she realized she had not even asked Juana if she would mind the additional duties, on top of Hannah's care, before offering her assistance to the housekeeper. "Is Hannah asleep?"

Juana nodded. "Mrs. Meyer said she would listen for her. I will fetch the lemonade and then you will tell me all, yes?"

"Yes," Maude agreed. "And thank you, lemonade sounds lovely."

And it was lovely, indeed, when Juana returned with

the two glasses moments later. After a few refreshing sips to restore her calm, Maude began her tale.

"He sounds proud as a Spanish grandee," Juana said sometime later, when Maude had told her the full story, from their meeting at the Spinsters' Club barbecue to MacLaren's final words about sending a man with a wagon to "collect" them.

"And yet he tolerates his mother behaving like a tyrant, apparently."

Juana shrugged. "She is his mother. He respects her." It seemed to be explanation enough for her.

"I wonder if that's the only reason? And why is he so high-handed about everything?"

Juana muttered something in Spanish. "That is our equivalent of your Anglo saying, 'The apple doesn't fall far from the tree.' If his mother likes to give orders, then perhaps that is why he does, as well. What he needs is a wife to keep him in line. I wonder why such a handsome man is not married? I peeked from the window upstairs when he was leaving," she admitted with a chuckle. "He is so tall…and his bearing—like a king!"

"Who'd marry such an arrogant man?" Maude retorted, though she had to admit to herself that Juana was right about MacLaren's appearance. It was a pity his personality wasn't as pleasing as his looks. "Even if some woman has considered it, his mother probably scared her off."

Juana laughed, and Maude let herself laugh with her. She felt her earlier tension dissolving.

"Maude, don't worry. It will be all right. You will

learn to deal with his mother, and little Hannah will have a place to grow up with you. And who knows? We may even come to like it there."

Maude blinked at the other woman's unquestioning acceptance. "You don't mind that I told him you would help the housekeeper? I'm sorry that I didn't even ask you first." She had taken so much for granted.

Juana shrugged. "I was busy from dawn to dusk running our household when Tomás was alive. I don't think I would enjoy being idle. I will be happy to help Senora Morales, when the little *niña* doesn't need me. And now, if you don't mind, I had better go tell my mother what I will be doing and take my leave of the family. I will take little Hannah with me. Mama will be so busy admiring her that she won't think to object to my going so far away, I hope," Juana added with a wink.

"And I had better tell Mrs. Meyer what we'll be doing, then check with Reverend Chadwick to make sure he can do the funeral service in the morning," Maude said.

Perhaps the preacher would have some wise counsel on how to deal with people such as the MacLarens, mother and son. What had she been thinking, to take on such a challenge? Was she at all suited to be a companion, much less to a woman of strong temper who would need soothing? She wasn't the sweet and agreeable type full of soft answers that turned away wrath. She could be as fiery as her red hair and as full of opinions as a cactus was of stickers. But she had to make a success of this, or she would have no place to live with little Hannah.

Lord, help me! I'm taking on the impossible!

She shook away the thought. She had to remember that with the Lord, all things were possible.

Even putting up with Jonas MacLaren.

Mrs. Meyer was predictably dismayed when she learned of Maude's plans. "Maude, I was planning on you inheritin' the boardinghouse when I die, since my children don't want to move back here and take it on. I thought of us as partners here. Was that nothing to you? Now you're going to go somewhere else, leaving me behind?"

She saw hurt and insecurity lining the woman's red-rimmed eyes, and felt a moment of regret at causing her pain. Truly, the woman had been kind and generous to her from the start. And the boardinghouse was a good, honest business. It just wasn't the *right* business for Maude—not right now, with the responsibility for Hannah's care resting on her shoulders.

"I'm sorry, Mrs. Meyer. I hope you still think the place would be in good hands if I managed it someday—and we all hope that's a very long time from now," she assured the boardinghouse proprietress. "No one's saying I will be living at Five Mile Hill Ranch for the rest of my life. I'm going to go *try* it. If I don't like it, I'll be back."

"'Like it'?" Mrs. Meyer responded with a laugh that edged on hysteria. "What is there to like? What sane woman would *like* living clear out there with that tyrant and his harridan of a mother? What could have induced you to make such an insane deal, girl?"

Just then Hannah set up a thin wail above them. After Maude went and got her, she returned to finish the conversation, picking it up just where they had left off. "This—little Hannah—induced me to take Mr. MacLaren's offer," she said, cuddling the sweet-smelling baby closer. "I want to give her a home, Mrs. Meyer, a home with me as her mother. It wouldn't be fair to you or the boarders to make that home here, not when she's up crying several times a night. And you wouldn't have let Juana stay indefinitely to nurse her, would you? She can't afford to pay rent."

Mrs. Meyer was too honest a woman to dodge the truth. "No, I haven't survived this long running a boardinghouse with butter for a heart, Maude. Nothing can be free forever, not if I'm to make a living. And you're right that the lodgers haven't been best pleased about the baby's cries during the night since she's been born. I should have realized you'd seek that baby's good over your own. But have you thought about what you're doing to your good name, taking on the raising of that child?"

Something in the older woman's tone made Maude bristle. "What do you mean, Mrs. Meyer?"

The other woman shrugged. "Well, what will men think of you? Will they be interested in courting a girl that has a child with no apparent father? You should have a care to your reputation, Maude."

A sharp bark of bitter laughter erupted before Maude could stifle it. "You mean, the hordes of men who hang around outside every night, just hoping for a kind word from Maude Harkey, will be discouraged and stop serenading me? Pardon me, but unless I'm mistaken, they stopped coming years ago, which is why I'm the president of a dwindling Spinsters' Club and still unmarried, years after most of my friends have achieved their happily-ever-afters.

"I believe thinking of how my non-existent suitors will react is what's known as a 'forlorn hope,' so yes, I'm not exactly worried about my reputation. I'm twenty-five years old, Mrs. Meyer, and I want to be a mother to this innocent baby here, who at this moment has no one in the world to care for her but Juana and myself. And anyone who wants to question her parentage can deal with me on that issue." She heard her defensive tone, but knew a foolish questioner would have a very poor time of it indeed.

"I—I *am* sorry, dear," Mrs. Meyer said. "You know, I only want what's best for you. If that big oaf of a Scotchman doesn't treat you right, you just come right back here. I'll hold your room open till we're sure it's going to work out for you to stay on the ranch."

It was no light promise. Mrs. Meyer usually had a waiting list of folks wanting to board with her. "Thank you," she murmured. It made Maude feel a little less fearful about being "collected" the next day to know that she had a place to come back to, if she needed it. But it didn't make it any easier to think of leaving the place that had been her home for so long now.

It was even harder to take her leave of Ella, who had been her best friend through all that time. "But if you're leaving tomorrow, you'll miss the wedding this weekend!" she wailed. "You were going to stand up with me! Can't you ask him to wait till Sunday to come for you?"

Hating that she had to say no, she shook her head. "I'm so sorry, really I am, Ella, but I need this new job in order to keep little Hannah," she said, nodding toward the infant whom she'd brought with her. "He wasn't pleased that I asked even for another day in town, to see to April Mae's funeral. I was afraid he'd change his mind about hiring me altogether if I asked him to wait any longer. From what I understood, they desperately need the help out at Five Mile Hill Ranch as soon as they can get it."

Ella nodded with a sad but accepting smile. "I understand, Maude. I just wish you weren't going so far away..." She took the contented baby onto her lap and smiled down at Hannah's happy face. "But looking down at this little one, I really do think the change you're going to be making will be worth it. This precious child deserves a mother as wonderful as you, and the ranch is certainly the best place for the two of you. I just wish Jonas MacLaren's mother wasn't notorious for being a shrew!"

Maude chuckled. "It'll be a challenge, I imagine, but that's why the job is available. If she were sweet-tempered, they'd have already hired someone."

"It'll be good for your character," her friend said, tucking a red curl that had fallen out of Maude's chignon back behind her friend's ear. It had always been a joke between them that Maude had a true redhead's temperament, just as Juana had said.

"It will," Maude agreed. "You'll see—I'll learn to hold my tongue and keep my temper. I'll give Mrs. MacLaren no reason to complain of me, no matter how shrewishly she behaves."

"Hmm," Ella said, noncommittally. Maude bristled.

"What's that supposed to mean?"

"Nothing of consequence," Ella said, mischief twinkling in her eyes. She focused her attention down on little Hannah. "You'll like it at the ranch, won't you, sweetheart? Yes, you will! You'll have lots of fun! Because watching your mama learn to hold her tongue and keep her temper should be quite a show, indeed."

Chapter Five

By one o'clock, MacLaren's man had still not made his appearance. "Shall we eat dinner? Once we depart, we will not have the chance to eat again for many hours. Yet what if he appears right in the middle of the meal and expects us to take off that minute?" Juana fretted.

"Never pass up food when it's available. It's a long ride out to Five Mile Hill Ranch, and if he arrives while we're eating we'll just invite him to sit down with us. Men never pass up a chance to eat."

Mrs. Meyer gestured them toward a table filled with steaming bowls of chili and bread still hot from the oven.

"I'm going to miss your chili, Mrs. Meyer," Maude told her.

"I've taught you how to make it, girl. Anytime you have a hankering for it, just stir up some. Remember to use good stewed beef and lots of chili pepper, and don't be shy with the jalapeños. If it doesn't bite you when you lay a spoonful on your tongue—"

"It's not Mrs. Meyer's chili," the two finished in perfect unison, then giggled.

Juana had still not taken her seat. "There he is, just as we figured," she said, staring out the window to where a cloud of dust heralded a wagon coming toward them.

A middle-aged man with thinning black hair and a dusty bandana slung low around his neck jumped down from the wagon with a lumbering grace, knocked hesitantly on the front door of the boardinghouse, then straightened and blinked in surprise as Juana went forward and opened the door to him.

"Buenas tardes," she said in lilting, melodious Spanish, and Maude was glad of all the Spanish words her father had made her learn so long ago. "I am Juana Benavides. You have come to take Miss Harkey, the baby and me out to Five Mile Hill Ranch, no? We were just having dinner. Won't you sit down and have some chili with us before we go?"

"*Mucho gusto,* senorita," the man murmured, and Maude could see that he was much taken with the sight of the pretty Juana. "I would be happy to join you for your meal, of course. I am Hector Gonsalvo, Senor MacLaren's *segundo*—his right-hand man," he added in English, for Maude and Mrs. Meyer's sake. "I did not know I would have the honor of *two* ladies' company today."

The man might as well have thumped his chest like a gorilla, he was so obviously impressed with his own importance.

Maude sniffed. MacLaren better not think he could

renege on the terms of the agreement, at this late stage. But perhaps he had just forgotten to tell Gonsalvo that he was hiring Juana, too. From the way the man was staring at Juana, it was clear that she was someone *he* would not quickly forget.

He'd better not think he was going to start up a flirtation with her friend right under her very nose the first afternoon they met, Maude thought, intercepting an approving look from Gonsalvo with a glare. She wasn't taking Juana Benavides away from all that was familiar to her to endanger her honor.

"My friend Mrs. Benavides will be caring for baby Hannah," Maude said tartly, nodding toward the cradle in which the baby lay dozing a few feet away. "She lost her husband and baby only a few days ago."

Gonsalvo blinked and looked at her, reminding her of a puppy who had just been scolded too harshly. "I can see the color she wears, senorita," he said, nodding toward the unbroken black of Juana's dress and the lace mantilla that covered her luxuriant mass of hair. "You need not doubt for a moment that I will treat her with utmost respect. I am a widower myself. I lost my Maria a year ago, but it seems like it was yesterday."

She shouldn't have said anything, Maude knew now. She felt very small just now, while she assessed the world of sorrow behind the man's dark eyes. When would she learn not to voice every suspicion she had in her head as soon as it bloomed there? Why didn't she give people a chance to prove themselves before she made judgments about their intentions and motivations? *Judge not, lest ye be judged...*

"I'm sorry for overreacting, Senor Gonsalvo. And I am sorry, as well, for your loss." She saw a quick forgiveness in the dark eyes in his weathered face, and was relieved to think she had not made an instant enemy. Life on the ranch would be isolated in the extreme—she needed every friend she could get.

"It's all right, senorita," he said. "It's wise for a young lady not to be too trusting."

Are you warning me about your boss now? she wondered, then realized she was speculating on his motivation again.

Stop it, Maude!

A few minutes later, Gonsalvo signaled he was done with his meal when he pushed his empty bowl away and wiped his mouth with the rough homespun napkin. After complimenting Mrs. Meyer on the food, he asked, "Was the burial of the unfortunate young mother of the baby accomplished this morning?"

Maude nodded solemnly. It had been a lonely affair, attended by just her, Mrs. Meyer and Juana. While Mrs. Detwiler had brought some of her late roses to beautify the grave and Reverend Chapman had been especially eloquent about how not even a sparrow falls without the Lord knowing it, it was hard to think of pretty April Mae Horvath lying alone under the cold sod.

"She has been laid to rest, yes," she said.

"The poor girl," he murmured, then eyed Hannah, who was drowsing in Maude's arms. "The poor orphan baby, as well..." The tall grandfather clock chose this moment to strike two, and Gonsalvo glanced meaningfully at it. "We must make preparations to depart very soon. It is a long way to Five Mile Hill Ranch, and there are some thunderheads brewing to the north that I don't like the look of."

They were loaded onto MacLaren's buckboard within the hour and said their last goodbyes to Mrs. Meyer and the others in the boardinghouse. Maude was touched by the solicitude Gonsalvo showed in making sure Juana and the baby were comfortably ensconced in a padded seat in the corner of the wagon bed with a canvas canopy over them, before MacLaren's foreman clucked to the horses. They set off at a spanking trot eastward out of Simpson Creek. Several people she knew—Mrs. Patterson of the mercantile, Mr. Wallace at the post office, Mr. Amos at the bank—waved at her as they went past. *How long would it be before she saw any of them again?*

They had not even begun the climb for which Five Mile Hill Ranch was named when the thunderhead let loose its burden, sending Juana whimpering as she dove farther under the makeshift canvas cover and clutched Hannah to her, while Maude held her parasol over the baby in an attempt to keep some of the icy November rain away from the quickly-sodden blanket. Gonsalvo tossed Maude his sombrero as a further shield for the baby, a gallant gesture, since it left the man's head at the mercy of the elements, but other than that, there was nothing he could do to help them other than flick the whip over the horses' shoulders to keep up their pace. There was nowhere for them to take shelter until they reached the ranch, which was still quite a distance away.

Hannah didn't approve of her dampness and let them know her displeasure in no uncertain terms. Time dragged at a snail's pace as they tried, in vain, to soothe her. But finally, the seemingly endless hours of the journey came to an end before the ornate wrought-iron gates of the ranch. Gonsalvo pulled up on the horses, bringing them to a halt. Seemingly shocked by the sudden end of the movement that had rattled her around for so long, Hannah's sobs cut off abruptly.

Dusk had closed them around them like a damp, foggy shroud, making the foreman specter-like as he faced them in the gloom.

"We are finally here," he said, pointing to an imposing fieldstone house. "Inside, the MacLarens will have a warm fire and dry clothes, as well as food for us. No doubt little Hannah will rest well once she is no longer cold and her stomach is full."

If she got the chance to lie down, she might never find the strength to rise again, Maude thought, dazed at the sudden cessation of motion and outraged wailing that had accompanied her past several hours of existence.

"Come in the house, all of you," called a woman who appeared to those in the courtyard only as a wavering shadow, backlit by the flickering of the fire inside. "Umberto is coming to care for the beasts, Hector. We've been looking for you these past two hours—Senora Coira's angry at the lateness, I warn you."

"The road's awash in several places between here and Simpson Creek, Senora Morales. Even their William Wallace couldn't have made better time."

So this was the housekeeper who'd been threatening to quit, Maude thought.

"Be careful of playing fast and loose with the name of their hero," the woman warned darkly.

Maude wondered where Jonas MacLaren was. So far he'd ruined his chance to give them a proper welcome, but she supposed the master of such a great estate didn't go wetting his precious head for just anyone. Besides, he couldn't have known exactly when to expect them, and likely had many duties that kept him occupied all over the ranch. But now, as Hector assisted first Juana and Hannah, and then herself, to descend the slippery sides of the wagon safely, she saw a tall, elegant figure emerge from the shadows at the massive carved-wood doorway.

"Welcome to Five Mile Hill, Miss Harkey. I trust you're none the worse for wear after your journey? Unfortunate weather you had, to be sure," he said, his rolled *R*s swirling around her like a velvet cloak warmed at the fire. "I imagine you're soaked to the skin."

"Thank you for the welcome, Mr. MacLaren. There's nothing wrong with me that dry clothes, a hot drink and a good night's sleep won't put right, I expect," she said, assuming a cheerfulness she was far from feeling. She had so hoped to make a good impression on his mother, but how was that to happen when her careful twist of hair had long ago devolved into a soggy wet mass that dripped a goose-bump-raising chill down the neck of her dress?

He made an attempt at a smile. "That's the spirit,

lass. Food and dry clothing are to be had in abundance inside," he said, gesturing that she was to hurry. "I trust the little one made the journey all right?" His eyes seemed to search the occupants of the buckboard, who were now all milling about under the shelter of the ranch house's eaves.

Maude found his mentioning Hannah without being prompted—for the babe had not resumed her wailing as yet—encouraging. "Well enough, though she's in sore need of the same creature comforts we all are."

"Come in, come in!" screeched a tall, thin woman swathed in a colorful length of plaid from the doorway. "No one's waiting for an engraved invitation, are ye? You'll only be getting wetter while you tarry there. Step lively, now—unless you like being cold and hungry!"

That must be the famous Coira MacLaren, Maude thought, as she swept forward with Juana and the baby and Jonas MacLaren toward the glowing maw of the door. Who else would suggest they *wanted* to linger outside in the cold and wet?

Maude felt the warmth of the house close around her like a well-fitting glove as she peered at the spare woman with the fading ginger hair and thin, bony neck. "Thank you, Mrs. MacLaren," she said, determined not to be a mouse in front of this formidable woman. "I'm Maude Harkey, and I thank you for being willing to have us come."

Cold blue eyes assessed her, then shifted on as if they'd seen enough. "And where's this squalling bairn of whom I've heard so much?" she asked.

Maude saw Juana grow rigid at the woman's labeling of the baby they had both come to love so dearly. Though she sympathized with her friend's sense of outrage, she still hoped Juana would let the remark pass. *Woman, you have no idea what you're missing*, she thought, then had to struggle not to smile. Her ears were still savoring the lack of strident noise. Juana straightened, and with grave dignity, presented the now quiet, alert child for the older woman's perusal. Maude gave thanks that the child had stopped the eldritch screeching that she'd been doing for the past few hours.

"Pretty little thing. Too bad about her parents," Coira MacLaren said with a sniff, after a quick examination. "Though it's still to be supposed, I'm informed, that the father will turn up?"

"Possibly," Maude said. "Or rather, eventually he's likely to pass through Simpson Creek—though we have no idea of when to expect him again. We're determined that she will not suffer any lack to the extent we are able to prevent it if he does not return, or does not wish to claim her."

"That remains to be seen, doesn't it?" Coira muttered cryptically, then exchanged a look with her son that Maude couldn't decipher. "The lack of a father is not easily made up."

When had Jonas MacLaren lost his father? To what extent did it explain his arrogance and distant ways? Would she learn the answer while she was here?

"This is Mrs. Juana Benavides," Maude said, realizing she had not introduced Juana. "She is Hannah's nurse."

"My sympathy for your loss, senora," Coira murmured, nodding toward her mourning.

"Gracias." Having gained the entranceway, Juana beckoned for Maude to follow, and within minutes they were shown to a room where they could remove their sodden garments and given dry clothing to wear. Finally, they were able to bask in the heat of a roaring fire.

Maude had no idea where MacLaren had obtained the clothing they now wore—a woolen shirt and skirt in her case. Did he have sisters who were now married? Or frequent guests of all sizes who left their clothing? There was no way to tell just by looking, and she was much too glad to be dry and warm to question it. Hannah, too, surrendered almost instantly, whimpering a little as her sodden garments were pulled off, then subsiding with a contented sigh as her petal-like eyelids drifted shut.

"There's hot soup and good fresh oat bread in the morning room," Coira said when they had all returned in dry clothes, and she chivied them all briskly into a great room with leather-backed chairs in front of a massive rectangular table. The soup was hot and nourishing, filled with shredded beef and stewed vegetables in a tomato-based broth, the bread and fresh butter filling, and Maude felt the last remaining icicles within her thawing.

"My son will give you a tour of the place tomorrow, when, with any luck, it'll be drier and sunnier," Coira MacLaren suddenly announced. "I take my tea and oatcakes at half six in the morning. Senora Morales will help you get it ready."

"Half six?" Did the woman mean six-thirty in the morning? Why on God's green earth did she rise so early? But it wasn't for her to question, Maude knew. This woman was her employer, and it was Maude's place to simply do as she was told. "I'll have them there for you."

Coira MacLaren's eyebrow rose. "Why can't Miss Juana do it, since you'll be my companion the rest of the day? If she's not suckling the babe, that's who I'll expect to see. Start as you mean to go on, that's what I always say."

Maude thought it was an attempt to put Juana in her place from the start, but she knew better than to answer for her.

"Of course, I will bring your tea, Mrs. MacLaren," the Hispanic girl said. "With the little one, I am naturally an early riser these days also. She has usually woken and gone back to nap by that time, so it will be no trouble."

"Well, we certainly don't want to put anyone to any *trouble*, that's for certain," came the matriarch's sarcastic retort.

"It will be our very great pleasure, ma'am," Juana said with a serene smile as if there had been no mockery aimed at her.

Good for you, Juana, Maude thought, and decided the honors for the first skirmish at Casa MacLaren had gone to them. As she watched, Jonas MacLaren's shoulders sagged as he let out a great sigh, as if he agreed and was content it should be so.

"Mama, perhaps we should show Miss Maude and Miss Juana to their rooms and let them make an early evening of it. I'm sure their bones feel fairly rattled from their bodies after their journey here today, not to mention their exhausting morning laying that poor girl to rest and then gathering all their things," Jonas MacLaren said. "No, stay seated, Senora Morales," he added, when the housekeeper would have arisen from her seat on the ottoman. "I can escort them upstairs to their room."

Out of the corner of her eye, Maude noted the narrowing of Coira MacLaren's eyes and knew she didn't like the idea of her son doing what was really something a servant should do, but there was nothing she could do about it without making a scene. And apparently Coira MacLaren picked her battles carefully. With a nod to Juana, Maude turned and the pair of them followed Mr. MacLaren from the room.

The chamber to which he showed them had an eastern exposure and a pair of beds, each with a pecan wood headboard and a canopy of the same yellow-threaded plaid she had seen his mother wearing downstairs.

"It's the same pattern," she observed, and saw his quick smile of approval.

"Miss Harkey, you have a good eye," he said. "Each Scottish clan has its own plaid, and the MacLaren one is storied indeed. After the battle of Culloden, it was illegal for a time to wear the clan tartan," he said, stroking the murky blue, green, yellow and red of the plaid with near-reverence. "Our motto in the Gaelic is *Creag an Tuirc*, or The Boar's Rock."

"I would love to visit Scotland one day," Maude said impulsively. "And learn more of its history."

"Perhaps you shall. And there are certainly those here who can tell you of its lore. 'Twill make my mother glad to hear you have an interest."

Maude nearly informed him she hadn't said it to make his mother glad, but realized there was no need to be confrontational. Her next impulsive question, though, was worse.

"Perhaps I shouldn't ask on my first night here, but I can't resist—why does everyone tiptoe around your mother so much? She seemed nice enough to me," she said, then watched for his answer. Coira hadn't been perfectly "nice," of course, but she wanted to let Jonas know she was up to the challenge of dealing with his mother.

"Do you never resist the irresistible, Miss Maude?" he said, his eyes kindling with a golden light. "'Nice enough,' is it? You have not known her an hour altogether. There's a fierceness to her you have not seen."

"Fierceness? Surely not. A little sarcasm, perhaps, but no more so than you might see in many ladies her age."

"Nay, 'tis far more than that, Miss Harkey, and far from common, as well. Indeed, I know of no one who is the match of my mother. And I'll venture it's safe to say you've never met a woman who'd kill to protect her child."

The words echoed in the air between them—*kill to protect her child.* She didn't know she had echoed the words aloud until he took a step back, shaking his head.

"Nay, Miss Maude. I've said too much. It's a tale you never need to hear. It's not conducive to a good night's sleep. I only hope I have not frightened you—there's nothing you need fear here, especially if 'a little sarcasm' does not bother you." He made a weak attempt at a smile and raked a hand though his red-gold hair, seeming to be calculating whether he had been gone too long. Maude guessed his mother was carefully monitoring the minutes since he had left the room. "And now I'll bid you good-night, and let you seek your rest, ladies."

"What do you suppose he meant by that?" she asked Juana, after he'd put the heavy oaken door between them and the sounds of his booted feet had died away on the stairs.

"Quién sabe?" answered Juana, who was busying herself with settling Hannah in the trestle bed she had pulled out from beneath her own. "Who knows? Perhaps we shall learn the truth of it someday while we are here. And if we do not, then perhaps we are better off not knowing."

"And ye shall learn the truth, and the truth shall set you free," Maude quoted, still seeing the bleak look on Jonas's face as he'd said, *You've never met a woman who'd kill to protect her child.* What child, she wondered. Was he speaking of himself? Was he the child who had needed such ferocious protection? He seemed so strong, so indomitable—it was hard to imagine him needing help or protection from anyone.

"Will that truth set us free?" she wondered aloud. Somehow, she doubted it. Jonas MacLaren knew the truth—and from the look she had seen in his eyes when he spoke of it, the memory haunted him still and would never let him free.

Chapter Six

Jonas MacLaren woke the next morning to the sound of heavy crockery splintering against the tile floor. "How dare ye bring me that heavy red mug, as if I was a loutish crofter who couldn't be trusted with the fine china?" demanded a shrill voice he knew to be his mother's. "I said bring the Royal Doulton cup, and that's what I'll have, girl!"

He heard footsteps, and a soft voice murmuring an apology. Senora Juana had just learned the importance of following Coira's instructions exactly, he thought, wincing at the earliness of her harsh lesson. It wouldn't surprise him if Senora Morales, jealously protective of her position in this strange household, had set the young widow up for failure by providing the exact opposite of what his mother had specified. The housekeeper's constant threats to quit would hold less sway over the household if Juana seemed poised to take her place at a moment's notice—hence the need to keep the newcomer in disgrace.

The polite Juana would not have wanted to argue when the housekeeper had not complied with her relayed instructions, and the sound of splintering crockery was the inevitable result. The poor lass. He should have warned her, he supposed. She had not asked for this new situation in her life and was the most essential of them under this roof, at least in baby Hannah's opinion.

His drowsy brain shifted to the last of the newcomers—Miss Maude Harkey. He could still picture her widened eyes the previous night when he'd said too much. What was it about the red-haired lass that had made him babble his secrets so? The one thing he had vowed never to tell anyone—how his mother had risked her own life to protect her young son's—and he'd jabbered it like a magpie her first night under his roof! She'd not forget he'd said it, and would require a full explanation in the not-too-distant future, of this he was certain. He *had* to regain his control over his willful tongue, or this situation would end in disaster. His mother would not thank him for letting someone else in on the truth of their shameful past.

In the meantime, the least he could do was to make sure Juana's second trip to deliver Coira's morning tea was more successful than her first.

Dressing quickly, he made his way down the passageway that led to the ranch house's kitchen, and was in time to meet the young widow, flanked by an indignant-looking Maude, who carried a disgruntled-looking baby Hannah, while Juana bore a steaming cup of coffee in the specified fancy china cup.

"I hear Mother's in her usual high spirits," he said wryly. "Sorry for a jolting beginning to your morning, ladies," he apologized, while his gaze found and silently accused Senora Morales of setting Juana up. The housekeeper had the grace to look abashed.

"If by that you mean she's like a spoiled child, you'd be right, Mr. MacLaren," Maude said. "Obviously she was given her way too often as a child. She's woken Hannah with her screeching, and for what reason? The mistaken choice of a cup?" Her eyes blazed with contempt toward Coira and indignation over the way her friend had been treated.

Jonas drew back. "And you're a bit too given to jumping to conclusions so early in the morning, Miss Harkey. Best have a care until you know the facts of the matter."

His remark was delivered just sharply enough that she realized that she did indeed owe him the roof over their heads—a roof that provided protection for Hannah, she reminded herself. *Servants, be obedient to your masters, serving them wholeheartedly*, Paul had written to the early church. She had to remember she was no longer Maude Harkey, pampered daughter of the late town physician, but a servant, whose continued presence in this house depended on pleasing her masters.

"I'm sorry, Mr. MacLaren," she said with all the meekness she could summon. "Of course you're right, and I regret my hasty words. No doubt we'll learn much in these first few days, and now we'd better hasten on to give Mrs. MacLaren her coffee and breakfast," she added to Juana, with a gesture for her to continue. She certainly didn't think the oatcakes looked very appetizing—nothing like one of Ella's hearty, appetizing breakfasts at the café. But again, it wasn't her place to say.

"'Tis all right, lass," he surprised her by saying, or maybe it was the softer look in his eyes that surprised her more. "I understand 'tis all new for ye, but 'twill soon become familiar."

She had to remind herself of her newly made resolve to be a perfect servant when she held the door open for Juana, only to hear Mrs. MacLaren greet her friend with a snapped, "Well, it's about time!" which set Hannah to whimpering all over again.

"What's the bairn fussing about?" Maude heard the woman ask.

"*Perdón, lo siento,* senora," Juana said politely. "She's a...bit late having her own breakfast."

"Well, aren't you her nurse?" the woman demanded, her tone holding a testy edge. "Why don't you go ahead and feed her?"

"Right here, senora? You do not mind?"

"Don't be silly," came the rapid retort. "I nursed Jonas when he was a wee babe, naturally. When a bairn's hungry, you feed it, or don't they believe that in this benighted Texas?"

"Of course we do, ma'am, thank you," Juana responded, and a moment after she settled herself in a nearby chair, the whimpering stopped. "And I promise your breakfast will be served more smoothly tomorrow."

"I imagine it will be," Coira replied. "You seem very competent with the babe, so no doubt it's just a matter of getting used to a new routine." Her calmer tone conveyed forgiveness for the way the morning had started off, and while it was not exactly an apology, it was more than Maude had hoped for.

"Yes, senora," Juana agreed.

"Is there…anything else we can get you?" Maude asked.

"Perhaps you could remind Senora Morales I'll need some hot water to wash with," Coira said in the same softened tone, though her voice warned that the housekeeper knew very well she needed it and should have brought it already. "And when you see my son, please remind him we need to discuss moving the cattle down from the hills. It's getting on toward winter."

To Maude's surprise, she found Jonas leaning against the wall outside his mother's room as if he had nothing else to do but wait on her reappearance.

"*Och*, but you look none the worse for talking to her," he said in mock relief. "I was worried for naught, it seems."

She felt a jolt of warmth that he had worried about her, though she figured he was really just exaggerating, and only meant to tease her.

"On the contrary, I think we understand each other better now," she told him, then delivered Coira's message about moving the cattle before she could forget to tell him.

"Aye, it's mid-November, so I suppose it is getting near to winter. Though winter in the Hill Country of Texas is a far different proposition, I've found, than facing a proper gale in the Highlands."

Maude was about to retort that he must never have seen a "blue norther" blow in, where the temperature was fully capable of plunging from blazing heat to an ice storm in mere hours, but before she could, he spoke again.

"Speaking of the weather, it's quite mild out there today—which leads me to what I waited to ask you. Would you like a tour of the ranch today? A proper horseback tour, not more jolting around in the buck-board in the midst of a rainstorm? You *do* ride, don't you?"

Maude still ached from the jolting, soaking ride yesterday, but after the way he questioned if she rode, she found she could not resist rising to the challenge. "Do I ride? Mr. MacLaren, I am a Texas woman, born and bred—of course I ride, sir. Just give me a few minutes to change my clothes and let Juana know what I'll be doing." She felt a guilty twinge, knowing Juana would have relished such a tour, too, but to fulfill their duties someone would need to stay with Mrs. MacLaren. And besides, unless she missed her guess, she thought Hector would offer to take Juana on a tour of her own before long.

He grinned at her words. "I'll tell Hector to saddle a mount for you."

He started to walk away to do as he said, but she called after him, "Oh, and would you tell him a regular saddle will be fine, rather than a sidesaddle? I have a divided skirt that I use for riding, Mr. MacLaren—unless you think your mother would disapprove?"

Jonas's eyebrow had risen at her request for a regular saddle, but she agreed with Coira's idea of "starting as you mean to go on," and she might as well make it clear that she had no intention of riding over the ranch using a fussy sidesaddle, especially on an unfamiliar mount. She'd had the divided skirt made for her by her friend, and the original founder of the Spinsters' Club, Milly Brookfield, after seeing the one she used.

"Good for you, Miss Maude," he said, giving her a mock salute. "How very sensible you are, to be sure. I'm sure my mother won't care either way. Very well, I'll meet you in the parlor downstairs in half an hour, if that's enough time for you to change."

He was as good as his word, appearing in denim trousers and boots, and gave her split skirt an approving look before presenting her with the floppy-brimmed hat he carried.

"You'll ruin that peaches-and-cream complexion, Miss Maude, if you don't shield it from the sun, even in mid-November. I'm surprised that a Texas woman wouldn't know that."

She would not have been female if she hadn't appreciated the compliment to her complexion hidden in his words and his having a care for the sun's effect on it. She started to say she hadn't been vain enough to worry about her complexion lately, but something stopped her and she merely said, "Thank you."

He led her outside to where Hector waited, holding the reins of a strapping sorrel as well as those of a gray gelding.

"This is Stirling, Senorita Harkey," Hector said, indicating the gray. "He'll carry you well. He hasn't a treacherous bone in his body."

"Sterling? Like silver? What an apt name." She stroked the horse's arched neck.

"No, like Stirling Castle, Stirling, with an I," Jonas said. With his accent, the word came out *Stirlin'*. Then, noticing her lack of reaction to the name, he added, "Stirling is called the Gateway to the Highlands. 'Twas the scene of a great battle many years ago between the English and the Scots."

Another bit of Scottish history she didn't know. Taking advantage of Hector holding the reins, she mounted the gelding, aware of Jonas's eyes on her as she did so, and proud that she accomplished the move with grace.

Once she had settled herself, she followed MacLaren as he led the way across a wide meadow that ended in a rise in the ground. As the foreman had promised, the gelding's paces were smooth, and he carried her without fighting against her directions or any attempts to trick her with a bit of bucking. They headed toward the hills that formed a ring around the ranch.

He led her first to a field where scores of longhorned cattle grazed.

"A fine herd," she commented, seeing that the varicolored beasts appeared fat and content.

"Aye," he said. "They'll be going to market the next time Brookfield organizes a cattle drive to Abilene or wherever he thinks best." Maude nodded at the reference to Milly's husband, who owned a nearby ranch. "'Tis good neighbors we have here, who work together for everyone's good."

"Nick Brookfield's a good man," she said, figuring MacLaren found much in common with his fellow British expatriate, for Brookfield had come from England only a few years ago. His marriage to Milly was the first success story for the Spinsters' Club.

As they climbed toward the ring of hills that surrounded the ranch, Maude spotted dozens of black-faced sheep with heavy wool coats, some with curling horns, all cropping what remained of the summer grass amidst the limestone hills. Here and there she spied small black-and-white collies and shepherds keeping a watchful eye on their charges.

"How heavy their wool looks," she commented. "What kind are they?"

"Merinos and Blackies—Black-Faced Highlands, mostly. We brought them with us from Scotland, since they're used to the hills. Everything woolen on this ranch—including our tartans—is spun from their wool. They're sheared in the spring."

"I imagine their lambs are darling," she murmured, picturing little black-faced lambs gamboling on the sides of the hills.

She'd forgotten how unsentimental a man Jonas was. "Aye, 'darling,'" he said. "I wonder if you'll still think so when you have a bleating orphan or two to raise and feed every few hours. There's always a couple that are rejected by their mothers or whose mothers die, for whatever reason. The lambs are too valuable to be allowed to perish with them, so it's up to everyone on the ranch to contribute to their care."

Thinking of hand-raising an orphan black-faced lamb made her smile. She'd never been able to have pets, growing up at the tiny doctor's residence. How fun it would be for Hannah to watch the little lambs grow from close at hand. This was a delightful aspect to becoming a mother—she was already looking forward to the wonderful experiences she could give her precious child. "I'll gladly help, if that happens," she pledged, and was relieved to see him smiling at her in approval again.

"So when was this battle of Stirling you named the horse for?" she asked, after the silence stretched on between them for a while.

"The battle of Stirling Bridge took place in 1297, and involved William Wallace. Nearby to it, the battle of Bannockburn happened in 1314, involving Robert the Bruce. Both men are considered great Scots heroes, as you'll no doubt learn, living here."

"Robert 'the' Bruce?" she said. "What's a Bruce?" she asked, thinking it was likely some Scottish nobility title she wasn't aware of.

MacLaren chuckled. "'The' means he's the senior member of his clan, the head of the household. I am considered 'the MacLaren' by my mother, or any other true Scot." There was a flatness to his tone then, and he avoided her gaze—an unusual shift, since prior to that he had seemed pleased and proud to tell her about Scottish history and customs.

"You seem so very Scottish at times," she observed. "How long has your family been in America?"

"Since the summer of 1863," he said. His tone was bitter. Clearly the memory was not a pleasant one. Had he suffered from a particularly rough or unpleasant crossing? Or was there something else behind his sour look?

"We landed at New York City just in time for me to be caught up in the draft riots affecting the city then," he continued. "Since none of my new countrymen could tell a Scottish accent from an Irish one, we were thought to be Irish, who were considered the scum of the earth there at that time. Thus I was swept into the Union Army like every other lad who didn't have three hundred dollars to buy his way out of the draft. I went from immigrant to cannon fodder before I'd properly lost my sea legs."

No wonder he was bitter. "Why would you choose to come from Scotland to a land in the middle of civil war?" she wondered aloud, and winced inwardly as she saw that wintry, distant look shutter his eyes again. When, oh, *when* would she learn to keep her thoughts to herself? Somehow, she had managed once again to ask a question on a forbidden subject.

"As dangerous as it was to be a new American, it would have been more dangerous still for my mother and I to stay in Scotland when we left it," he said, lips thinned and tight. She waited, hoping he would explain further, but he clucked to his horse and the big sorrel stated moving again. Evidently the interview was at an end—*the maddening man*!

"So how did you end up in Texas, after starting out in New York?" she persisted, kneeing her horse to follow his.

Perhaps he sensed her exasperation with his earlier vague answer, for he answered readily enough. "I was mustered out of the army after Appomattox, of course, and I returned to our tenement in New York City to find Mother more than ready for a change of location," he said. "She longed to be away from the noise and bustle in New York, and wanted to live somewhere that wasn't flat, where she could enjoy a climate that wasn't so bitterly cold in the winter as New York City. We chose the Ozark country of Missouri at first, because it was most like the highlands, but it didn't seem like a good fit. 'Twas a border state in your war, aye? Too many folk there seemed to be still fighting the war."

"So you chose the Hill Country of Texas, after living in Missouri for a while, you said. Why would you choose one of the conquered, beaten states of the Confederacy after leaving the Union Army?"

"Since the 'Fifteen' and the 'Forty-Five'—the big battles between Scotland and England in which Scotland took a thorough drubbing—a Scot is used to living in conquered territory," he said. "Not being Southerners, though, we were able to come and buy land at a reasonable price, thanks to the last owner of Five Mile Hill Ranch being a thoroughgoing scoundrel, as I understood it."

"Drew Allbright?" she said. "Calling him a scoundrel is the understatement of the year." Briefly, she told him how the once-respected newcomer to Simpson Creek had nearly murdered Nick's sister Violet Brookfield—now Violet Brookfield Masterson—and Raleigh, who won her love and saved her from Allbright's clutches. "He's now serving time at Huntsville Prison," she concluded. "And Violet's married to her Raleigh."

"Just in time for me to buy Five Mile Hill Ranch at a bargain price," he said. "How convenient for me. And Raleigh won the fair maiden. Love conquers all," he said as if concluding the tale for her. His old mocking tone had returned.

What female made him so cynical? Maude wondered, not for the first time. She sensed he hadn't told her half of what he could have about his history and what brought him here, but the edge in his voice and that guarded look in his golden eyes warned her not to probe further just now.

They stopped to water their horses at a branch of the Colorado that wound its way through the low hills at the boundary of the ranch. "No tour of Five Mile Hill Ranch can be considered complete without enjoying the view at the overlook here," he said, reining in and pointing back the way they'd come.

She gasped as she looked in the direction his finger pointed. Below them, Five Mile Hill Ranch was spread out before them, the ranch house looking sturdy and yet elegant even from a distance, with smoke curling from its chimneys and the bunkhouse lying at a right angle to it, behind the barn.

"What a view—it's beautiful," she said sincerely. "Are you glad you've come to Texas?" she dared to ask.

He shrugged. "Time will tell, I expect. So far, I like it. There are good people here, and my mother seems content—as content as the woman can be, I suppose. I'm not sorry to have left New York City, that's for sure. I'm not a man for the big city—I feel trapped when I can barely see the sky for the big buildings, let alone breathe the air."

She knew he was telling the truth. He seemed to *fit* here in Texas, somehow. She hoped he would find happiness here. He seemed sorely in need of it. "What's that little cottage there?" she asked, indicating a smaller building to the left of the ranch house.

"That's Senora Morales's house," he told her. "No doubt she'll invite you and Miss Juana for tea and *dulce de leche*, once she knows you both better."

Maude had tasted the sweet confection as a child, thanks to a Tejana housekeeper that had worked for her father and mother, and she gave an unconscious sigh of delighted anticipation.

He smiled at her reaction. "I see you're acquainted with it. So tell me, how is it that you're not living on your own ranch or a house in town, with your own Mexican housekeeper to make *dulce de leche* for you?"

She was surprised that he had asked her such a probing question.

"Come now, Miss Maude," he teased. "Turnabout is fair play, surely," he said in a mock-chiding tone. "I've answered your questions about my personal history—surely 'tis fair for you to answer one or two of mine."

It was fair, she supposed. "All right," she agreed. "Though I haven't figured out the answers completely myself. I grew up the pampered daughter of the town doctor, and the picture you just painted was certainly how I pictured my life at this stage."

"And what transpired to prevent it?"

"The Comanches," she said. "They raided one day, and Papa was killed along with a few other unfortunate Simpson Creek citizens. I went from being the doctor's precious daughter to being an orphan, for my mother had already passed on. When Dr. Walker came to be the new doctor, I lost my home."

"I see," he said, and she was relieved to see compassion but no pity in his gaze. It was always painful, retelling what had happened, and she could not have borne pity from him, especially since she now knew that he and his mother had lost their homeland, thanks to whatever had caused them to flee their beloved Scottish Highlands.

"But you told me you're the leader of an intrepid band of ladies called the Spinsters' Club," he went on. "And the purpose of the group is to make matches for its ladies, which it has done with some success since the war left the town without eligible young men."

He turned to face her directly then, and there was an edge of disbelief in his voice when he spoke.

"Yet there was no happy match for you? Are the men of this part of Texas *blind*, then? How is it you're still *Miss* Maude Harkey? These hills should be watered with the tears of your disappointed suitors."

His questions provoked the old pain within her.

"A gentleman never asks a lady why she is not wed, Mr. MacLaren," she said archly. "It calls for her to confess all her failings, all the faults that have kept her from becoming the light of some man's life."

"Forgive me," he murmured. "But who said I was a gentleman, Miss Maude?" he asked her then. "And apart from a tart, too-ready tongue, I have not seen any faults in you…just yet."

His remark stole her breath. He hadn't seen any faults in her? What about her temper, and her tendency to argue and to be opinionated? Was he being sincere now? There was no shadow in those golden eyes, no quirk of his mouth to suggest otherwise. Did that mean he found her…*fair*? *Attractive? Worth knowing?*

The idea flustered her to the point where she almost didn't know what to say. She was so accustomed to being overlooked by men that having that sharp focus directed at her left her shaken. Should she be flattered? Perhaps. But instead, all she felt was unsettled. She prided herself on being capable and calm in nearly every circumstance. She could face a bleeding wound without flinching, could sit by a deathbed with quiet resignation. She did not panic or lose her poise during any manner of sickness or injury. Medical emergencies were familiar to her and therefore held no fear for her. But a man's admiration…that was new and strange. And in that moment all she wanted was to put some distance between them so she could recapture her sense of self-possession, which had mysteriously vanished.

"Thank you, but perhaps we had better return to the house," she said quickly. "The afternoon is getting late, and little Hannah can be very fussy at this time of day. I wouldn't want to overburden Juana," she added. She reined the gray around, and nudged him into an easy, rolling canter in the direction of the barn.

The rest of the tour could be postponed for now.

While she would like to see more of the place that was now her home, she knew she'd be far more comfortable in a setting with a little *less* of this puzzling, discomfiting man.

Chapter Seven

After making sure the scent of horse was washed away and changing her clothes, Maude found Jonas—the MacLaren, she reminded herself, amused at the idea of the title—along with his mother and Juana cozily ensconced in chairs in the parlor in front of a roaring fire. Juana looked not in the least "overburdened" with the care of Hannah; in fact, Mrs. MacLaren was holding the baby and smiling as fondly as if she were the child's grandmother as she clapped the baby's hands together and hummed some nonsense song.

Hannah seemed to be enjoying being the center of attention; one of her precious moments of focused alertness lit her baby features. Maude wondered why Juana wasn't helping the housekeeper prepare supper, since her friend was not currently occupied with the baby, but she supposed she'd find out about that later.

"I hope you're being agreeable, young lady," Maude greeted the baby. "She *can* be a little cranky in the afternoons," she explained to Mrs. MacLaren.

"So Juana was telling me. Nothing unusual about a little colic in a newborn bairn. It's probably just that you two are new at mothering and indulge her fussing. She likely only wants the attention," Coira MacLaren opined, with the calm assurance that this far from her childbearing years, she must be right. She apparently had no idea how condescending she sounded. Or perhaps she knew and simply didn't care. "But we're having a marvelous time, aren't we, wee lassie?" She looked back at Maude. "My son tells me you're quite the competent horsewoman, Maude."

Maude couldn't help the way her eyes widened and her gaze involuntarily flew to Jonas. "It was kind of him to say so," she said, surprised to learn he had been speaking about her, and in a complimentary way, too, in front of his mother. "But I'm afraid it's not such a remarkable accomplishment here. Most Texans, men and women, learn to ride before they can walk properly." She remembered following her father's buggy out into the country on her pony when he'd go on doctor calls.

She turned back to Mrs. MacLaren. "I really enjoyed the ride—especially the lovely view of the ranch house from the overlook. It was marvelous, seeing the ranch and its outbuildings spread out like that, and the livestock… I've never seen such thick-wooled sheep before." She'd never seen many sheep at all before, truth be told.

"Aye, our Scottish merinos and Blackies," Coira MacLaren said, her face proud. "All our tartans are spun of their wool. I don't know why you Texan ranchers are so anti-sheep, when they're so useful, both for food and clothing."

Maude knew why. This was cattle country. Ranchers claimed that sheep poisoned a pasture so that their cattle wouldn't graze on it after sheep had been there. There was nothing poisonous about the sheep, of course. It was only that they tended to graze so thoroughly that they consumed the grass down to the roots, so that there was no grazing to be had for weeks. As for the benefits to come from raising sheep, Maude didn't personally care for the taste of mutton, and she couldn't stomach the idea of eating a sweet little lamb, either, no matter how much more tender it was than the mutton from a sheep full grown.

"She's already volunteered to foster an orphan lamb or two, come spring," Jonas said.

His mother gave an unintelligible grunt—*was she skeptical that Maude would even be here that long*?

Coira MacLaren cleared her throat. "Well, if it wouldn't be too much trouble, would one of you ladies fetch me some hot tea, and find out when Senora Morales means to serve supper?" she asked, a pettish tone creeping into her voice. "You two weren't around at noon—you've got to be hungry, even if you took some oatcakes to munch on," she said to Maude and her son.

"I will, Senora MacLaren," Juana said, rising gracefully and leaving the room.

Maude couldn't help but notice the way Jonas MacLaren's gaze followed her friend. Was he, too, becoming attracted to the pretty Mexican widow? Little Hannah noticed that her nurse was leaving, too, though, and let out a little wail that escalated in seconds to full-scale distress.

"Ah, *niña*, I wasn't going to be gone for long," Juana said, returning and reaching out to get the infant. "Would you like to come, too?"

"I can hold her, Juana," Maude assured her, and held out her hands but Hannah refused to accept a substitute, crying disconsolately until Juana retraced her steps for her.

"See, I told you—spoiled rotten, already," sniffed Coira MacLaren as she relinquished the fretful baby. "Scottish babies are not so cosseted, I promise ye. They spend hours outside in the fresh air, no matter the weather and with no heed paid to their whims, so they grow up tough, not always expecting a woman to be comforting them."

Maude was careful to keep her face expressionless, but she couldn't help but wonder, *Was that what had caused that hardness within Jonas MacLaren? Had this woman never given him the assurance that he could count on her love and care, through thick and thin? And yet he'd said she had killed to protect him...*

Juana returned before Maude managed to dismiss that thought, and reported that supper was indeed ready, according to the housekeeper. She seemed amused by something, but she didn't let on what it was.

"Why didn't you help with the cooking?" Maude whispered as they arose from their seats and headed for the dining room. "If it was because I was gone, I'm sorry."

The secret smile faded from her friend's lovely features as she whispered back, "I tried, but nothing I did suited her! She threw me out of the kitchen! She's *impossible*, that one! And the food is, too—you'll see!"

When they got to the dining room, the first dish that was passed to her was stewed mutton—hence the reason for Juana's expression during the earlier conversation in the parlor, for Maude had told her of her dislike of mutton. But she had no idea what the next dish was. It had a savory aroma, but she'd never seen anything like it. She looked up to find Mrs. MacLaren watching her with great anticipation.

"Wondering what that is, are ye?" she asked. Now it was she who wore a secretive smile. "'Tis a very traditional Scottish dish, known as haggis. 'Tis the minced-up lungs, liver and heart of a sheep, mixed with oats and seasoned with onions and spices, and cooked in the sheep's stomach."

For a moment, Maude could only stare at the woman in horror. Surely she was teasing her and would admit she was joking in a moment.

Mrs. MacLaren grinned openly at her discomfiture. "I'm sorry ye shan't have the proper experience for yer first time trying it, 'tis supposed to be piped in—brought in to the music of bagpipes—but we're short of a piper, here in Texas," she said.

She stared across the table, first at Juana, who mouthed the word *loco*, and then to Jonas, who to her surprise, actually looked sympathetic.

"I'm sorry," he said, "'tis a rite of passage, I suppose you might call it, that Mother enjoys putting non-Scottish guests through. 'Twill be all right if you'd rather just eat the mutton and the soup—that's called 'cock-a-leekie,' but 'tis just chicken broth and onions, there being no proper leeks to be had here," he said, his golden eyes reassuring, but also retaining a glint of amusement.

It had been a long day, full of new experiences and the exertion of riding, and Maude was tired of being the MacLarens' source of enjoyment. "No, I'm sure if it's good enough for a Scot, it's good enough for a Texan," she said, and helped herself, a little defiantly, to the unimaginable concoction.

"That's the spirit," Jonas approved, even as Juana said she'd just have the soup.

Maude glanced over in time to see a look of admiration on Coira's face, too, and was surprised. So serving her haggis had been a test?

Maude found the strange concoction not too bad, once she got past the idea of its ingredients. She supposed Texans ate some strange things, too—she'd consumed fried rattlesnake, as well as candy made of cactus and the so-called "prairie oysters" obtained when young bull calves were made into steers.

At least dessert was pleasant and easily enjoyed—freshly made buttery shortbread cookies. Afterward, everyone retired to the parlor, and Mrs. MacLaren picked up a thick leather-bound volume and handed it to Maude.

"Have you read aught by our national bard, Robbie Burns?" Mrs. MacLaren asked.

Maude had to admit she had not, but looking over poems titled "To a Mouse" and "Scots Wha Hae," she found some of the Gaelic spellings of words incomprehensible.

"Perhaps Mr. MacLaren should read it to give it the proper flavor?" she asked, offering him the volume, then realized she didn't even know if he could read.

Evidently he'd had some schooling, though, for he accepted the book and she found she understood the stirring lines quite easily when he read them.

At one point, though, he laughed as he looked over at Juana, who was holding Hannah.

"Looks like Robbie Burns and I have bored the wee lass into slumber," he said, smiling as he gazed at the sleeping baby.

"I'll put Hannah to bed," Juana announced, "and return in just a bit."

Maude was torn, wishing she could be the one to put her baby to bed, for there was nothing sweeter than the way Hannah clung to her before surrendering to sleep. But this time, at least, it was probably better that she stay with Jonas and his mother.

"Do ye like our national bard, then?" Mrs. MacLaren said as Juana took the baby away.

"I do," Maude agreed, "very much." Burns was an excellent poet, but if she was honest, she had enjoyed Jonas's musical voice even more than the words themselves. It had been a good decision to hand him the book.

"What about Sir Walter Scott, then? Have you read anything by him?"

Maude thought Violet, Raleigh Masterson's English bride, had brought a book of his or two with her, but she had to admit she hadn't read them as yet. Her life at the boardinghouse helping Mrs. Meyer, as well as assisting Ella with cooking and service at her café, hadn't left her much time for reading. She shook her head.

"Are you willing to read aloud for a while?" Mrs. MacLaren asked with surprising eagerness. She handed Maude another leather-bound volume, and Maude read the title, *Ivanhoe*, in gilt lettering across the front.

"Certainly, if you don't think my Texas drawl will mangle Mr. Scott's prose," she said.

"It might make an interesting mix," the older woman said with one of her all-too-rare smiles.

Maude began reading, and was soon caught up in the stirring medieval tale. But it was apparent by the end of the first chapter that Mrs. MacLaren was drowsy. Maude laid the book down and offered to help Mrs. MacLaren get ready for bed.

"It's been a pleasant evening," Coira MacLaren murmured as she allowed Maude to lead her away. She sounded almost surprised. "A taste of home, between the haggis and the Burns and Sir Walter. You've been good to put up with it all, Maude, hasn't she, Jonas?"

Maude had thought Jonas's mind far away, but he nodded his agreement. "Here in Texas, they'd say she has sand, aye?" he said with a wink.

"Why, thank you, Mr. MacLaren. Mrs. MacLaren, would you like me to comb out your hair?"

"That would be very nice. Senora Morales doesn't offer to do that very often. I suppose that Juana has gone on to bed?"

Maude knew how easy it was to grow drowsy, as

one rocked and soothed a tired baby who wasn't quite ready to surrender to sleep. "I think she must have. Will you mind if I help you, this once?"

"No, that would be fine," Coira MacLaren said with surprising flexibility. "Any lass who can down haggis with as little missishness as you did is welcome to help me."

Jonas carried his mother up the stairs with the apparent ease of long practice.

Coira's room was as austere as her heart, plainly though comfortably furnished. But she was surprised to notice a little anteroom leading out of the bedroom, and while Jonas assisted his mother to bed, Maude went into it and found a small room lined with large windows and filled with a multitude of potted plants of all varieties, including several types of cactus and some which would have flowers in the warmer seasons. There were herbs of all kinds and aloe with big fleshy leaves.

"I see you've found Mother's greenhouse," Jonas said, coming up behind her. "She has quite the green thumb, my mother does. Always ask her before you water something—she kens which ones need it and which do better with less, aye?"

Maude nodded her understanding.

"I'll leave you to your duties, then," he said.

After he left, Maude found there was something soothing about combing out and replaiting the older woman's faded ginger hair. Mrs. MacLaren seemed to think so, too, for she was quiet and looked content as Maude worked her way through the task.

"You're a good girl, Maude Harkey," Jonas's mother said a few minutes later, once Maude had helped her into a nightgown and into her bed. "You've made a good start today. Jonas did well to bring you here, I think."

Blinking at the unexpected praise, Maude decided she *had* made quite a bit of progress toward acceptance by her new employers during her first full day at Five Mile Hill Ranch, especially since the day had begun with shattered crockery thrown in a fit of temper, yet was ending so tranquilly.

"But tell that Juana she is to bring my tea on time and in the proper cup in the morning," Coira ordered, just when Maude was feeling very satisfied with herself. A perfect illustration of pride going before a fall, Maude thought ruefully. Clearly it would take more than one day to soften the imperiousness out of Coira MacLaren.

When Maude left the old woman's room, she wondered what to do next—return to the parlor or seek her own bed? The idea of being with Jonas MacLaren, alone, in front of the fire, was a puzzling contradiction for the way it made her feel. On the one hand she was drawn to him and wondered if more time alone with him would incline him to provide more pieces of the puzzle about himself.

On the other hand, the idea of being alone with him made her nervous. He looked at her too closely, and saw things other men had never bothered to see. She had no experience with handling such intense attention, and she wasn't certain she entirely liked the flustered way it made her feel.

No, she would not rejoin the bewildering Mr. MacLaren tonight. Instead, she headed to the bedroom she shared with Juana.

Her friend had indeed fallen asleep next to baby Hannah and was snoring softly. Maude lifted Hannah into her cradle, then spent a few moments staring down at the child. She had taken this position for the child's sake, and she did not regret the decision. Hannah would grow up healthy and happy here, she was sure. But when she had agreed to take the post, she had spent so much time considering what life on the ranch would be like for Hannah that she had devoted little time to what it would be like for herself. It was…not quite as she had anticipated. Maude kissed the baby's tiny forehead, then knelt by her bed to say her prayers.

Climbing into bed, she closed her eyes and ended her day wondering what she and Jonas might have talked about if she had returned to the parlor instead.

Chapter Eight

The next two days passed so peacefully that Jonas kept looking around to see if he had somehow wandered into the wrong house. Coira's explosions of temper, such as the one that had marked the morning of the ladies' first day at the ranch, had decreased to one or two a day, and seemed more a matter of fretful habit than anything else. The housekeeper had stopped threatening to leave. Jonas even caught her humming.

Not that his mother's character had been transformed overnight. She still wanted what she wanted, when she wanted it, and quickly, too, but both Maude and the little Tejana widow had lost no time in learning how to please her new mistress. His mother had become quite besotted over the "wee bairn in the house," almost as if little Hannah were her granddaughter, and was not content unless the baby was present, either awake or sleeping, near her. She loved having Maude read to her, which the girl willingly did, apparently without tiring, for hours.

Saturday morning continued mild, warm and sunny

as it had been, and immediately after breakfast Hector appeared and invited Juana to take the same tour of the ranch that Maude had enjoyed two days before. He was quite willing to take baby Hannah with them, but at the suggestion of it, Coira MacLaren jumped up, eyes flashing and asked if everyone had gone quite mad to even consider it. *She* was not about to trust the wee little bairn to the vagaries of a horse's temperament, even if *he* was, for "weren't the daft beasts always spooking and bucking at the least little thing?"

Jonas suspected his mother's real reason was that she didn't want the baby away from her for so much of the day—but he held his peace. It would harm little for his mother to get her way in this, and anyway, she had a point about the ride not being fully safe for a child so small.

The plan was soon amended so that Juana and Hector would go on their tour, but would take care not to be gone that long. Hannah would remain in the ranch house with Maude. Juana promised to return before the time Hannah was usually waking from her afternoon nap and needing to be nursed.

Jonas was amused to see that Hector, heeding Juana's insistence that she was not the horsewoman that Maude was, had brought the tamest, most docile mare in the barn for the nursemaid to ride, and helped her mount as gallantly as a knight of old. *Oh-ho! So that's the way the wind blows!* Unless he was very, very mistaken, his foreman was already rather smitten with the young widow. Jonas wasn't averse to the idea of romance developing between the two, but he hoped his *segundo* would keep in mind how recently the young woman had lost her husband. Juana did not seem quite as smitten as Hector, but he reminded himself she had lost her husband recently. She accepted Hector's courtly attention with a gracious smile, leading Jonas to believe that she might warm to Hector in time, if the man was patient.

Juana Benavides was indeed a pretty woman, and he knew his foreman had been lonely since the death of his wife. Perhaps, when the time was right, Hector would take another bride.

He could hardly fault his foreman for being quickly attracted to the slim, dark Juana, since his own eyes searched the room for Maude whenever he entered the house. Maude, with her dark red hair and flashing blue eyes, seemed to glow in the dim interior of the thick-walled ranch house. Despite his earlier scornful words on the subject of romance, he still had trouble believing what fools these Texas men were for not plucking Maude from the vine long ago.

Yet perhaps he had no right to condemn them, for he would not be courting her, either. Much as he enjoyed the sight of Maude in his home, he was resolved to keep his distance and guard his emotions. He still had no intention of trusting his heart to another female.

But even if he would not let himself love her, he could still appreciate her. He had done a good thing in bringing Maude here. The peace that he had hoped for had seemingly settled on the ranch house at long last. His mother had something new to focus on besides her own aches and ailments, thank the good Lord above.

"Mr. MacLaren, may I ask you something?"

Jonas had just settled down to a noontime bowl of soup in the dining room, and here was Maude with her own bowlful of the same.

"Of course," he said, hoping she couldn't see how glad he was of her presence. "Sit down, Miss Maude. Is the wee one napping, then?"

"Yes, and here's hoping she'll sleep till Juana returns. Your mother sang her to sleep and is dozing by the sunny window in her chair with Hannah in her lap."

"You and Mrs. Benavides have accomplished quite a lot in a short time," he said as she settled herself across the table from him. "I thank you for the calm and quiet, which was all too rare here before your coming. What was your question?"

He liked the way her blue eyes shone at the compliment. It was a peculiarity he had noticed in the lady over the past few days. Praise for being clever, capable or practical were accepted with pleasure. Compliments to her beauty or charm threw her into confusion, as if no one had ever said such things to her before. Yet how could that be?

"Thank you," she said. "This being Saturday, my question was whether anyone would be riding into Simpson Creek for church services on the morrow. The good weather seems to be continuing."

She paled a little as she asked him the question, and he became aware that she'd been apprehensive about asking it. But she looked him right in the eye as she did so, without ducking her head. Aye, she had sand, all right. But he'd have to quash her notion, unfortunately.

"No, no one will be going into town for church tomorrow," he told her. "I'm afraid you might say we're not exactly devout, God-fearing folk, my mother and I…and even if we were, 'tis just too far to be practical. You'd have to rise before dawn and ride hard to make it there in time for the service, and by the time all the pious folk quit yammering prayers, it'd be nightfall before you returned. 'Tis not for me or my mother. And if you were to go alone, who's to do your job while you're gone? Nay, I'm afraid you're needed too much here to go gallivanting off to chapel."

He hated to dim the bright hope in those blue eyes—hated it even more than he hated the feeling of bitter resentment that he always felt when the subject of church was broached. He was bound and determined never to darken the doorstep of a church again…and yet for all that, he was sorry to disappoint Maude's hopes of being able to attend.

"Does no one *ever* go to church from Five Mile Hill Ranch?" she asked, wistfulness clouding over the hope that had bloomed on her face.

"No. We'd have to stand the expense of a hotel room and go in on Saturday, and the MacLarens' purse strings have never extended to such things."

"Did you ever think of building a Sunday house, as some of the ranchers have in Simpson Creek?" Maude found herself asking. "A little cottage, just for staying in on Saturday nights to make attending worship easier? Some of the ranchers in these parts have constructed such places—they learned it from the German settlers around Fredericksburg, I'm told. There are several such cottages down the road from the boardinghouse."

He could feel his jaw tighten and his lips flatten into a hard line, and despised the way he could hear the chill in his voice when he spoke. Yet he could not stop himself. "Evidently the prosperous burghers from Germany left the Old World with more gold than the Scots, Miss Maude. I'm afraid you'll find no extra money here for the extravagance of constructing a separate house to inhabit once a week. Some of the servants say their prayers and sing a hymn or two in the kitchen on Sunday mornings. You and Juana could join them, if you're so inclined." He felt his lip curl as he said it and heard the derision in his voice. He made a conscious effort to soften his tone for his next words. "I'm sorry, Miss Harkey, but you knew how far this ranch was from town when you signed on to work here."

"I know, and I'm sorry, too," she said quietly with downcast eyes. "I don't mean to sound as if I'm eager to shirk my duties."

"No one accused you of trying to get out of work, Miss Maude," he said, a little more sharply than he should have. But he felt so awful at dimming her joy, after she'd done so much to bring peace to this once-contentious house. "Perhaps in time, something can be worked out, especially after winter is over. Mother and I wouldn't want to chance you getting stuck in town due to bad weather rolling in—one of your infamous 'northers' for example."

"I see," Maude murmured, looking wan and diminished now. Why would the idea of dressing up and listening to a parson drone on for an hour or more bring her such joy? It had never done so for him or his mother. The church had never been there to help when they'd so desperately needed it, back in Scotland, so he'd never seen the point of attending church in the New World, either. A parson was just another greedy fellow with his hand outstretched, Jonas thought, to dip into pockets already bare. What little money his father had possessed had been used to buy their passage to America, and their first property in Missouri. The sale of that had purchased Five Mile Hill Ranch, which had been a bargain because of its notorious previous owner.

Clearly, though, Maude got something more from church attendance than Jonas ever had. Something that lit her up all the way through when she thought of it. Suddenly he would have given anything to see that bright gladness on her face again.

"Perhaps next Sunday, if the mild weather continues..."

"We'll see," she murmured as if she knew how little such a vague promise was worth. "There's no guarantee about the weather, this time of year, but at least the cold never lingers long here."

He hoped that was true of her mood, as well. He'd discovered he much preferred a happy Maude.

The little gathering in the kitchen on Sunday morning was halfway through a dirge-like rendering of a hymn when Juana and Maude joined them. Hector and three cowboys were there, in addition to the housekeeper, but that was the total attendance. Maude had seen more cowhands around the ranch than what she saw here, but possibly some of them were not church attenders or had duties that kept them from coming.

It could hardly be called "making a joyful noise to the Lord," she thought dispiritedly, *but Lord, You promised to be in the midst of "where two or three are gathered in Your name."*

"Welcome, Maude and Juana," Senora Morales greeted them. "We're glad you could join us. At this point we usually read from the Scriptures. Would you care to do the honors?" she asked, offering a Bible with a tattered leather cover to Maude. "We've been reading from Genesis."

"I'd be happy to, senora," she said, accepting the book.

Maude was surprised that the first book in the Bible was as far as they'd gotten. The MacLarens had been at Five Mile Hill Ranch for over a month. If the Sunday meetings had been ongoing throughout, then their progress through Genesis must have been very slow, indeed. *And no wonder,* she thought, when she realized that the passage was a chapter with nothing more than who had begotten whom among the old patriarchs of Israel. She struggled through it, trying to read with animation and expression despite the dry nature of the text.

"Thank you, Maude. That will have to conclude our service, for I've got to get this pot on the boil for dinner," Senora Morales announced, indicating a kettle on the stove. "And I'm sure you all have duties to go back to." Her remark and pointed look seemed especially aimed at Maude and Juana.

That was it? There was no prayer, no concluding words of any kind? Maude had to smother a squeak of dismay. Even more than before, she longed for the chance to attend church in town, where Sunday services were truly a blessing, joined together with devout friends and led by a wonderful minister. While she'd been reading the chapter in the Scriptures, Maude had imagined Reverend Gil's fine, resonant voice bringing life to it. Even the driest of passages gained energy and meaning when he read them.

"Have a nice Sunday, Senora Benavides," Hector murmured, and moved forward toward the door.

Ought she to offer to say a concluding prayer? Maude wondered. But no, Senora Morales might well think it presumptuous of her to put herself forward in that way since she was a newcomer, or might take it as an implied reproach. The woman was doing the best she could. It would have been easy, in the absence of a formal church in the vicinity, not to do any kind of worship service at all.

In any case, the housekeeper had already turned to the stove and was laboring to lug the pot of peeled potatoes in water to the waiting hook over the fire. And Hector was shuffling out of the kitchen, after his words to Juana, along with the other ranch hands.

"May I help you, Senora Morales?" Juana offered, coming forward. "That looks heavy."

"I could have used the help earlier, when I was peeling all those potatoes by myself, while you two dallied with the baby," Senora Morales snapped. It was clear that despite all this time of complaining at the lack of help, she felt a little threatened by the arrival of these two young women, and the popularity of little Hannah. Finally reaching the fireplace, her skirt whirled as she hefted the pot onto the hook that would suspend it over the fire.

One moment all was well; the next, her skirt had flicked into the fireplace. A tongue of flame licked up the heavy serge fabric with a hiss.

Senora Morales screamed and ran toward the door as the flame crackled and widened its swift march up to her waist.

Instinctively, Maude dashed after her, knowing she had to stop the woman and smother the growing fire or she would die. Running only fanned the flames.

She was instantly transported back in time, when one of her father's patients, a rancher's wife who lived east of Simpson Creek, had caught her skirt on fire in the hearth, too. She had been hideously burned over most of her body, for she had also run, feeding the fire that damaged her so severely. Maude knew her father would not have taken her along if he'd had any idea how extensive the burn would be. She still remembered the odor of charred flesh and the dreadful sight of the blackened, peeling skin.

There had been little her father could do for the woman except leave a bottle of laudanum with the family to ease her pain. He had returned every day or so to change the dressing, but the burns were too deep and extensive to easily heal. The woman had died of infection after a painful fortnight of agony.

"Senora Morales, stop!" Maude cried, but the housekeeper, crazed with fear and pain, paid no heed. Maude kept running, shouting, "Hector, bring me the pot of water!"

She was a lot younger, and many pounds lighter, than the housekeeper, and she caught up before Senora Morales escaped the kitchen. With a desperate lunge, she tackled the housekeeper; bringing both of them crashing heavily to the floor. Then she whipped off her shawl and began to beat at the flames.

"Hector!" she cried without looking up from what she was doing, but she heard the foreman's heavy booted feet nearing them, as well as the water splashing from the pot he carried.

"I have the pot, senorita!"

"Pour it on her!" The water would not have had time to heat to a dangerous temperature in the brief time it had been over the fire. It would douse any remaining sparks on the woman's skirt that sought enough air to reignite and cool the scalded flesh.

With a mighty heave he upended the pot. Peeled potatoes cascaded over the woman along with the water. Juana reached them then, and whipped off her own shawl, wrapping it around the shuddering, drenched woman.

"You saved my life!" Senora Morales sobbed. "*Ay yi yi*, the pain! I hurt, I hurt!"

Had she saved the housekeeper? Maude wondered. *Or would the woman linger in agony for days, only to lose her fight in the end as the ranch wife had done?*

Hardly breathing in anticipation of what she would see, Maude lifted the blackened edges of the skirt.

It was bad, though fortunately not quite as bad as

she had feared. Blisters were already forming like pale whitish-gray islands over the reddened skin. Reddened—not blackened. That was good. Unaware that she was sobbing herself, Maude wet Juana's shawl in the what water was left in the bottom of the pot and laid it gently over the blisters, careful not to press too hard.

"Blisters are God's own perfect bandage," Maude could hear her father saying. *"Try to leave them intact, if possible."*

"Juana!" she called. "I need you to fetch me clean cloth for bandaging, and those pots of aloe from Mrs. MacLaren's plants—all of them. And hurry!"

But Juana only stared at her. "Maude, she has so many different plants—I'm afraid I don't know one from the other," Juana confessed, dark eyes huge in her frantic, pale face.

"They're the ones with the big fleshy spears of leaves," Maude told her, but Juana's face remained uncomprehending.

"I know this plant," Hector said. "And where to find clean linen for bandages. Come on, senora, I will help you," he said as he pulled Juana to her feet from where she had been kneeling next to Maude and the housekeeper. Together they ran from the kitchen.

They had been gone only a moment when Jonas appeared in the kitchen doorway.

"What's the meaning of all this caterwauling? And what's that awful stench?" he demanded. Then his gaze found his housekeeper lying on her back on the floor, with Maude holding the wet shawl over the charred remains of Senora Morales's skirt. "What on earth happened?"

There was silence in the kitchen. Even Senora Morales's moans of pain and fear had ceased as she saw the master of the house staring down at her with that fierce expression on his face. Maude realized it was going to be left up to her to explain.

She did so, her voice shaking as she described the frightening event. "I've sent Juana and Hector to fetch your mother's aloe plants—their liquid will provide some pain relief when I bandage the burns. But I think Dr. Walker should be sent for, too," she added.

He'd said their pockets weren't deep—would he refuse to pay for the doctor to come?

To her relief, Jonas replied immediately, "I'm sure you're right, Miss Harkey." His face was somber—it was clear he understood the seriousness of the situation. "I'll send Hector." Jonas said. Then he turned to a ranch hand standing close by. Though they had left at the end of the service, the men had apparently returned at the sound of the shouts. In the rush of events, Maude hadn't noticed their presence until now. "Someone run out to the barn and get his horse saddled."

They heard a cry of outrage then, from upstairs, followed by the thudding of feet down the stairs toward them.

Hector and Juana burst back into the kitchen, their arms loaded with pots of aloe plants as Maude had requested. They were closely pursued by a staggering, wild-eyed Coira MacLaren, who was yelling in some incomprehensible tongue—Gaelic?—and shaking a clenched fist.

When she caught sight of her son, Coira switched to English. "Jonas, they're stealing my plants! They burst into the greenhouse room and started carrying them off! Tell them they can't have my plants!"

Quickly, Jonas crossed to his mother and spoke to her in the same exotic-sounding rapid-fire speech. Then he instructed Hector that he was to ride for the doctor.

"You and you," Jonas said, selecting a couple of male servants standing at the back of the throng. "Help me carry Senora Morales upstairs to her bed. Maude, come with us, please, and help me get her settled."

It was nearly dark by the time Dr. Walker arrived. He immediately examined the housekeeper, and gave her laudanum for her pain. He praised Maude's quick action and her use of aloe beneath the dressings.

"I couldn't have done better myself, considering what you had at hand. Oddly enough, raw potatoes are an old wives' remedy for burns, so they likely helped somewhat, as well. I'll stay the night, and see how this looks in the morning. Unless infection sets in, though, I think she will fully recover with nothing more than a few scars—"

"Thank God," Maude breathed.

"Thank God you're here to nurse her," Dr. Walker replied with a smile. "It's a mercy your father was a doctor, Miss Maude, and that he taught you what he could. Otherwise, I'd be forced to move her into town, and I shudder to think how hard that trip would be on her. You two ladies will have your hands full, between caring for her and Mrs. MacLaren, won't you? I'll have to come out frequently to check her. I'll leave bandage material for you. Do you have enough aloe to keep dressing the wounds?"

"Only enough for another dressing change or so," Maude said. Senora Morales was a large woman, and the burns covered an extensive area. Maude had squeezed dry half of the aloe leaves already.

"I'll leave you some salve I have in my bag, then," Dr. Walker said. "When that runs out, spread egg whites over the burns—also an old wives' remedy. But the aloe plants are best—use them first."

"I'll do my best, Dr. Walker," Maude said, her mind already awhirl with how to handle her added responsibilities. Besides the cooking, there would be cleaning and laundry to do. She and Juana would really have their work cut out for them, now that they would have to tend both the housekeeper and Jonas's mother, and keep the household fed. And they'd have to make nourishing broths for Senora Morales, who would be laid up for some time.

She was aware of Jonas lingering nearby. He had come to hear what the doctor had to say about his housekeeper.

"Don't worry about the house servants," he told Maude. "They can take their meals in the bunkhouse. One of my ranch hands has been a trail cook, and he's used to cooking for the cowboys. He can just add more beans to the pot."

"Thank you," Maude murmured, grateful for this

practical solution. Now that the worst of the crisis had been handled, she felt exhausted.

"It is I who should be thanking you, Miss Maude," Jonas said, his eyes warm. "You're a braw lass. I ken you handled the situation with skill and courage this morning. It's fortunate you were here, or we'd have been preparing to bury Senora Morales, not planning how to cope without her for a time."

His praise, spoken in that rumbling brogue, made her suddenly feel she could handle anything.

"We'll manage. It won't be forever," she told him, keeping her head turned away and her tone businesslike. She was inwardly dismayed at how avidly she'd drunk in his praise. *He was acknowledging a job well done, nothing more. She had to stop feasting on his approval!* He was a man who saw no value in tender feelings, who scorned the idea of love. She must not let herself think his words meant he was softening in his outlook. He had praised her for being practical and brave—for being useful. That was how he saw her. The same way Dr. Walker saw her, and every other man she'd ever known. She was useful. She was practical. And she inspired not an iota of softer or more tender admiration in anyone.

Especially not in Jonas MacLaren.

Chapter Nine

Thank You, God, for seeing to it that I had the experience of helping Ella with the cooking when she opened up her café, Maude cast upward as a brief prayer three days later, making her way down the steps from Mrs. MacLaren's room to the kitchen. If she'd had to take over the cooking for the ranch house before learning Ella's cooking secrets, it would have been a disaster.

Her mother had died before she could teach Maude how to cook, and the housekeeper her father had hired afterward had always shooed Maude out from underfoot when she hovered in the kitchen, hoping to learn. Later, in the boardinghouse, Mrs. Meyer would rarely accept help with the actual food preparation for the tenants.

Yet from Ella Maude had learned how to make a variety of dishes, as well as mastering the speed and efficiency needed to get everything ready at approximately the same time. So far, Jonas, his mother and Senora Morales had all expressed approval of what she'd cooked. It had helped that Juana had stepped in to make the tortillas when needed, for the MacLarens had learned to like many of Senora Morales's Mexican dishes. Maude's first attempts at making tortillas had resulted in corn disks as heavy and tasteless as leather.

Senora Morales was healing well and had no sign of infection, thanks be to God. The doctor had been out to check on her yesterday, and had pronounced himself satisfied with her progress, enough that he could stay away unless they sent for him to report a problem. He decreed the housekeeper should stay off her feet and out of the kitchen for another day or so, though, much to Senora Morales's displeasure.

Maude suspected the other woman was feeling insecure because Jonas had complimented Maude's fried chicken so highly last night. Could it be that the housekeeper feared Maude wanted her job?

The thought made her chuckle out loud. Far from wanting to be a full-time cook and housekeeper, Maude couldn't wait for the older woman to return to the kitchen and cut her workload in half. Because of the time she'd spent cooking the ranch house's meals, she'd had only a scattering of moments to spend with Hannah. By the time she finished with her cooking duties in the evening, she was too tired to do more than kiss the baby goodnight before Juana laid Hannah in her cradle.

Just stopping to think about Hannah made her smile, though. The child was growing like the proverbial weed—before long they'd have to sew her some more clothing. The next thing they knew, she'd be crawling, then walking…

The knock at the front door startled her so badly she nearly dropped her tray full of dishes. *Who could be calling? They weren't expecting Dr. Walker today. And with the ranch so far from the nearest neighbor, it was unlikely anyone would just drop by without a very good reason.*

She saw a dark-coated, chestnut-haired figure through the window in the door, but the glass was too wavy to identify who it was. Setting the tray down on the landing, she ran the rest of the way, hoping the knocking hadn't awakened Mrs. MacLaren.

It was Reverend Gil, the preacher from the Simpson Creek Church.

"Come in, come in, reverend!" she said as she pulled the door open. "What a nice surprise. There… Nothing's wrong back in town, is there?" she asked, after a sudden thought struck her that he might be here to summon her back to Simpson Creek for some emergency. "Is Mrs. Meyer all right?"

"Mrs. Meyer is right as rain," Gil Chadwick assured her. "Everyone said to tell you they missed you. Your friend Ella's wedding went off without a hitch, and she and Nate Bohannan are off on their wedding trip now."

Being reminded of the wedding she'd had to miss caused a twinge of pain, but she covered her inward wince with a cheerful smile. "Yes, I was sorry not to be able to attend."

"I spoke with Dr. Walker yesterday," Gil Chadwick went on, "and he told me about the housekeeper's accident, and all the burdens you've had to carry since then.

I figured you had your hands full, so I thought I'd come out to check on you, see if you were doing all right."

"Why don't you have a seat in the parlor, Reverend, and I'll bring you a cup of coffee? That's a sharp wind out there today."

"That's a fact," the preacher agreed, and then added, "Coffee would be most welcome. It's nearly Thanksgiving, so I suppose we should expect the cold."

When she pushed open the door to the parlor, though, she found Jonas sitting at his desk, poring over his ledger. She blinked, not having known he was there. He'd come in for the noontime meal, but she'd assumed he'd gone back out to the corral afterward, where he had been working with a young gelding all morning long. Apparently he had decided the accounts needed his attention more than the animals this afternoon.

Jonas looked up from his ledger in surprise, but Maude didn't miss the way his eyes narrowed when he noticed the preacher.

"I'm sorry, Mr. MacLaren," she said quickly, "I didn't know you were in here or I wouldn't have disturbed you. Reverend Gil Chadwick's come to call—would you rather we sit in the kitchen? I was going to get him some coffee."

He rose. "There's no need to take him elsewhere—what I'm doing can wait. I wouldn't mind a cup of your coffee, Miss Maude. Reverend Chadwick, I'm Jonas MacLaren." He held out his hand and the preacher clasped it with a friendly smile. A smile that was not returned by his host.

"Welcome," Jonas said, in a voice that fully contradicted the word. "Is there something I can do for you?"

"No, no, I just thought I'd come out to check on Miss Maude," the young preacher told him. "And your housekeeper and your mother, too, if they're able to have visitors. Dr. Walker told me about your housekeeper getting burned, so I knew Miss Maude and Mrs. Juana would be keeping very busy. I came to see if there's anything we could do to help. My wife's ready to pack her valise and move out here as long as you need her assistance if you're feeling overburdened, Miss Maude."

"Oh, that's so nice of her to offer," Maude said. "But no, Senora Morales is healing nicely and is allowed to resume her duties in a couple of days, so I think we'll be all right until then. Excuse me, gentlemen, I'll just be a minute getting the coffee."

Should she rejoin them when she brought the coffee? Reverend Gil was here to see her, not Jonas, but perhaps this was a good opportunity for him to get to know the preacher and perhaps see how appealing his faith was. And in any case, she had very little time to spare from her many tasks. She knew Jonas had very little regard for churchgoing in general, and wondered if that same disinterest extended to preachers, as well. Certainly he had not seemed well pleased when she had walked in with the preacher. But after Gil had explained the purpose of his visit, Jonas had seemed to relax. Maybe he had feared that the minister had come to chastise him for not attending Sunday services. That might explain his relief at learning the true reason the reverend had come calling.

Still pondering Jonas's behavior, she set two china cups on a tray, poured coffee from the pot on the stove, poured a little milk into a small pitcher and added the sugar bowl to the tray, then went back down the hall toward the parlor.

"Maude Harkey works harder than any three women," she heard Jonas say as she drew near. "She's taken on an amazing load, and all without a word of complaint. I'm not sure how we ever got along without her. And everything she does, she does well. Her cooking is delicious—but don't tell Senora Morales I said that, will you?"

Maude froze just outside the door, her face aflame. Could she have possibly heard him correctly? He'd given little indication that he thought so highly of her.

"Miss Maude's always been a good woman," Reverend Gil said then. "I've known her for years, ever since my father came here to be the minister before me. As the doctor's daughter and the minister's son—for my father was the pastor of Simpson Creek back then—our paths often crossed. I'm sorry to say I was away at seminary when her papa was killed by the Indians a few years ago and could not offer her any help or comfort during that difficult time, but I've seen her shoulder her responsibilities and make a new life for herself since then. You're lucky to have her here."

"Don't I know it," MacLaren agreed. "My mother thinks she hung the moon, and Senora Morales is convinced Maude saved her life, running after her and tackling her like she did so she could beat the fire out.

It's a wonder she wasn't burned herself, but she didn't hesitate to place herself in harm's way."

The constant stream of compliments was making her heart race and her face flush. Maude waited until she felt her pulse slow to a more normal pace and the men began to speak of other things before taking the coffee in. Fearing her face would still betray what she had overheard, she avoided looking at Jonas. She didn't want him to realize that she'd been eavesdropping. And most of all, she didn't want him to guess just how much those words of praise meant to her.

Jonas watched Maude's graceful movements as she poured the coffee and offered each man a cup. How did a small-town girl, from what was still a very wild and sometimes lawless part of the United States, come to possess the poise of a duchess? She excused herself as soon as she had served both men. He found himself wishing she would stay. But he could not think of a pretext to ask her to do so and regretfully allowed her to excuse herself.

As he focused his attention on the man in front of him, he at least had the comfort of feeling something other than the suspicious fury that had sprung up instantly when Maude had entered his parlor with a caller.

Gil Chadwick was young for his pastoral responsibilities, and not a bad-looking fellow. Until he'd mentioned a wife, Jonas had been sure the preacher had come here out of romantic interest in Maude. His hands had clenched into fists at his sides at the thought of it.

The nerve of the man, to come sniffing around right under Jonas's nose! So Chadwick had missed Maude being in town, close at hand, and traipsed clear out to Five Mile Hill Ranch to see her?

Chadwick's casual mention of his wife—who was apparently a friend of Maude's—had thrown water on the flame of Jonas's sparking ire. He found himself feeling downright cordial to the young parson. But now that the anger had cleared from his mind, the vehemence of his initial reaction made him wary. *What difference should it make to him whether Chadwick was a would-be suitor of Maude's or not?*

He'd told Maude the day he met her that the last thing he was looking for was a wife. He'd learned his lesson with Annabella, hadn't he, that females were not to be trusted?

Then why had he felt a completely unreasonable surge of jealousy and possessiveness when he'd thought the young preacher was sweet on Maude?

He realized the preacher had made a comment and seemed to be waiting for some response from him. "Pardon me, reverend. You were saying—?"

Gil Chadwick smiled, not at all perturbed that his host's attention had wandered. "I was saying, we've been missing Miss Maude's fine singing on Sunday mornings," he said. "She has a beautiful soprano voice. She's graced us with solos a time or two. Have you heard her sing?"

Jonas had to admit that he had not. Now he couldn't imagine anything he wanted to experience more. *Would she sing for him, if he asked it of her? Did she sing to put the wee bairn to sleep?*

It was a moment or two before he realized the implied question in the preacher's praise of Maude's voice. "Aye, well, I'm sorry she's so far from the church now—the distance makes attending impractical. Perhaps some Sunday, when the weather is cooperative, she can come back for a visit. And I don't suppose she'll be here forever…"

But he couldn't imagine her *not* living here always.

"I'm sure she'd be welcome to stay overnight with a family in town…" the preacher murmured. "Or at the boardinghouse. So far, Mrs. Meyer hasn't rented Miss Maude's old room."

Jonas wasn't interested in sharing Maude with the town. *What if she found she missed it so much that she didn't want to return to Five Mile Hill Ranch? What if there was some young swain who realized what a prize she was and took advantage of her brief return to strengthen their relationship or declare his intentions? She had come to the ranch to have a home for Hannah, but a husband could give her and the bairn a proper home easily enough. She hadn't mentioned anyone, and she was part of that spinsters' group looking for spouses, but that didn't mean there wasn't someone interested in her, did it?*

"We'll have to see," he said vaguely. "Right now, my mother needs her at her side. It would not suit her at all to have Miss Maude absent for most of Saturday and Sunday. And there's the bairn to be tended. The servants conduct their own service on Sundays, which

Miss Maude has attended, so you needn't worry she'll become a heathen while she's here."

Did he sound defensive? Jonas wondered. Perhaps he *was* rather jumping to conclusions. And, indeed, perhaps the reverend's question had been perfectly innocent. The preacher was just worried about Maude because she was one of his flock, a single female living far from her home, working for a man she'd barely known before coming to live at his ranch. *It was admirable in a way, knowing someone cared about Maude like that, wasn't it?* Made him feel almost *charitable* toward the man for valuing Maude in a way she clearly merited.

"Of course, of course," Chadwick said, looking not the least offended by Jonas's verbal jab. "Well, I've taken up enough of your time, Mr. MacLaren. It was good to meet you at last. Perhaps you could call Miss Maude, and she can take me up to see your housekeeper and your mother so I could pay my respects?"

The two men shook hands. Then Jonas called Maude and watched her climb the stairs with the young reverend. He went back to the ledger he had been working on, but he found the figures before him blurred together like a black sea of ink.

It was time to admit to himself that he was starting to care for the winsome red-haired Maude, that he wanted her to play a larger role in his life than just a caretaker for his mother.

The question was, was he ready to act on his feelings? Could he put his heart at risk yet again? The last time had been so disastrous that it had just about killed him. He had truly thought he was done with love and romance for good—and had relished the knowledge. If he never opened his heart to another woman, then he would not have to fear it getting trampled again.

Should he hold strong to that resolution? Perhaps he should just enjoy the time that she was here and appreciate what she was doing to make his mother's life more pleasant, knowing that someday she would leave and return to her life back in Simpson Creek. He found he could not bear that idea.

Maude took Reverend Gil to visit Coira first, knowing Jonas's mother was more likely to be awake and would see it as her right that a visitor would pay his respects to her first.

"So you're the minister o' th' kirk in Simpson Creek?" Coira asked, after Maude had gone in first and made sure the older woman was presentable for a visitor. Now, seated in a rocking chair, her hair neatly combed and tucked under a lace cap, and smelling of lavender water, she blinked and smiled delightedly at her visitor. "That is to say, the church, no' the kirk. I am a Scottish lady born and bred, y'see, and I suppose a church will always be a 'kirk' to me."

"It's just fine to call it a kirk if you wish, Mrs. MacLaren, and yes, I minister at the Simpson Creek Church, though my father still has the official title. He's had an apoplexy and finds it difficult to speak, though, so I do the preaching."

"'Tis delighted I am to meet ye, Reverend Gil," Coira said with a bright smile. "So 'twould have been yer father and not yerself that brought our Maudie up to be the fine Christian lass she is?"

Maudie? Maude could hardly believe her ears, hearing Coira MacLaren use an affectionate form of her name. Her father used to call her Maudie.

Reverend Gil beamed. "It's true that I've only been ministering in Simpson Creek for a relatively short time, but even my father wouldn't take credit for Maude's character. He always said what a fine Christian man Miss Maude's father, Dr. Harkey, was. And her mother was a good, faithful woman. It was a very sad loss when she was taken from us, though nowhere near as tragic as the loss of Dr. Harkey. But I know they would both be proud of their daughter. And yes, I heard the story of Miss Maude courageously coming to the aid of your housekeeper. Simpson Creek is very proud of her."

"Aye, and so it should be. She's a braw girl. Though she's decimated my aloe plants to help Senora Morales," she said with a wink at Maude. "I'm grateful for her healing skill."

"Thank you, Mrs. MacLaren," Maude said, feeling flushed at the unexpected praise. "I'll just leave you two to talk for a while, while I go see if Senora Morales is up to a visitor. Then I'll come back and take you to see her, Reverend Gil." She had to smother a smile as she left. From the eager look in Coira's eye, Maude had a feeling the old lady was going to talk Reverend Gil's ear off.

Senora Morales was thrilled to hear that she was to have a visitor, and required Maude's assistance in combing her hair and donning a fresh wrapper so she would be fit for company. Maude smile as she left the housekeeper. All in all, she figured the reverend would be savoring the blessed silence during his ride home, while she was unable to get over how Jonas had praised her to the preacher.

At supper time, all Coira and Senora Morales could talk about was how nice they thought the young minister had been, how kind, what a good listener, and how much they wished they lived closer to town so they could attend services and hear him preach.

"Aye, well, I don't mind saying I was pleasantly surprised at him, too," Jonas said. "The entire time he was here, he didn't stick a hand out for so much as a penny. Most unusual for a cleric, in my experience."

Maude couldn't stifle a small cry of exasperation. "Reverend Chadwick wouldn't think of asking for money during a pastoral call," she protested. "Are you saying that's what you're used to, Mr. MacLaren?"

"Aye, 'tis generally what the clergy are after, when they come calling. Oh, they do not ask for funds in so many words, they don't," he said with a cynical twist of his lips. "But in my experience they always manage to ask for money in some way or another. And who can blame them, living poor as church mice? Dinna fash yerself, Miss Maude," he added as she opened her mouth to protest. "I'm sayin' yer Reverend Gil is a fine man, a credit to his kirk. And nary once did I feel he was here for any cause but to pay his respects to us all, and ensure your good treatment at our hands. 'Twas a fine visit."

Maude sighed. She had enjoyed it, too, not only because Reverend Gil had prayed for her before he left and blessed little Hannah, but because of the cheering effect he had had on both Jonas's mother and the housekeeper. He had also brought news of the life she had left behind her in Simpson Creek, though, that had her feeling a bit homesick. Mrs. Meyer had a new tenant in one of her rooms—likely the room Juana had occupied, since Maude's old room was still vacant. Jane Jeffries, as the new president of the Spinsters' Club, had announced a Christmas party to be held in the church social hall. All of it made Maude miss the life she had left behind. He had brought some good news that related to her directly, too—Felix Renz, Hannah's father, hadn't returned. Hannah was still safely hers.

Three days later, the weather defied the calendar and was warm as a day in spring. Restless when Coira announced she would take a nap and had no need of her for a while, Maude decided to take a walk to have a closer look at some of the small cottages she had seen nestled against the hills when she'd toured the ranch. Senora Morales had said her daughter lived in one of them and would welcome a visit. Thinking Juana could probably use some time to herself, Maude tied Hannah onto her back with a shawl and, wearing sturdy boots in case she encountered any rattlesnakes enjoying the sun, she set out.

She had a wonderful time singing aloud and enjoying the fine day, and she could tell from the pleased note of Hannah's little cries that she was having a good time, too.

"Ah, Hannah, just wait until spring," she told her. "I'll bring you with me and we'll watch the newborn lambs frolicking in the sunlight," she murmured. She could imagine Hannah's excited chuckles. She would be several months older, and would doubtless be reacting to the world around her even more noticeably.

Half an hour's walking took Maude past the corrals and the bunkhouse and into the scrubland of mesquite and pecan trees, cactus and rock that led upward to the limestone hills. It felt good to get out and stretch her legs, breathing air free of the smell of the salve she applied to the housekeeper's healing burns and the faint camphor scent of Coira MacLaren's clothing. Even Hannah seemed to enjoy the outing, cooing contentedly on Maude's back and chuckling when a startled turkey sprang up out of the brush and took wing directly overhead.

The sight of the bird made her think of how close it was to Thanksgiving. Was Jonas a hunter? If not, could Hector be sent out to bag this fine bird for their table? She was not about to eat haggis on Thanksgiving Day. She'd seen a pumpkin or two in the housekeeper's kitchen garden; hopefully Senora Morales would make it into a pie.

She wondered if Jonas MacLaren had ever had a proper American Thanksgiving feast.

Nearing the cluster of cottages on the side of a hill, Maude stopped by a small creek surrounded by tall cottonwoods and live oaks to rest. She had untied Hannah—who was fast asleep—from her shawl and was leaning over to cup some of the cool water into her mouth when she heard footsteps approaching.

Who could it be? Maude wondered, suddenly realizing how alone and defenseless she and Hannah were. She crouched over her baby, whom she'd laid on a grassy area, still wrapped in the shawl. *And her without so much as a big stick to defend herself. What kind of fool went walking in the brush without a weapon?*

But the girl who entered the shaded grove would be no threat. No more than sixteen, dark haired and dark eyed, she carried a bucket. She gave a little cry of surprise as she spotted Maude.

"*Ay de mi!* Who are you?" she asked, clearly poised for flight. She brandished the empty bucket as if she intended to bash Maude over the head if Maude gave an unfriendly answer.

"I'm Maude Harkey. Might you be Senora Morales's daughter? She sent me to visit you." Now it was apparent why the housekeeper was eager for Maude to meet the girl, for she was hugely pregnant.

"Oh! Yes, I am Dulcinea Alvarez, Dulcy for short. Pedro the shepherd is *mi esposo*, my husband. You came to visit *me*?" The girl seemed childishly pleased at the prospect. Then she caught sight of Hannah, who had awakened at the sound of her voice. "Oh, but you have a baby! How pretty she is! May I hold her?"

Maude nodded, thinking the girl was young to be not only a wife but soon, a mother. Though April Mae had been even younger, she remembered—just fifteen when she'd given birth to Hannah.

"I see you're expecting a wee one of your own. You should not be carrying heavy buckets of water. Let me fill the bucket for you and carry it back to your cottage."

"*Gracias*. It is very kind of you. Yes, Pedro is so happy that he will soon be a father. Please, follow me, and I will show you to our casa," she added, when Maude straightened again after dipping the bucket into the water.

She followed the shorter girl up a narrow deer track that led to the cottage, a white frame lean-to perched against the wall of a limestone cliff. Inside, the furnishings were humble, but Dulcinea showed her to a rickety chair as proudly as if the cottage was a palace and the chair a throne. Then she reached onto a shelf and brought out some carved wooden animals and placed these in front of Hannah, whom she had laid on her tummy on a tanned goatskin on the floor. Maude placed one of them, a figure that looked like a goat, into her hand.

"Pedro made these for the baby already," Dulcey announced, a proud smile creasing her face.

The animals were carved with amazing skill. Maude could clearly see that one figure was a sheep, such as the wooly creatures she had seen clustering on the hillside. When she picked it up, its carved curly fleece looked so real she could practically feel the wool beneath her fingers. Another was a ram with curling horns. There was a crouching dog, its mouth carved open as if it was barking, and a shepherd with a crook.

"He's quite a skilled wood-carver," Maude praised, then saw the girl clutch her abdomen, her face creased with distress. "Dulcinea, what's wrong?"

"Dolor," the girl ground out. "The pain comes again."

"'Again'?" Maude echoed. "Dulcey, when did the pains start? How long do they last?"

But Dulcinea's eyes were squeezed shut, and she moaned too loudly to hear Maude's questions.

Maude waited until the contraction loosened its grip on the girl's abdomen, then asked her questions again. "Have you seen a doctor since you learned you were with child? When did he say your time would come?"

"No, no doctor…"

Maude realized the question had been foolish. This daughter of a servant wouldn't be taken into town to see Dr. Walker. Her mother would merely help her figure out when her baby was to come, and try to be present to help when it was time.

"The pains started this morning," the girl went on, "and they come…every few minutes. They last for as long as it takes me to say a *Padre Nuestro* or two…"

Padre Nuestro—Our Father—the Lord's Prayer. Maude thought about how many seconds it would take to recite the prayer, then came to a conclusion she really didn't want to face.

The girl was in labor.

Chapter Ten

"Dulcey, I think the baby is coming," Maude said as calmly as she could manage. "We should get you into bed..." Searching with her eyes, she found an alcove at the end of the room, separated from the rest of the room by a screen made of tanned goatskins stretched on a frame.

Dulcey's eyes widened. "The baby? Now? *Ay yi yi!* Pedro isn't here...it's too early! The old woman told me it would not come until the *luna llena*—the full moon," she added, when she saw that Maude didn't understand. "But she also said first babies have a mind of their own."

Maude thought for a moment. The last time she had looked at the moon was the last evening she had spent at the boardinghouse—had it only been a week ago? What had the moon looked like then? Then she remembered the sight of the half-bright orb.

"Dulcey, the time of the full moon is late this month, so it's all right if the baby is coming now," she said, keeping her voice calm. "It's not that early. And who is this old woman you speak of?" she asked, hoping the girl would say there was an experienced midwife nearby.

"The *curandera* lives up the hill a ways," the girl said.

"Curandera?" Maude asked, unfamiliar with the word.

"The healer," Dulcey explained. "An old wise woman."

The thought that there might actually be an experienced helper nearby was the only thing that kept her from full-blown panic that would have spread to Dulcey, who already looked apprehensive.

But even knowing that there was someone nearby who could help did not banish her panic entirely. Maude could not believe she was being asked to experience such an ordeal again. It hadn't been that long ago that she had delivered a baby whose birth had resulted in her mother's death, and now she would have to deliver another baby. *Lord, what are You thinking, to put me in this position? I wasn't equal to the task before!*

The answer came immediately, as she recalled to mind verses from the Bible that told her that God's grace was sufficient for all things. Even for this. Even for her. She could let go of her fear and turn it all over to God.

Hannah gave a little squeal of protest just then, for she had dropped the toy Maude had placed in her hand. The reminder of Hannah's presence gave her new cause for alarm.

Lord, if I'm to stay and attend this birth, what of Hannah? She'll get hungry, and Juana isn't here.

They don't know where I am, back at the ranch house. Please, Lord, help me!

Maude rose and went behind the screen. Dulcey had changed into a simple night shift and had gotten into bed.

"I'm going to examine you now, Dulcey," Maude told her, and began to palpate the girl's abdomen to determine the position of the baby.

The results were not reassuring. Instead of being head down, deep in the pelvis, Maude felt the hard round prominence of the skull at the top of the rest of the soft mass of the baby's body.

It was going to be a breech birth—that is, the head would be delivered last. A very dangerous sort of birth, because nature intended for babies to born headfirst, so that the largest part of the baby's body was released first. When the head was delivered last, all sorts of disasters could happen—especially when the mother was both young and small, as Dulcey was.

Dear Lord, I need Your help.

"The baby will come soon, yes?" Dulcey asked, smiling up at Maude with utter trust.

"Yes, with God's help," Maude told her. *God, help me!*

All might still be well unless the umbilical cord came first—or the head was too large to pass after the baby's legs and body had been delivered. And Dulcinea was so small…

She settled down to time Dulcey's contractions as best she could without a watch. They were coming every five or so minutes now, and lasting about sixty seconds each. During each one, Dulcey would grip Maude's hand so tightly Maude was sure her hand would break, but no cries passed the girl's lips.

"Breathe with the pains, Dulcey," she told her, and the girl smiled weakly and tried to comply.

After the tenth contraction, Maude noticed the shadows lengthening outside the dwelling's only window. It was late afternoon, and they would be worrying about her back at the ranch. With a first baby, there was no telling how long this could take. The delivery might be hours away. And since she didn't know where to find the nearest neighbor—even if she had been willing to leave Dulcey's side—there was no way for her to send word. *What would they do when she failed to appear by nightfall?* Hannah had fallen asleep on her goatskin, and Maude had covered her with one of Dulcey's skirts, but when she woke, she would be hungry—and furious when she was not fed.

After the tenth contradiction, there came a knocking at the door. *Thank You, God! Deliverance was at hand!*

It was an old woman, but it was not the *curandera*, Maude learned after the visitor and Dulcey had spoken a few sentences—just a neighbor from one of the other crude lean-tos clustered on the hill who'd come to check on the young mother-to-be.

"Can you ask her to summon the *curandera*?" Maude asked, when the old woman seemed about to leave. "And can you ask her to get word to the ranch house that I am here?"

After a rapid exchange in Spanish, Dulcinea smiled. "She will send her grandson for the *curandera*. Then, afterward, he will run to the ranch house. He can run very fast," she added, when Maude allowed her dismay to show. It was already suppertime, and they were relying on a child's legs to run so far?

Meanwhile, Dulcey's labor was progressing. The pains were closer together and lasting longer. Maude had managed to light a fire in the hearth, and was boiling a knife in a pot over it. Dulcey had asked for a second knife to be placed under her pillow—"to cut the pains." Bowing to the superstition seemed to bring her comfort, and Maude saw no harm in the idea.

Hannah, however, was not comforted. She had begun a fretful fussing, which Maude knew was only a prelude to the wailing that would soon come if she was not fed. Between contractions, Dulcey suggested that Maude take the corner of a clean cloth and dip it in the honey Pedro had brought her in a jar. Sucking on that seemed to satisfy Hannah for now, but how long would that last?

As the pains grew closer together, Dulcey began to get fretful, too, calling for Pedro.

"Does he come home in the evenings?" Maude asked hopefully. She didn't want to leave Dulcey alone, but if she had to go get help, at least the girl's husband would be with her.

Dulcey shrugged. "He comes when he can…" she said vaguely.

Maude felt her fists clenching in frustrated worry. What kind of a husband left a young wife with child alone, and assumed she would be all right?

"He comes when someone else can watch the sheep,"

the girl explained further, perhaps sensing Maude's frustration. "Someone must protect the young lambs against the coyotes, the *cuguar*."

It was all very well to protect the lambs against the coyotes and cougars, but who would protect the little lamb Dulcey was struggling to give birth to?

A verse from the Psalms came to her—*I sought the Lord and He heard me, and delivered me from all my fears.*

Thank You, Lord. May I ask that You send help quickly?

Dulcey was moaning in the throes of a contraction again. She kept getting out of bed to crouch beside it, instinctively seeking the position in which gravity helped the laboring woman.

The light had faded from the window now, and Hannah was no longer content with sucking the honey rag. In between contractions Maude tried to soothe her baby, but Hannah was hungry and she was not willing to be pacified.

Dulcey had gone to the window after her latest pain, and she turned to Maude, hopelessness shadowing her face.

"The *curandera* will not come now that it is dark," she said. "She is old, and she worries about falling against the rock and breaking her...how do you say?" Dulcey asked, pointing to her upper leg.

"Her hip? She worries about breaking a hip?"

"*Sí, sí*, her hip."

What sort of a healer worried about darkness when a patient needed her? Maude wondered irritably. Her own father had left his home at all hours, and even in all sorts of foul weather, to see patients, trusting in his buggy horse to use the light of the lamp or the moon to guide him. Yet she didn't know if a healer had any tricks for breech birth that she didn't know, anyway. There weren't any tricks for that, just prayer, and she was already "praying without ceasing," as the Scriptures suggested.

Her own father had said he didn't believe in trying to turn a breech baby to face head down before labor. If it did not happen naturally, the way it was supposed to before labor began, then he believed in leaving the baby where it was. Even if the physician was successful, he had told Maude, all too often the baby stubbornly turned back into the head-up position before birth.

Dulcey was moaning through another contraction now, crouching and grabbing her abdomen. When it was through, she clutched at herself.

"Something has come," she said, looking alarmed. "It is sticking out."

Lord, let it be a leg, or both legs, Maude prayed, trying to ignore the increasing volume of Hannah's wails. If the legs were showing, perhaps she could gently pull this baby into the world.

"Dulcey, I am going to wash my hands again quickly," Maude told the girl, striving to keep her features calm and her voice cheerful. "And then I'm going to check. You should lie down now, please."

Obediently, Dulcinea lay down on the now-rumpled sheets, and after Maude had washed with the crude lye soap and water she had poured into a basin, she went to examine her patient.

It was as she had feared. The umbilical cord was protruding from between the girl's legs. It pulsed faintly with Dulcey's heartbeat. When a contraction seized the girl, though, and caused the muscles to tighten, the circulation provided through the cord would be cut off, leaving the baby with no air for the length of the contraction.

This could cause the baby to be stillborn. It would be up to Maude to insert a finger against the punishing pressure so that the cord's blood—and air—supply was not cut off for vital seconds.

"Dulcey, you're going to have to stay in bed for the rest of your labor," she told the weary girl as she wiped beads of sweat from Dulcey's forehead with a cloth. "And I want you to lie down on your left side. We'll prop you so that your hips are higher than your head." In simple terms, she explained why—because the baby's head was not coming first, gravity would become their enemy instead of their ally, pressing on the endangered cord.

Maude saw a single tear slip out of one of Dulcey's eyes, but then she nodded and obediently lay down again. There was only one large pillow in the humble dwelling, so Maude used every blanket she could find to prop the girl's hips up and take pressure off the cord.

With the next contraction, Maude inserted a finger into the birth canal, keeping the intense squeezing pressure off the cord, and it kept pulsating, though she thought for a moment the force of the contracting muscles against the pelvic bone would surely break her finger. After the contraction was over, she inserted her finger farther, hoping she would feel a foot, but she could find nothing yet. The feet were probably tucked up around the chest, which would make it harder to deliver the baby, for there was nothing she could grab on to and pull.

Lord, stay with me, she prayed, steeling herself to ignore Hannah's crying. *Let this baby come quickly but safely.* She had no idea how much longer this labor would take or how she could help the baby or the mother if it took too much longer.

She lost track of time, and her entire world became a series of contractions and prayers she said out loud, knowing that Dulcey was in too much pain to really comprehend them. Like many laboring mothers at this stage, the girl despaired of the ordeal ever being over.

Then suddenly Maude caught a glimpse of the baby's buttocks coming, but the contraction didn't move them farther downward.

Don't pull, or get in a hurry. Remember the cord. She heard her father's voice as if he were in the room. *It could be caught around something, like the baby's neck.*

The cord that protruded was slack and not pulsating, an ominous sign. *Lord, help us! Save this little life!* Keeping the fingers of one hand against the part of the cord she could feel, she inserted the other fingers up alongside the cord, feeling along the baby's buttocks, then chest. She wished praying could give her instantly longer fingers…

Handle the cord as little as possible. You don't want it to spasm...

There! As Dulcey's body began to push again, she felt the baby's neck, and the cord wrapped around it. She inserted a finger under the cord, lifting it away from the neck. It began to pulsate again.

Lord, we can't accomplish this without Your help. Please aid us quickly.

Dulcey grabbed her free hand then with a strength and fierceness that belied her small size. "I have to *push...*" she cried, panting.

"Then push, little Dulcey, push, and the Lord will help us," Maude told her. She was ready, having put a clean cloth underneath the girl's hips. She held another one to receive the baby.

She could see the baby's slick, tiny buttocks, protruding a little farther with each breath's pushing.

An eternity later, the wet, blue-red baby boy slid into the cloth Maude held ready and began to squall in protest at the indignity of his birth.

Maude hadn't realized she was weeping until she tried to find her voice. "It's a boy, praise God! A healthy, very angry boy, Dulcey!"

"Gracias, Dios!" Dulcey cried, sagging back on the bed, grinning. "Pedro will be so happy..."

"Yes, thank You, Lord," Maude murmured, swaddling the baby before handing him into the embrace of his exhausted mother. The delivery wasn't quite complete yet, so she waited until it was before cutting the cord and wrapping mother and baby against the chill. The angry wails from the newborn had stopped mingling with Hannah's fretful cries, for Dulcey was already nursing him.

Maude pulled Hannah close to soothe her as much as she could. No sooner had she realized how exhausted and drained she was than a pounding sounded at the door.

Who—? Had the curandera *finally come, now that the crisis was over? Unlikely, given what Dulcey had said about the woman's refusal to travel after dark. Was it the baby's father? But why would he knock at the door of his own dwelling?*

"*Maude!* Maude Harkey, are you in there?" shouted a very familiar voice.

Maude jumped upright and tottered to her feet, feet that threatened to collapse beneath her, and somehow made her way to the door, carrying Hannah.

When she pulled it open, she was surprised to see it was dawn. A furious-faced Jonas stood there, holding a blazing torch.

"Put that out before you set the house on fire, and stop shouting," she said, holding a finger to her lips, for Dulcey and the baby were already asleep.

Jonas laid the torch down on the rocky ground where it could do no harm, then rounded on her. "What in the name of— What do you mean, sneaking off like that with a baby, letting no one know where you were, taking your child that needs to be fed? We were frantic by the time the lad reached us and told us where we could find you, woman! Juana is beside herself!" He was shouting so loudly that Maude flinched from him, and baby Hannah began to wail anew in her arms.

"Stop yelling!" she yelled back. "You're frightening everyone! I had no choice but to stay and help your shepherd's wife deliver her baby!" She pointed at the screen that stood in front of Dulcinea's bed. "She would have given birth all alone if I hadn't stayed, and the baby might well have died—maybe even the mother, too!"

Incredibly, Jonas obeyed her and not only stopped shouting, but turned around and began descending the slope again. Maude thought he must be so angry that he was leaving her there. "Jonas, wait—" she began.

But then she heard him calling down the hillside, "I've found her! She's here!" Then he turned to look back up at her. "I've brought Juana in the wagon, so she can feed poor Hannah," he said, his tone softer, and nodded at the baby who was crying inconsolably in Maude's arms. Then he was clambering back down the hillside to assist Juana to climb up to where they stood.

Maude caught sight of the little Mexican boy who'd fetched them entering one of the other lean-tos now that his task was done. She hoped he'd try to get word to Pedro about his newborn son after he'd rested.

Maude sagged in relief, the tears flooding down her cheeks again as Juana, helped by Jonas, reached them and, going inside, settled herself down to feed Hannah. While she did so, Maude told them about the difficult birth, and when she was done both Juana and Jonas tiptoed over to take a peek at the new baby.

"Maude, you are a heroine!" Juana proclaimed. "My sister died in childbirth because her baby came the same way, and the baby died, too. How frightened you must have been!"

"You have no idea," Maude agreed, smiling now. "I just thank God all ended well."

"Aye, a true heroine," Jonas said. He had listened quietly, but a warning glint in his eye told her he wasn't completely done with his anger. Maude felt sure he was just waiting to speak to her privately. She was certainly not looking forward to that conversation, though she was grateful that she didn't have to bear it just yet. She thought if he spoke sharply to her now she might dissolve into a puddle.

"I suppose we'd better get back to the ranch house," Jonas said a little later.

"But we can't leave Dulcey here alone to fend for herself," Maude protested. New mothers who had had long, difficult births like Dulcinea were especially prone to childbed fever, she knew. "We must take her and the baby back to the ranch house with us," she told Jonas. "Do you think you could carry her to the wagon?"

She could see he was about to refuse, then, to her relief, Juana chimed in, too. "She's right, Senor MacLaren. The young mother is much too weak to care for herself and her baby after such an ordeal. She will want her mama—and Senora Morales will want to have her close by, too."

"But her husband—"

Juana made a dismissive gesture with her hands. "He's a man. He won't know what to do. And he is busy minding the sheep, so he would not be home often regardless. Besides, it won't be for very long."

Maude could see he was still tempted to refuse, and the thought panicked her. She felt a tear slide down her cheek and impatiently swiped at it, not wanting him to think she was trying to manipulate him through the use of tears that were only escaping because she was so tired. "Please, Jonas, I can't let another woman die like Hannah's mother did," she pleaded, impulsively reaching out a hand to touch his wrist. "In fact I'd like to get the doctor out to check her, but don't worry, I'll pay for his visit," she told him.

He looked deeply into her eyes then. "All right, Maude. It seems I can refuse you nothing. On your head be it when my mother learns what we've done."

"Your mother would be the first to want to help a young mother and her 'wee bairn' as she'd call it," Maude insisted, relieved.

"You are a good man, Senor MacLaren," Juana told him, her eyes shining.

"Occasionally," he agreed.

Chapter Eleven

As her son had predicted, Coira MacLaren was not pleased when she learned that a Mexican peasant girl and yet another crying baby had taken up occupancy under the MacLaren roof.

"I don't recall being consulted about my own household being transformed into bedlam," she raged, when Hannah and the newborn boy began wailing simultaneously on their arrival back at the ranch. "I won't have it!"

Quickly, her son filled her in on the circumstances of the baby boy's birth.

Coira turned to Maude, whom Jonas had just helped to descend from the wagon, Maude's limbs having turned to jelly from exhaustion. "And ye, ye irresponsible slip of a girl, to go waltzing off into the hills without a thought for the needs of yer own babe," she said, gesturing toward Hannah, who had ceased crying and was now rubbing her eyes sleepily. "The poor wee thing must have come close to starving while you tended this—this peasant girl! And then there's my own needs that you were hired to see to, and have woefully neglected today."

"I agree, I should not have taken Hannah with me," Maude admitted. "And I apologize for being gone so long. But we were just taking advantage of the nice weather and had not intended to be absent for more than an hour or so. I'm sorry, Mrs. MacLaren," she said, knowing she was blessed that everything had turned out as well as it had. "It won't happen again. And Dulcinea and the baby will just be here until I am certain she has recovered from the childbirth. After such a difficult delivery, I couldn't leave her up there alone," she said, jerking her head back in the direction of the hillside hut.

"It better not happen again," the older woman snapped. "Well, I suppose ye'd best be about readying a guest room for yet another noisy guest."

"They can use the east room, Mrs. MacLaren," Senora Morales said, still moving gingerly because of the healing burns. "It's made up and ready. Ah, my grandson, what a darling little one!" she exclaimed, peering over the wagon bed where Dulcinea still rested in a nest of blankets with her newborn. "I'll have Hector send word to your husband that you're here, Dulcinea. Then he will be here fast as the wind to see his *hijo*!" She chuckled as she took charge. "You look about to collapse, Senorita Maude. To bed with you!"

Since Senora Morales was taking charge of her daughter and new grandson, Maude gladly obeyed the command from the housekeeper to seek her bed, knowing Juana would watch over Hannah.

Jonas touched her shoulder lightly as she started to walk toward the house. "We'll speak when you've rested," Jonas said.

Was that a threat or a promise? Maude wondered, but she was too tired to worry about it. She used what remained of her energy to climb the stairs to the room she shared with Juana.

Exhausted, she slept straight through dinner and supper and didn't wake until Senora Morales brought a plate of sliced beef and soup to the room.

"Senor MacLaren said he'd be waiting for you in his study, but that you were to take your time and eat first," the housekeeper said after Maude had sat up at the side of the bed.

A shiver of apprehension slid icily down Maude's spine, but the beef smelled too good to let fear ruin her appetite. She ate as if she hadn't seen food for a week, then put on a fresh dress and descended to the study, wondering what the man would say.

While he waited for her, Jonas pored over the account book, but as soon as he heard her soft footsteps in the hall, he dropped the pretense that he was doing anything more than killing time till she arrived.

She'd changed out of the rumpled, stained clothing she'd come back to the ranch in and was now wearing a dress of some soft rust-colored fabric with black trim that went well with her red hair and turned her eyes a more vivid blue.

What a beauty she was, he thought. "Ah, there you

are, Miss Maude," he said. "Did you have a good rest? Get enough to eat?"

She blinked as if the kindness of his tone surprised her. "Yes, Mr. MacLaren, thank you," she said. "Again, I want to apologize for worrying and inconveniencing you and your mother by my actions. I really did not see that I had a choice. But I'll understand if you've decided I cannot be trusted to work here anymore."

"Miss Maude, what kind of self-centered tyrant do you take me for?" he asked her, a little indignantly. "Indeed you did not have a choice," he said, and met her gaze with his. "No decent person could have left that girl alone under the circumstances, especially when you knew that you were the best suited for the task of helping her bring her baby into the world. But I need to let you know that my primary concern when you went missing was not any inconvenience to myself or my mother—and yes, I'm aware that my mother made it sound as if that was *her* sole concern," he added, when she merely raised an eyebrow and continued to study him. "But it wasn't mine."

He took a deep breath, knowing what he was risking but knowing he'd gain nothing without taking a chance. "Ah, Maude, don't you see? I'm starting to care about you—very much. It's not a feeling I recognize easily, or am very comfortable feeling. I know what I said at the barbecue makes it sound as if I'm a crusty confirmed bachelor, but I *care* about you. And because I care, I was worried about your safety."

Her jaw dropped, and she stared at him, eyes wide as English pennies. "You care. About me. The man who said seeking love was nothing more than claptrap."

"Go ahead, laugh if ye want," he told her. "I reckon I've earned it. I've said many foolish things over the course of my life. Surely you won't hold that particular thing against me forever? Aye, I care about you. I've seen what a fearless and brave lassie ye are, and skillful as well as kind and gentle. I find myself wanting to be around you more and more."

Maude closed her mouth, but kept staring, as if she thought any moment now the cynical Jonas MacLaren would reappear and make fun of her for her gullibility. "Mr. MacLaren—" she began.

"Do you think you might call me Jonas?" he dared to ask. "At least when 'tis just us?"

Her eyes bore a guarded glint now. "I'll call you Jonas if you wish," she said, in that delicious Texas drawl that made everything she said land pleasantly on his ears—even what she said afterward. "But, Jonas, what do I know about you, really? You're a man of secrets—you keep more than you give up. How am I to trust you?"

He saw it as she must see it—he was asking her to trust him without any basis, without any transparency on his part. His cryptic announcement the first night Maude was here, about his mother being willing to kill to protect her child, hadn't helped, especially when he'd refused to give her any explanation afterward.

"Trust doesn't come easily for a MacLaren," he said. "Not after what we've been through."

"Without trust there can be no honest caring," she told him. "If you don't trust me enough to show me your true self, how can I know who I'm caring for in return?"

The idea that some part of her, at least, *wanted* to care in return gladdened his heart, if only for a moment. *But how could he bare his soul to her, knowing that if she knew everything she'd whirl away from him in horror and disgust?*

He cleared his throat, which suddenly felt thick with emotion. "I…I'll think about what you've said, Miss Maude. Will you give me some time?"

"Time?" She looked confused—or was she wary, wondering if he was trying to distract her from her quest for the truth?

"Aye, time. Time to show you who I am, time to get to know you, to trust you, too?"

She studied him, her clear blue eyes penetrating to his soul. "Yes, Jonas."

He was so pleased—and relieved—he wanted to kiss her right then, but knew it was too soon. She'd run screaming from the house and take Juana and Hannah with her.

"I'll make sure you're not sorry," he told her. Should he sit down with her now, and try to begin telling her about his past? Not yet. He had to think about how to do that. "And now," he said, "but only if you're not too tired, my mother was wondering if you would you have a few minutes to read to her before she sleeps? She's been missing her daily dose of *Ivanhoe*."

She smiled and said, "Of course. I'll go right to her."

Figuring Coira MacLaren wouldn't mind if she was five minutes later, Maude checked on Dulcey and the baby. She was pleased to find the girl lying in bed, smiling down at her sleeping baby, and relieved when she placed a hand gently on Dulcey's brow and felt only a normal amount of warmth, rather than feverishly hot skin. *No sign of childbed fever after the difficult birth—at least, not yet. Thank You, Lord.*

"How is your little son?" she asked the new mother. "Is he still nursing well?"

Dulcey nodded with enthusiasm. "*Sí.* I have decided to name him Pedrito—little Pedro—after his father. I can't wait for him to see his son."

"I'm sure he will think him the finest baby boy ever born in San Saba County," Maude agreed. "Did you know where my room is, just down the hall? Please let me know if you need anything during the night."

Then she went to Coira's room. The old woman smiled as she entered. "All recovered from your adventure, Maude?" She held out the leather-bound volume of *Ivanhoe*. "Please read me a chapter—I can't wait to see if Ivanhoe marries Rebecca or Rowena, can you?"

Maude was happy to lose herself in the compelling story—anything to keep from obsessing about how her relationship with Jonas might change after their talk earlier. After reading for an hour, Maude finally bade the woman good-night and was free to go to her room. She expected to find Juana already sleeping, but although Hannah was snoozing away, safely tucked in her cradle, Juana was sitting up in the bed, a shawl around her shoulders. Maude was glad to have a chance to talk with her friend.

"I want to apologize again for worrying you so by taking Hannah with me and staying gone so long. Does she seem all right?" she asked, glancing once again at her sleeping daughter.

"She seems none the worse for wear," Juana said, her face serene. "But you look like there is something on your mind—something pleasant," she added with a wink. "Your talk with Senor MacLaren went well? He is no longer angry with you?"

Maude shook her head. Remembering what he'd said, about why he'd been angry because he was worried for her safety, because he cared about her, and the conversation that had followed, sent pink heat flooding her cheeks. "He said he understands I had no other choice."

As she feared, Juana's bright eyes hadn't missed the sudden flush of color in Maude's face.

"He said more than that, didn't he? Maude, what did he say? Hector said Senor MacLaren was like a man possessed, once he realized you were missing—pacing up and down on the carpet as if he wanted to wear a furrow into it, searching the barn again and again to see if you were there. He said he feared the man would go loco..."

At the mention of MacLaren's foreman, Juana's eyes brightened. Yes, it had not been very long since her own husband's death, but Juana found Jonas's right-hand man interesting, and it said much that the foreman had confided in her. But Maude forbore to tease her friend right now, thinking she'd tried Juana's patience enough today.

"Juana, he said he was angry because he was worried—because he *cares* for me," she told her friend, allowing her amazement to show.

"Aahh," Juana said, infusing a world of meaning into the drawn-out syllable. "He *cares*. I thought so, *mi amiga*. What will you do now?"

"Do? There's nothing I can do as long as he keeps so many secrets. How can I let myself care for a man who's as secretive as he is? How do I know he's not wanted for murder or something equally horrible back in Scotland?"

"What an imagination you have, Maude!" Juana cried, laughing. "I think you should give the man a chance. After all, look how kind and understanding he is to his mother, who can be difficult at times, yes? *Mi madre*—my mother—always said that a man who treats his mother well will treat his wife well, too. Jonas MacLaren will show you what he is, if you give him time—and you're right here under his roof, in a perfect position to observe. You don't have to be in a rush to decide."

Maude dropped a quick kiss on Juana's brow. "You are very wise, my friend. Thank you. And now I'm sure we should get some rest, or tomorrow will come before we are ready."

Because she had napped earlier, Maude lay awake for a long time that night, listening to Juana's and Hannah's even, soft breathing. What would Jonas do, now that he had made his surprising declaration of caring for her? But she found no answers in the darkness. As Juana had indicated, she would have to wait and see. She finally fell asleep until Hannah woke to be nursed near dawn.

* * *

Jonas had no easier time than Maude in finding rest. How did a man go about courting a girl like Maude in his own home, under his mother's eagle eye? It wasn't as if he could bring her flowers—even in the relatively mild climate of the Hill Country there were no roses or wild flowers blooming in November to be picked for her. And he suspected it would take more than flowers to cause Maude Harkey to drop her guard with him.

It would take nothing less than the full truth to gain her heart, he knew that now. But before she learned the full truth, he needed for her to like him, or nothing would persuade her to stay with him another moment once she learned the whole story. Yes, making her like him would have to be the first step toward love…and the more he thought on it, the more he realized just how hard he would have to work to reach it. The first day they'd met he certainly hadn't charmed her with his cynical remarks about love. He knew she never would have come to Five Mile Hill Ranch to tend to his mother if baby Hannah hadn't come into her life, and with her, the need to find a new home. No, he was not off to a promising start on his goal of making her like him. He would have to work harder—show her that there was more to him than the curt man she met at the barbecue.

He suspected he would also have to improve his relationship with the Lord. Maude was a woman of faith, so she wouldn't ally herself with a faithless man like himself. *But how could he believe in a heavenly Father, a God of love, after the example his earthly father had set?*

Lord, help me, show me the way, he prayed, then marveled that he had addressed words to Heaven. *Was there anyone to hear them? And would God have any interest in answering the prayers of a man like him?*

"Might ye be free for a little while this afternoon once you're finished with your other tasks?" Jonas asked.

His question surprised Maude, but she laid down her soup spoon and considered. Mrs. MacLaren had been served her noon meal and was now dozing in her chair, so she was free of any duty toward her for a while. Senora Morales considered herself fully healed and had resumed her position as queen of the kitchen and denied needing any help.

Pedro the shepherd had shown up this morning, and with a shy pride had indicated he was here to collect his wife and baby son. His joy when Maude had taken him to see them was enough to bring tears to her eyes. Hector had allowed him to borrow a wagon to take his wife and child home, and he had done so with touching gratitude. Dulcey had given Maude an affectionate farewell, and had only left after Maude had promised to pay a visit to her and Pedrito at her earliest convenience. She could tell the young shepherd's wife felt a deep admiration toward Maude for saving hers and her baby's lives.

"I just have Hannah to watch, but otherwise, yes," Maude said, nodding in the direction of the baby, who was toying with a crust of bread, hoping Jonas wouldn't ask why Juana wasn't available to watch her. Juana had fed the child and then gone off to have the midday meal with Hector, but Maude didn't feel free to discuss this with Jonas. She knew Juana wouldn't be gone too long, anyway.

Jonas MacLaren smiled at the baby, who grinned back like a born coconspirator. "The wee lass is no problem. In fact, I think she might like what I plan to be showing you."

"Oh? And what would that be?"

He waggled a finger at her. "You'll just have to wonder until you come with me," he said with maddening vagueness. "'Tis out in the barn."

Maude stared at him, but his hazel eyes gave no clue. If he was encouraging Hannah's presence, he could hardly be planning anything scandalous. Besides, during the day there were apt to be cowhands coming into the barn to take a horse out of a stall or to retrieve a saddle or bridle from the tack room, and Jonas had to know that their solitude might be interrupted.

"I'm finished now," she said, gesturing at her empty plate. "There's no time like the present to see what you're being so mysterious about."

Grabbing her shawl from its hook by the door, she followed him as he led the way across the courtyard toward the barn. Walking into the shady interior of the barn, she smelled the characteristic odors of horses, hay and leather. When he got to the tack room he pushed open the door.

As the door creaked on its hinges, a big tabby cat streaked past him and out toward the sunlight.

"Need a bit of time away from your bairns, Tiger?

Never fear, we've only come to admire them," Jonas said as a protesting chorus of mews erupted from the far end of the room.

The tack room was big enough for a semicircle of old chairs beyond the racks of saddles and bridles. It looked like a gathering spot where the vaqueros might sit and trade yarns and laughter while they cleaned tack.

And here, Maude saw as her eyes adjusted to the shadowy room, Tiger had left her litter in a box of old rags.

"Kittens," she breathed in delight, hurrying forward to kneel in front of them, grinning at the squirming mass in the box—black, white, orange, gray tiger like their mother, and one spotted with patches of black and brown. There had to be at least half a dozen, though they were so close together and constantly moving, it was hard to count.

"Let me hold the lass while you get a closer look," Jonas said, taking Hannah from her.

Once her hands were free, Maude impulsively picked up the spotted one and held to her cheek, giggling as it wriggled and mewed, its little paws scrabbling for something to hold on to. She let it perch on her shoulder, then giggled as it began to purr and lap her neck with its sandpaper-rough tongue.

"Aren't they a bonny sight?" Jonas asked, sitting down on the rough board floor so that Hannah could get a closer look from his lap. The sight evidently pleased the baby, too, for she squealed in excitement as one of the bolder kittens drew near, climbing over Jonas's leg.

"But I thought kittens were always born in the spring," Maude said.

Jonas grinned. "So their mother's a wee bit daft and chose to have her babies in the fall," he said with a shrug. "Who can tell a cat what to do?"

She chuckled, then nearly lost her breath as she watched Jonas holding Hannah, an arm protectively curved around her to hold her upright. The sight sent an odd surge of tenderness racing through Maude. He looked so natural with the child, as if Hannah were his daughter and he had planned this treat just for her.

"They're darling," Maude murmured, sighing in delight as the kitten she held kept purring. She remembered a cat she'd had as a child, colored very much like this one. "I wish Hannah and I could keep one. But they're probably not old enough yet to leave their mother, are they?"

Jonas looked thoughtful, staring at the far end of the room. "If I ken aright, they were born two months ago at the full moon, so aye, they could leave. I've already found a couple of the rascals out exploring in the stalls. Pretty soon they'll all have scattered around the barn, doing what cats do. I had nae thought of bringing one into the house—Mother has a weakness for wee things like kittens, but she'd have a conniption the first time she found one sharpening its claws on her sofa leg." He looked momentarily regretful, then brightened. "Now that you mention it, though, Senora Morales was just wishing for a cat to keep the mice away from the pantry," he said. "I believe we'll take the kitty for a visit into the big house, after all," he said. "I'll leave the decision to you as to which kitten to choose. Mother will get used to the idea. She wouldn't like mice in the oatcakes, would she? We'll do our best to keep the animal away from the furniture. The worst Mother can do is to banish the creature from the house," he added with a grin that was so infectious Maude couldn't help but grin back while her heart did a funny little flip-flop at the sight of "the" MacLaren's upward-curved lips.

Then she saw that he had seen her smiling, and there was a sudden intensity to Jonas's gaze. He leaned toward her…

Hannah shrieked in protest, for the kitten had climbed down from Jonas's arms and was out of Hannah's reach. It was now stalking Maude's fingers in her lap.

It was enough to interrupt the moment, and to stop Jonas from…*kissing her? Was that what he had been about to do, or was she only imagining the intent that had gleamed in those golden eyes?* Surely she had seen something that wasn't there, she told herself, yet a smile of regret—at the interruption?—curved his lips now.

"Perhaps we'd best be getting back to the house so our new 'guest' can get settled in the kitchen. Is this the kitten you've decided upon, then?" he asked, nodding toward the one in Maude's lap, then back at the surging, meowing mass of half a dozen kittens of various colors.

"Yes. Mama always said to pick the one that picked you first," she told him, dredging up a memory she hadn't even realized she still had of the day she had adopted a kitten so long ago.

"Good advice, I'm sure," he murmured, and handing

Hannah back to Maude, hoisted the kitten to his chest. The image was every bit as unexpectedly appealing as the sight of him cradling Hannah in his arms.

Maude looked away before she could do something foolish—like ask him if he'd wanted to kiss her after all.

Chapter Twelve

Coira MacLaren watched with narrowed eyes as Maude and her son approached her bed.

"What have ye got there?" she demanded. "And why are ye bringing it into my room?"

"We just thought you'd like to see one of the barn cat's new litter, Mother," Jonas said, holding it close to the old woman. The calico kitten chose that moment to let out a plaintive meow as Jonas laid it gently on her bed.

"Ah, the wee sweet creature!" Coira cooed, reaching for it and astonishing Maude at the transformation in her mood. "What are ye doin' in the house now? So soft ye are! Are you a boy or a girl kitty?"

"Maude informs me calico cats are almost always female," Jonas told her. "Senora Morales was saying she needed a cat in the kitchen to keep away the mice—"

"Och, 'tis not for me?" protested Coira, pouting. "But it's so bonny and lively..." She picked up a loose ribbon that had bound her braid of gingery hair, and trailed it in front of the kitten. Instinctively, the kitten coiled and pounced, capturing the end of the ribbon in its tiny paws.

"Well, I suppose we could always get another kitten for the kitchen," Jonas allowed with a grin.

"No, one cat in the house is enough," his mother said. "I suppose she's a bit wee yet to be catching mice, so she can stay and distract an old woman from her pain. When she gets older, 'twill be time to think of putting her to work. Mind you, Jonas, she'll need a box of dirt so she can mind her manners. And while you're seeing to that, why don't ye fetch a saucer of milk up from the kitchen. Such a tiny thing's bound to need nourishment. Are ye sure she's old enough to leave her mother?"

"Yes, she is, and I'll go fetch the milk," Jonas promised, and with a wink at Maude, he left.

"You said you're in pain, Mrs. MacLaren," Maude murmured. "Do you need some more of the willow bark tea?" She'd been giving the older woman some with her breakfast every morning, and Mrs. MacLaren claimed there was nothing like it to make her aching joints less swollen and painful. Occasionally she needed some later in the day, too, but Maude was careful not to give it to her too often, knowing the tea contained a powerful medicine that should not be overused.

"Nay, I'll be all right now, with this wee sprightly thing to distract me," Coira said. "Come sit with me for a moment, till my son returns."

Bemused at their unexpected success with convincing Mrs. MacLaren to allow the kitten to stay in the house, Maude sank into the bedside chair.

Coira turned on her side to face Maude. "I know what you're about, you know."

Maude was so surprised at the woman's sudden change of tone she could only goggle at her. "About? Whatever do you mean, Mrs. MacLaren?"

"You're scheming to capture my son's affection, and you've certainly got an advantage, living under the same roof and constantly showing yourself off as a heroine."

Sensing the change in the atmosphere, the calico kitten dashed off the bed and darted underneath it.

Maude felt the sudden kindling of her famous temper at the unexpected, undeserved attack. "Scheming? Mrs. MacLaren, I seek nothing but your son's well-being, and yours, too," she said hotly. "Jonas has made no commitment to me," she said. *A man saying he cared for you wasn't a commitment, was it?*

Coira pounced on her use of her son's first name much as the kitten had. "Jonas. Ye call him by his first name, then deny you're after him?"

Maude was past caution now. "If you no longer need my services, then please have your son take me back to Simpson Creek. But first tell me why you'd deny your son the right to happiness, to a life of his own."

"I? I would deny Jonas nothing," the woman hissed. "But he was happy once, aye, and in love, too. The love of his life, Annabella MacKenzie was. And then he had to bury his love and leave her in a Scottish grave—all because of his father. How much of a heart do ye think he has left to give anyone? Ye might say I'm lookin' out for your good, too, girl."

Maude could only stare at the woman lying in the

bed. Then she staggered unsteadily from the room, intent on reaching the sanctuary of her room before she gave way to tears.

He'd been expecting the knock on his door since he'd returned to his mother's room and found Maude gone and the kitten hiding under the bed.

"Where'd Maude go?" he asked as he set the saucer down on the floor. The kitten crawled out from its hiding place to lap at it.

Coira shrugged. "How should I know? She's a moody creature, that one."

Jonas leaned over his mother with both hands resting on the bed. *"What did you say to her?"*

His mother's sudden defiant expression confirmed his worst suspicions. "Nothing she didn't need to hear, my lad."

Aghast, he stared at her, then turned on his heel and walked quickly down the hall to the room Maude shared with Juana and Hannah.

He knocked. There was no answer. He called through the door. No answer still, but he heard Hannah commence a fretful crying. Finally, just as he was about to start shouting, Juana quietly opened the door a crack, just enough to give her room to step out into the hall, shutting it behind her before he could see inside. She held Hannah, who was rubbing her eyes and whimpering.

"I'm sorry, Miss Juana. I've wakened the bairn, haven't I? Sorry," he mumbled again.

"Yes, you did," she said, but gave him a small smile

of forgiveness. "I'm sorry, Senor Jonas, but Maude is in no condition to talk to you right now. Perhaps mañana—tomorrow."

Wait until tomorrow? Impossible. He wanted to tell Juana what she could do with her mañana, but he reminded himself that this situation wasn't her fault. She was only trying to protect her friend by relaying a message. But there was no way he could endure a night without knowing what his mother had said to Maude, or whether she hated him now and would announce her departure tomorrow.

"Miss Juana, please," he said, letting Maude's friend see the anguish that he felt, "I can't wait that long. I must speak to her. Please tell Maude—that is, please *ask* Maude—to meet me in the parlor tonight, after the household is quiet. After the grandfather clock in the hall strikes ten, say?"

Juana studied him with unblinking black eyes. "I will ask her." Then she backed into the door, never taking her gaze from his as if she feared he would try to force his way in after her.

He heard murmuring as he waited, seemingly for an eternity, and then Juana reappeared again, without Hannah.

"She says she will come," Juana said. "But before I let my friend do that, senor, I shall require a promise of you." Again, her stare was steady and unblinking.

"Anything, Miss Juana."

"I require that you will respect Maude's decisions, even if you do not like the response she gives you to whatever questions you have for her. While you are her employer, that does not give you the right to overrule the choices she makes with her life. I must know that you will honor that."

"I promise. I wouldn't dream of forcing any decision on her, no matter what she says to me. I will respect whatever choice she makes. You must believe me." He prayed she would accept his word, though he would not swear on anything holy, or on his father's grave—he wasn't worthy to make such a vow.

"I do believe you, senor," Juana said. "I wish you well." Then she disappeared behind the door again.

Somehow, Jonas managed to contain himself until the hour arrived, listening as the myriad sounds of the big ranch house gradually devolved into silence as the household retired. He felt simultaneously eager to see Maude and tempted to run—to shut the door to his room behind him and pretend he had never arranged this meeting. What if his mother had revealed everything to Maude, and she came to this meeting to tell him she hated him? Could he bear to hear such a thing from her? But he would not for the world have her show up in the parlor, only to find it empty. She may choose to turn herself away from him, but *he* would not voluntarily turn from her.

He heard the soft sound of her footsteps approaching down the hall before the grandfather clock had struck its last tone, and then Maude was in the parlor. She carried a single candle, which wavered in its pewter holder and cast a quivering light on her.

Maude wore a simple, high-necked white shirt with her usual dark skirt, but her hair was down, an impossibly glorious dark red bounty spreading across her shoulders. He wished he could just go to her and bury his hands in it.

"You…you wanted to see me, Mr.—that is, Jonas?" she quavered.

"Yes. Sit down, won't you?" he invited, gesturing to the big horsehair sofa drawn up before the fire.

He waited until she did so, then sat down next to her—close, but not so close that she would feel threatened by his nearness.

He waited only a moment, until he felt her expectant gaze fasten on him.

"Maude, I wanted to speak to you because I believe my mother said something to upset you this afternoon, am I right?"

Eyes downcast, she nodded. "She thinks I'm scheming for your affection."

"You? A schemer?" He chuckled. "You don't have a scheming bone in your body, Maude Harkey."

"Nevertheless, that's what she thinks. And she says you have no affection to give me after losing the love of your life, Annabella MacKenzie."

Hearing Annabella's name on Maude's tongue stole Jonas's breath for a moment. But Annabella was gone, and he was not, and here was a living, breathing woman whose honest feelings shone from her blue eyes. A woman whom he sensed was not capable of hurting him as Annabella had.

He took a deep breath. "'Tis time for the truth you asked me for once, if you're willing to hear it, Maude."

Slowly, she nodded.

"Back in Scotland, I didn't grow up with a father

like yours, Maude, a father who loved me and wanted to teach me things."

He saw that she was listening intently, no doubt wondering why he was speaking of fathers when she was expecting to hear about Annabella. He looked away from her clear, trusting eyes so he'd have the courage to say what must be said.

"James MacLaren, my father, was a hard man, a tavern keeper who loved his whiskey much more than he loved his wife and son. I was an only child. I'd had a sister who died young of a fever before I was old enough to remember her. Ma said Katie was the apple of Father's eye, that he only grew harder and meaner and more given to drink after she passed."

He saw pity fill Maude's blue eyes then.

"Jonas…" She reached out a hand to him. He took it, and was surprised by the strength it gave him to be touching her.

"He was selfish as the day was long, my father. Always insisted that he have the best chair, the best cut of the meat, the best clothes, never mind what was left for Ma and me, and there was a beating for us if we so much as looked at him cross-eyed. Anything he wanted, he took, whether 'twas rightly his or not. He could charm where he pleased, when he had a mind to, but the charm always turned sour in the end. He had an easy time making friends, but as you can imagine, he never kept them for long. There were none my mother or I could turn to for any help against his cruelties.

"I grew up running the wynds, the narrow streets of Edinburgh, a wild young lad, seizing any chance I could find to be away from my home. Then I grew up and met Annabella MacKenzie. She was a pretty thing, and I fell in love as only a foolish boy can do. I thought she hung the moon and was pure as its light. We were to be married, Annabella and me. And then she…she met my father."

Nausea churned inside him. *Did he really have to tell her this?*

He'd gone too far to turn back now. He had to rid himself of the secret that was poisoning him.

"It was hard to wait for our wedding day—for our wedding *night*," he admitted. "I was not religious, as you know, and cared little for the idea of the sin in it. But I was resolved to wait, because I respected Annabella's honor and wanted her to know it. But something changed in Annabella after she met my father. She became—what was your word?—*secretive*. Something was wrong, I knew it deep in my bones. And then she told me she was with child."

He heard Maude's gasp, her whispered, "Jonas, *no…*"

"She wouldn't tell me who the blackguard was, not until she lay in childbed, dying, and the babe perishing along with her. It was my father. He'd come to her with sweet words and little presents, using that fiendish charm of his to get what he wanted, promising her the earth, until she'd given in to him."

He felt as if the remembered rage and grief was about to swamp him. Her grasp tightened in his, as if he was drowning, and her hand was the only thing that could pull him to safety. He didn't dare let go.

"I waited till she breathed her last, and then I ran down to our home over the tavern and confronted him.

Unfortunately he'd heard that Annabella was in labor and wasn't doing well, and he was sodden with drink. I went after him with a poker from the hearth, though my mother screamed at me to stop. My father was too startled to retaliate at first—I'd never fought back against him before. But when it sunk in that I had 'dared' to raise my hand against him, his temper boiled over. I was no match for my father in one of his whiskey rages—he yanked the poker from me and began to beat me with it. I remembered him yelling that he was going to kill me. He would have, too, but there was another poker that my mother grabbed. In his rage, my father did not notice when she came up behind him. The last thing I remember before I passed out was the sight of her raising the poker over my father's head..."

"Jonas..." Maude whispered, and he realized he'd been staring into the flames.

"The next thing I knew," he said with a lifeless voice, "was my mother waking me with a cold wet cloth to my face and saying that she'd killed my father and we had to flee or she'd be hanged. We threw what clothes we could quickly gather into a valise and ran for the docks, determined to take the first ship out of port that would let us aboard before the body was found and the hue and cry began. We finally found a ship that would take my mother's ring in exchange for passage for the both of us, as long as she agreed to cook for the crew and the other passengers. We'd have sailed no matter where the ship was going, but fortunately for us, it was bound for New York."

Maude buried her face against his chest, then, and wept. He held her until the storm passed.

"Oh, *Jonas*. How unspeakably horrible for you," she murmured, when she could talk again.

How horrible *for* you, she'd said. Not, how horrible *of* you. And he noted with dazed amazement that she did not pull away from him, as he had expected her to do.

"That cannot have been easy for you to tell me," she said at last. "Thank you."

"I'll…I'll understand if you don't feel you can stay, after what I've told you," he said, wanting to make it easier for her to utter what she must surely be trying to find a way to say.

"I…I'm not going anywhere," she said. "Why would I? Nothing you told me about is your fault. What a burden you've been carrying all these years."

He hadn't realized it, but she was right. The burden of his guilt had weighed him down ever since that night of horrors.

"Shouldn't I feel guilty? If I hadn't gone after him, my mother wouldn't have had to intervene, and she wouldn't have had to flee the gallows."

"No provocation on your part justified what he did. He would have killed you," she pointed out. "Surely it wasn't wrong for a mother to save her son's life."

He allowed himself a mirthless bark of laughter. "I doubt the magistrate would have seen it that way, but bless you, Maude, for saying that. You're a sweet, innocent girl, always trying to see the best in a person."

She turned to look at him full in the face. "I see a good man when I look at you, Jonas MacLaren," she said to him. "But it's time to lay your burden of guilt down. There's someone willing to take it for you."

At first, he misunderstood. "*You* can't make up for what I did, Maude. How could you?"

She smiled a gentle smile, despite the tinge of disbelieving scorn in her voice. "No, not I, Jonas. The Lord will take your guilt, if you'll give it to Him. He's been waiting all these years to take it from you—to heal your heart and make you feel whole again."

All he could do was stare at her. "I know you're a woman of faith, Maude Harkey. But I would have killed my father, and I'm not sorry he's dead. I don't believe there's anyone up there," he said pointing toward the ceiling, "who cares what happens to me."

"But you're wrong, Jonas," she insisted. "I understand now why you'd have trouble believing in a loving heavenly Father when your earthly father was so horrible to you, but He's there, Jonas, just waiting to hear from you."

There was silence between them in that moment, and only the hiss and pop of the flames in the fireplace punctuated it. Maude rose.

"It's late, and you've given me a lot to think about, Jonas, so I'll bid you good-night. Please think about what I said, too. But don't be afraid you'll awake to find me gone in the morning."

Chapter Thirteen

She understood so much more about these bewildering MacLarens now, Maude thought as she lay in bed that night, listening to Juana and Hannah's soft, even breathing.

What she had learned explained so much about this troubled household and the man and woman who owned Five Mile Hill Ranch.

First, she now knew what Jonas had meant that first night about Coira being a woman who would kill to protect her child. Perhaps fury about her own treatment at the hands of her husband had lent her the strength to make that fatal blow, but Coira MacLaren had completely believed her husband would kill her son if she allowed him to live. She had acted to save his life, to protect him from being hurt. And she had continued to act that way in regard to Maude, worrying that Jonas's trust might be betrayed again, as it had been by Annabella. She understood now why Jonas's mother was so jealous and possessive of Jonas—and why he was so cynical about tender relationships between men and women. Love—or at least, any love other than the love a mother had for her son—seemed to bewilder him.

Had Maude gone too far, though, when she'd tried to explain that the love of the heavenly Father was nothing like what a far-from-perfect man might feel for his son? Surely a man's relationship with the Lord was something that should be explained to Jonas by Reverend Chadwick or some other official religious figure who was way more qualified than she. Surely she'd overstepped her bounds, and should have waited until she could arrange for another visit from the Simpson Creek preacher.

But when could that happen? She had no way to get a message to Gil Chadwick, and Jonas might refuse to see him anyway. Surely she had done the right thing to speak the truth at the time when it had been so sorely needed. Perhaps, when she next saw Jonas, she would be coldly told to mind her own business in the future, or that she no longer had a job at Five Mile Hill Ranch. She didn't think that was likely, based on what he had said, but she knew she had taken a risk.

Hannah made a grab for a tendril of Maude's hair that had escaped its knot at the back of her head, and she chuckled. "Oh, no you don't, little Miss Clever One," she murmured, feeling a surge of love for this child as she pushed the lock of hair back into place. Even if she was shown the door by the MacLarens, she would do whatever she must to provide a home for this child.

But she knew now she would regret it if she never

got to see what came of the promising feelings that had sprung up between Jonas MacLaren and herself.

She heard a light step in the hall and then Juana, fresh from taking Mrs. MacLaren her breakfast, entered.

"Did I hear you laughing?" she asked, smiling down at Maude and the baby.

Maude nodded. "Little Miss Mischief is trying to pull my hair down already and it's not even nine o'clock."

"Ah, she's full of tricks, that one. And here's something that might make you smile some more," Juana added, pulling a folded piece of paper from her apron. Maude could see her name inscribed on the front; on the back it was sealed with a blob of wax with the MacLaren seal impressed into it. "Senor Jonas gave this to me to give to you as I passed him in the hall," she said.

Maude froze. Was this written notice that she was being fired?

"Don't think the worst, *mi amiga*. Senor Jonas looked happy, not like a man handing out bad news," Juana said. "Besides, you know he is a direct man. If he was going to fire you, he'd tell you so to your face, no? Not on paper. Now, open it and tell me I was right."

Maude's hands shook as she obeyed her friend, unfolding the stiff writing paper. It took a moment before his elegant copperplate script arranged itself into comprehensible words:

Mr. Jonas MacClaren requests the pleasure of Miss Maude Harkey's company on the veranda at two of the clock today for a reading of the poetry of Robert Burns. Refreshments will be served.

Wordlessly, she handed the missive to Juana.

Juana grinned as she read it. "*Ahh*...I guess we're not being fired, eh? Quite the contrary—he is *courting* you. He didn't tell me what he wrote, but he did say to tell you that his mother would not be needing you this afternoon. *I* will be listening for her bell."

"Ah, Miss Maude, I'm glad you could make it," Jonas said, rising as Maude came out onto the sunny veranda at precisely two o'clock.

"I had many invitations, but I'm glad I was able to fit you in," Maude quipped. She had dressed with care and wore a becoming gown of rust-colored nun's veiling, a lightweight wool-and-silk blend that perfectly suited the sunny day, but was warm enough for the occasional chill breeze.

Jonas grinned in response to her teasing tone. "In all seriousness, I wanted to do something approaching what I would have done if your parents were still living and I was paying you a proper call—after asking your father's permission, of course. We would sit on your veranda and have genteel refreshments just as Senora Morales has provided," he said, gesturing to the plate of cookies and cold tea that sat on a little table in front of the chairs, "and make discreet conversation while your mother frequently looked out the window. This is as close to such an experience as I could manage."

Her heart warmed as she understood his endeavor to provide her with what could have been, what *should* have been, had death not intervened and taken her parents from her too soon—the ordinary ritual of courting. His understanding of what she had missed touched her, so much so that she found herself momentarily at a loss for words and hoped her smile was enough to convey what was in her heart.

"I thought I might read a poem by Robbie Burns that I always liked," he said, and began to read.

"O my Luve's like a red, red rose,
That's newly sprung in June:
O my Luve's like the melodie,
That's sweetly play'd in tune…"

She began to blush as he read the next stanza.

"As fair art thou, my bonnie lass,
So deep in luve am I;
And I will luve thee still, my dear,
Till a' the seas gang dry…"

Was it possible that he was letting the poet make his declaration of love for him? Could he really love *her*, Maude Harkey?

"That's beautiful," she said, when he had finished, loving the way his voice had caressed the Scottish words, such as *gang* for *go*.

He smiled at her. "Perhaps you'd pour me a glass of that tea? My mouth's gone dry, but I thought you might like to hear 'A Rosebud by My Early Walk,' as well."

She poured the tea, and he drank, then began to read the next poem, only to break off as they heard the sound of horses' hooves coming up the lane from the road.

Hector Segundo rode at the side of a man Maude didn't recognize at first, not until they drew up in front of the veranda. Hector said, "I'm sorry, Senor MacLaren. I suggested this man send a message, but he insisted he must see Senorita Harkey at once."

The man, who wore a travel-stained, mud-spattered duster over denim trousers and a striped shirt and leather vest was the very man Maude had hoped never to see again—Felix Renz. Hannah's father. He jumped off his horse and stood facing her, reins clutched in his hand.

She felt Jonas stiffen beside her as she said, "Mr. Renz, I'd like to present you to my employer, Jonas MacLaren. Mr. MacLaren, this is—"

"Where is she?" Felix interrupted her, his voice frantic. "I just got back into town late last night, and Miz Meyer told me April Mae was dead, and that I had a kid…"

"Mr. Renz, let Senor Gonsalvo take your horse, and why don't you sit down?" Maude said, rising. She saw out of the corner of her eye that Jonas was fetching another chair from against the wall of the house.

"Where's my girl? Mrs. Meyer said it was a girl," Renz said as he collapsed into the chair Jonas set down for him. "And what happened to April Mae? Mrs. Meyer wouldn't tell me much…"

Maude thought about offering him some tea, but he looked too panicked to be capable of swallowing anything or holding on to a delicate china cup.

"I'm so sorry, Mr. Renz. April Mae arrived at the boardinghouse in labor, delivered a baby girl and died two days later of childbed fever. It…happens to new mothers sometimes…" she murmured, realizing how inadequate the statement must sound to someone who cared even as thoughtlessly as Felix Renz had for April Mae Horvath.

Renz was as pasty pale as the belly of a fish and stank of spirits. His red-rimmed eyes stared blearily at her.

"But how did she get to Simpson Creek?" he demanded, taking hold of her hand and clutching it desperately. "I left her on a ranch 'bout fifty miles from there. I went there to see her when I came back through, and her people shut the door in my face, sayin' she'd run off."

There was a whining note in his voice that was causing her to lose pity fast. "She *walked*, Mr. Renz. She came looking for *you*," she told him without trying to soften the facts.

"But I *told* her I'd be back to see her," he insisted. "I didn't know I'd left her expectin'…"

"Her parents threw her out when it became obvious she was with child," Maude told him. "She didn't have a choice about waiting for you. She came to the boardinghouse hoping to find you."

"And I was gone."

Maude nodded.

"So where's my baby girl?"

That wasn't the question she'd expected to come next. She'd thought he'd ask, *Did April Mae suffer? Did she have a decent burial? Did she ask you to try to find me?* Maude seethed inside at the man's omissions and his disregard for the sorry state in which he'd left that poor girl.

"I have been caring for the child, Mr. Renz. Hannah is well."

"Hannah? Hannah is what you named her?" He looked around them frantically then, as if baby Hannah might be sitting quietly at the front door, just watching the proceedings, or peeking from Maude's front pocket or Jonas's shoulder.

"April Mae named her," Maude told him.

"I wanna see her. I'm her pa."

"I think not," Jonas said, standing and putting an arm protectively around Maude's shoulder. "At least, not today. If you want to see her, you will sober up and bathe, and return with clean clothes on."

Renz drew himself up to his unimpressive height. "You can't keep a man from seeing his child!" he shouted, lurching unsteadily toward Jonas who showed no signs of backing down.

"The same child you *abandoned*, along with her mother, before she was even born?" Maude asked in an icy tone. "You haven't even asked where April Mae is buried. You forfeited any rights you might have had, Mr. Renz."

Renz gaped at her as if he might be trying to focus. "I was comin' back, I told you..."

Hector, still holding Renz's horse's reins with one hand, caught him before he could get any closer. "My boss has spoken. You must leave, senor."

"All right, I'll leave," Renz said, shaking off Gonsalvo's grip. "But I'm comin' back. An' when I do, little Hannah's leavin' with me. A man's got a right to his child!"

Renz staggered toward his horse, seized the reins ungraciously from Gonsalvo and somehow managed to mount. The horse rolled its eyes and did a little protesting crowhop, nearly unseating his rider.

"Show him the horse trough at the side of the barn before he goes, Hector," Jonas said. "He's ridden all this way and hasn't given a thought to watering his horse. Clearly he doesn't think any more of his animal than he did of his woman."

Hector obeyed, and Maude and Jonas remained on the veranda, frozen in silence, until Renz and the horse returned from the other side of the barn, then trotted down the lane that led to the road. Then Maude, her face awash in tears, turned to Jonas.

"He can't take her, can he? *You won't let him take my baby*?"

From his shirt pocket he produced a handkerchief, which he placed in her hand. He waited until she swiped at her eyes and cheeks, then said, "Of course I won't let him take her, Maude. The man's no more fit to be a father to Hannah than a pig is." His face was grim as he added, "But don't worry yourself—with any luck the horse will buck him off on his way back to Simpson Creek and break his neck, and that'll be the end of it."

Maude could tell he was completely serious about his wish, and couldn't find it in herself to blame him for it. She was just thankful she had left Hannah with Juana, rather than bringing her out to sit in the sunshine where Renz would have seen her immediately. In his worked-up state, he probably would have grabbed for her. She wished they didn't have to face the prospect of his return, and she knew instinctively that he *would* return, despite the distance of the ranch from town. The man wandered all over central Texas selling his wares—what was an extra ten-mile trip?

Jonas must have been thinking about it, too, for he turned to Hector, who had remained where he had been holding Renz's horse and said, "I want two hands on watch at night until I say otherwise. If you see that man again, you're to notify me immediately, no matter where I am on the ranch, you understand? Do not let him anywhere near Miss Maude or her child unless I am there."

Hector nodded, his black eyes liquid with earnestness. "Of course, senor. That *serpiente*—that snake—will not get close to that sweet baby or Senorita Harkey. This I vow. I will go and alert the rest of the vaqueros." He bowed, then walked his horse toward the bunkhouse.

She believed in that moment that Jonas's foreman would give his life before letting Hannah's father get past his guard, but she still wasn't easy in her mind.

"Jonas, I'm afraid," she said, turning to the man next to her. "What should we do? *Does* that man have a right to his child, just because he fathered her? He's done nothing to prove himself a responsible parent," she said. "He didn't even know he'd left her mother with child, and he's got no job in Simpson Creek to provide a stable home for her. He doesn't even have anywhere to take her other than back to the boardinghouse—and I doubt he's bothered to consider how he'll take care of her once she's there. He's not a man who thinks things through, which is why he's always going to be nothing but a drummer, carting his pots and pans from town to town. But what if he insists, and brings the sheriff out to make us give Hannah to him?"

Again she felt those strong arms go around her and pull her close. In the circle of his arms she felt protected and safe, and knew that he would see Hannah was protected and safe, too.

"I've only met Sheriff Bishop once, but he doesn't seem the kind of man to suffer fools like that man gladly," Jonas said. "Still I think it might be prudent to let the good sheriff know what's going on, and your Reverend Chadwick, too. Would you like to see the preacher, and hear his advice?"

Tears streaming down her face, she nodded, amazed that he had discerned the very thing that would bring her at least a measure of peace.

"Then I'll send for them, sweeting," he said. "Right now. I'm going to have Hector send one of the hands into town directly, and tell them we'd appreciate the two of them calling on us as soon as possible. Until they come and we hear their counsel, rest easy, but do not leave the house without someone with you. And keep Hannah in the house. I won't be leaving the ranch till this is settled."

"I'll be careful," she promised. "Thank you, Jonas."

He put his arms around her again. "Don't worry, Maude. After suffering so much at the hands of a bad father myself, I will not allow it to happen to a sweet innocent like little Hannah."

Felix Renz's bad example was one more reason Jonas would use to keep from believing in a heavenly Father who cared about him, Maude thought grimly, even as she rejoiced that he was here to protect them. *Please, Lord, change his mind about Yourself. Show him Your love.*

"I'm going to go tell Juana what happened and see if your mother needs anything," Maude said when he released her.

"'Tis well for Juana to be aware, too," he said approvingly. "And while I wouldn't worry my mother with Renz's threat—she never leaves the house and I would never permit him inside, so she won't be crossing his path—I will say she'd die before she let anyone harm a hair on Hannah's head. She's very taken with the wee lass." Then, astonishingly, he leaned over and kissed the top of Maude's head.

"All will be well, Maude. Trust me," he murmured. Then he turned and headed for the barn. Too dazed to speak, she watched him go until he was out of sight, and then she went into the house.

Chapter Fourteen

When Maude went to attend to Coira the next morning, she was quickly made aware that her son had told his mother of yesterday's visit by Felix Renz.

"I wish I'd been there to greet him," the older woman grumbled. "And if he comes back, I'll bash him over the head with my cane," she said, pointing with a bony, shaking finger at the polished mahogany cane with its silver-knobbed head that lay propped by her bed.

Maude, who'd been brushing the old woman's pale ginger hair, paused and said carefully, "I hope we won't have to resort to any violence to make the man see sense. Reverend Gil and the sheriff have been sent for, so hopefully they can give us wise counsel on how the situation should be handled."

"If that man comes and thinks to do anything but leave the wee bairn here where she's loved and safe, I won't be responsible for the result," Coira harrumphed. "Though my son would probably take action before I could."

Maude couldn't help but smile at Coira's assertion

that Hannah was "loved and safe" here. "I thank you for giving us a home, Hannah and I, and Juana," she murmured, her fingers moving deftly to braid Coira's hair before winding it into a thin coronet at the top of her head.

"You earn your keep," the woman muttered. "But how do you feel about serving a murderess, now that you know what happened to Jonas's father back in our homeland?"

Startled that Coira knew that Jonas had told Maude of their past, she dropped a handful of hairpins, which fell to the floor with a tiny, tinny clatter.

"I don't think of you as a murderess, Mrs. MacLaren," Maude said honestly. "To me, you're a mother who did what she had to do to protect her son. I wasn't put here to judge you." How could *she* decide that there was some way Coira could have handled it better? Maude hadn't been there and didn't know what Coira's choices could have been. *Yet didn't the Commandment say Thou shalt not kill?*

"You're a good girl, Maude Harkey," Coira murmured, placing a hand on Maude's wrist. "I wish I could have your peace of mind."

"Would you like me to have Reverend Gil call on you when he comes? I'm sure he would pray with you and help you find the peace you're looking for."

Coira uttered a short, bitter bark of laughter. "As simple as that, ye think? Girl, I *killed my husband.* Do ye think it's as simple as saying, God I'm sorry, please forgive me?"

"Yes, I do," Maude said. "The thief hanging on the cross next to Jesus wasn't able to atone for his crimes, but he asked our Lord, and Jesus took him with Himself to heaven that same day, didn't he?"

Coira stared at her for a long moment. "So the Good Book says, child, so it says." She didn't sound convinced. But she didn't sound scornful, either. It was a start.

Hector returned to the ranch at midday the next day with Sheriff Bishop and Reverend Gil in tow. The two were shown into the parlor of the ranch house and given coffee, and Maude and Jonas sat down to hear what they had to say.

"I've spoken to Gabe Bryant, whom you'll know is Simpson Creek's only lawyer, Miss Maude," Sheriff Bishop said. "And he's of the opinion that having abandoned the baby's mother, no court would order that a helpless infant be given to such a person, especially seeing as how he has no fixed residence, no wife and makes his living traveling all over Texas," he said. Hannah, who was sitting in Maude's lap, chose this moment to gurgle happily at him, and Bishop smiled, reminding Maude that the hard-faced, grim sheriff was a loving father, too.

"That's reassuring," Maude murmured. "But what if he comes and tries to insist on taking her?"

"Then Mr. MacLaren has every right to throw him off his property," Bishop said. "I've already put Felix Renz on notice in Simpson Creek that I'm watching him and won't stand for any shenanigans. One wrong move and he'll be enjoying the hospitality of my jail. You just send me word if he comes out and harasses any of you. But I think the reverend might have some good advice worth listening to," he said, nodding at Gil Chadwick.

"If it involves turning the other cheek while that blackguard tries to take the wee bairn, forget it, parson," Jonas warned, his voice a rumbling growl.

Gil Chadwick smiled. "Oh, I don't think it'll come to that. I've been praying about the matter, and here's the approach I would suggest..." He laid out his plan as Jonas and Maude listened attentively, asking questions to work out all the details.

When it came time for the sheriff and the preacher to return to Simpson Creek, Maude felt only a trifle more confident about following the preacher's suggestion. What if it didn't work? She wanted to beg Sam Bishop to stay and guard her child, but she knew that was impossible. The sheriff had a whole town to guard, several miles away. She needed to remember that Jonas, as the owner of Five Mile Hill Ranch, would protect those who lived here. She owed him her trust that he would do as he promised.

And perhaps she was worried about nothing, in any case. Felix Renz might have realized on his own that he had no real means to provide for a child, and never return to Five Mile Hill Ranch. But still she thought she'd better cover her worries with prayer, and did so that evening with Juana. Juana had not been present when the preacher made his suggestions and was a great deal less confident that they would work.

Maude's hopes were dashed the next morning when Felix Renz, freshly bathed and shaved and wearing clothes that must have been newly purchased in the Simpson Creek mercantile, rode up to the ranch house and announced he was here to see his child and wouldn't take no for an answer. There was at least this much to be grateful for—he was sober this time.

True to his word, Jonas had remained at the ranch house in case of this visit, and grudgingly escorted Renz to the parlor. Maude had gone to wait there, and now greeted the man as civilly as she could, hoping he didn't see just how nervous she was about the prospect of letting this scoundrel near her child. But like it or not, he was Hannah's father and had the right to see her—even if she had no intention of letting him take the baby away.

"Make yourself comfortable, Mr. Renz, and I will go and get Hannah."

"You tell my baby girl her *papa* is here to see her!" Renz crowed with a smirk as if he was well aware of Maude's and Jonas's discomfort at his presence and enjoyed every minute of it, despite Jonas's glowering.

A few minutes later, Maude shakily descended the stairs, accompanied by Juana, who held baby Hannah.

"*Amiga*, are you sure this will work?" Juana hissed as they hovered outside the parlor. "That our Hannah will be safe?"

"Have faith, Juana. We prayed about it, didn't we?" Maude said, though she felt far from perfectly assured herself. "Besides, Jonas will be here the whole time. He won't let anything bad happen. I think it was wise to dress her as you did."

Juana winked. "A father must learn certain realities, no?"

For anyone else who'd come to admire baby Hannah, Maude would have made sure Juana was dressed in her best, a long gown with lace trim that Senora Morales had stitched, and would have wrapped her in the crocheted blanket she'd made herself out of the ranch's softest wool. But Maude would not dress Hannah up like a gift for Felix Renz.

"Here she is, Mr. Renz, your daughter, Hannah," Maude cooed, taking Hannah from a shaking Juana and bringing the baby forward, though she wanted nothing more than to run out of the room and barricade herself and her child in their bedroom.

"Come to Papa, sweet girl," Renz said, grinning as he stood to admire his child. "What a beautiful little thing you are! I believe you have April's blue eyes, daughter."

Maude stiffened at Renz's mention of Hannah's late mother, for she had last seen April's blue eyes clouded with pain and fever before they closed forever. She steeled herself to keep smiling as she held out the baby.

"Why don't you have a seat in that big leather chair behind you, Mr. Renz, and you can hold Hannah," Maude suggested.

"I'll just do that," Renz said, grinning ear to ear as Maude settled the baby in his lap. "What a lively little girl you are—and I think you got your papa's nose, little Hannah, and his hair color," he murmured. Then his eyes narrowed.

"What is this on the front of her shirt?" he inquired suspiciously.

Juana glided forward. "Oh, senor, I'm sorry," she said in a sweet voice. "But the *niña* was so excited to hear that you had come to see her that she spit up her milk. I did not want to make you wait even longer while I changed her clothing, so I just brought her as she was. I knew a *father* would understand."

Renz nose wrinkled in obvious distaste. "Yes, well, of course I do," he said in a tone that was far from convincing.

Hannah didn't like being handed off from Juana's familiar arms to those of a stranger whose arms were stiff, and decided to protest as only a baby could, setting up a loud wail of protest that quickly turned to howls of rage as Renz, unfazed at first, began to bounce the baby as if he thought he could jolly her out of it.

Maude had to struggle not to seize Hannah from her so-called father's arms and comfort her. She could tell from Juana's rigidly set jaw that her friend was fighting the same internal struggle. Deliberately, she made eye contact with her friend and winked, and Juana relaxed.

Just then Hanna decided she had had enough of this pomaded stranger and threw up all over the man's store-bought shirt.

Renz's reaction was everything she could have hoped for. He jumped up and held the squalling baby out in front of him as if to lessen the chance of any further such damage before indignantly turning to Maude.

"Is she sick?" he demanded.

"Not at all," she said, keeping her tone carefree. "Just not enthusiastic about being bounced around by a stranger right after she's eaten. She'll be all right now."

Renz's attempted smile was sickly. "I—I see. Of course. But..." He looked down at the spit-up milk on his shirt and turned a sickly green.

"We must wash your shirt for you, senor," Juana purred soothingly. "I'm sure we can find something for you to wear meanwhile. I'll be right back with it."

Minutes later, Juana brought down a cast-off shirt of Jonas's to lend Renz while she scrubbed the sour milk out of Renz's garment. Jonas must have intended the borrowed shirt for the roughest, dirtiest work around the ranch, for while it was clean, it was also threadbare and showed clumsily mended repairs. After putting it on, Renz looked even more pathetic, for he didn't have Jonas's long arms or broad chest, and the shirt was hopelessly baggy on him. But it was free of spit-up milk, and Renz made a valiant attempt to pretend he was taking it all in stride.

"Goes with the territory, I reckon," he said with false cheerfulness, once he returned wearing Jonas's old shirt. "Suppose I should get used to it if I'm going to be a good papa to my girl."

Maude darted a glance at Jonas, who had taken up a position in the corner of the room, leaning against a wall as if he was too restless to sit. She saw that his jaw was rigidly set as if he dared not relax it for a moment for fear of what words he might utter. Indeed, he had maintained a stoic silence since Renz's arrival, though the tension in his face and his shoulders showed what a strain it had been.

"And about that," Renz began. "I'll need you to pack up all my girl's things so I can be headin' back to Simpson Creek with her."

Maude did her best not to gasp, but out of the corner of her eye she saw Jonas's face lose several shades of color before it flushed with anger.

"And where were you going to live with her? When you're in town, that is?" she asked.

"Mrs. Meyer always keeps a room for me. You know that, Miss Maude."

So he was just assuming that Mrs. Meyer would take Hannah back in, Maude guessed, without considering the inconvenience it would be to the rest of the household. Did he think he possessed that much charm that he could convince Mrs. Meyer to agree to such a thing?

"And what are you going to do when you have to go sell your pots and pans, Mr. Renz?"

He grinned. "Ah, you know Mrs. Meyer. She's an old softy, and she's always loved babies. I'll bet for a little extra cash she'd love to keep my little April till her papa could come back. And it wouldn't be long before my little sweetie could go traveling with her papa. I'll wager the old ladies I call on would buy twice as much if they could dandle my daughter on their knees."

His bold assumption that he could take Hannah out on the road like some kind of a good luck charm, ignoring the baby's comfort and feeding schedules for his own profit, made Maude want to slap him for being such a fool.

"And what were you planning to feed her, Mr. Renz? Hannah is still nursing and hasn't started on solid food yet. That's why I brought Juana with me when Hannah and I moved here," she added, nodding toward the Mexican girl.

Renz's eyes shifted to Juana, and a sly look came over his face. "Well now, I could make it worth your while, senora," he said. "You could stay at the boardinghouse, handy for my daughter when she needed you—I'm sure Mrs. Meyer could find an extra room for you, and you could help her mind the baby while I'm away. And when Hannah's big enough to go on the road with me, you could travel with us, too, if you was of a mind to."

"You would have to pay for Juana's room," Maude reminded him.

"And how could I travel with you, an unmarried man? What of my good name, senor?" Juana demanded, her dark eyes flashing. "I am a respectable widow."

For a moment Renz looked to be at a loss, but then he eyed Juana up and down in a way that made Maude's skin crawl. "Well, I reckon we could get hitched for a while, at least, you and I. That'd make it all respectable, sure enough."

"For *a while*?" Juana echoed. "What are you saying, senor?"

Renz shot her an easy grin. "Well, my little Hannah won't be needin' you to feed her forever, will she? One a' these days soon she'll be eating regular food, and when that happens you can go your own way, if you like. But you never know—you might begin t'like bein' married to me. I make good money in my travels, I'll have you know."

"That is out of the question, as my husband died only recently and I am still mourning him, but I thank you for the proposal," Juana told him with much more courtesy than Maude could have mustered in a thousand years. But there was a dangerous glint in her eyes.

"But there must be a way," Renz blustered. "A man has a right to be a father to his child."

Maude wanted to shout that he'd missed his chance to act as a true father to this baby by not staying with her mother. Just then, however, a noise erupted from Hannah that was unmistakable and signaled a need for a change of her diaper.

Maude and Juana exchanged knowing looks.

"Senor Renz, why don't you come with me?" Juana said. "Your daughter needs some cleansing and a fresh *pañal*—a diaper."

Renz had risen and approached, but as soon as he got close and caught a whiff of the tell-tale odor, he backed away.

"No thanks, Miss Juana. I'm sure you're much more capable..."

"But I insist, senor," Juana said sweetly. "It's something any good father should know how to do."

With the offer framed that way, there was no way he could gracefully refuse, and he knew it.

When he came back down, minutes later, the green tinge to his complexion had deepened.

"Mr. Renz," Maude began, "we were thinking you might like to stay with us for a few days and learn how to care for your daughter, so that if you *are* able to come to a solution as to how she will be fed, you'll know how to be a father to her."

"Stay? Here?" His gaze darted around the room, then settled back on Maude.

She'd already discussed this with Jonas and knew he would permit it for the reasons she'd explained, but she didn't want to be around when someone told Coira about the presence of this disreputable scoundrel under her roof. Ah, well, it was easier to ask for forgiveness than permission.

"I…I suppose I could do that," he allowed.

Maude guessed he'd been planning to go to the saloon when he returned to Simpson Creek, and he was probably regretting the loss of an evening spent over cards and whiskey bottles. *Too bad.*

"While you're here, you'll assume full care of Hannah," she informed him. "You'll do all diaper changes, her bath…we'll wake you in the night when she gets up to nurse, and you'll stay awake until she goes back to sleep." It would mean one of them would have to be with the man and his child as long as Renz remained at the ranch house, and in all likelihood neither she nor Jonas would sleep a wink until he had gone, but if it worked to convince him that he wasn't suited for fatherhood, it was worth it.

His face was a study in suspicion, but he only said, "I understand. It's very good of you to be so hospitable."

Hospitality had nothing to do with it, and they both knew it, so she settled for uttering a noncommittal "You're welcome," and showed him to his room.

She wondered if there was time for Senora Morales to make haggis for supper.

Chapter Fifteen

Jonas watched them go, marveling at Maude's calmness with wee Hannah's scoundrel of a father. She was quite a braw lass, his Maude. He wished he could go and tell her how much he admired her right now.

If it had been left up to him, he would have saved the trouble of Renz's visit and thrown the man bodily out of the house as soon as he arrived, hoping he'd meet up with a pack of Comanches on the warpath before he made it back to Simpson Creek. But this had been the minister's plan, and Jonas had to admit he could see the logic in it. If Renz decided on his own that he wasn't up to being a father, then they'd never have to worry about him returning.

By the time two full days of Renz's presence had passed, the ranch house's inhabitants' tempers were on a razor's edge. Jonas noted deep shadows under Maude's eyes. Juana had told him that every time she got up to nurse Hannah, Maude sat with her and Felix Renz so that her friend would not have to be alone with the man while she performed such a personal task.

At first, Renz apparently thought it was a good idea to use the time to make flirty conversation with Juana while he sat up with them, which had the effect of thoroughly waking Hannah up so that she stayed awake far longer into the night than she would have otherwise.

After two or three attempts at sparkling repartee, however, Maude had had enough and finally told him to hold his peace. "Mr. Renz, the object is to get the baby fed and back to sleep, so that we can go back to sleep, too," she growled. "Not to convince her that the middle of the night is an entertaining time to be awake."

"Sorry," he said with obviously false regret. "I'm just trying to keep myself awake. After all, it was *your* idea that I be present for my daughter's feedings, Miss Maude."

By the third afternoon, when Jonas went to visit his mother's room to see if Maude would like to get some fresh air, he found her dozing in the rocking chair by his mother's bed with *Ivanhoe* still spread open on her lap.

"Look at the lass," his mother said. "So busy guardin' the wee bairn that she's not getting any sleep of a night. Ye must do something, Jonas."

Maude had stirred slightly at the sound of Coira's voice, then settled back into sleep.

"He'll be gone tomorrow," Jonas promised. He knelt by the side of the rocker. "Maude. *Maude*," he whispered, touching her forearm gently.

She startled awake, her limbs flailing, eyes darting wildly around.

"Jonas...Mrs. MacLaren...I—I fell asleep. I'm so

sorry," she said, sure despite the kindness she saw in Jonas's eyes, that his mother had called her son into the room to reprimand her.

"Och, dinna fash yerself, lass. It's obvious you're dead on your feet, so it is," Coira said from her bed.

"Go take a wee rest," Jonas said.

"But I can't!" she protested. "It's the middle of the day. Hannah—"

"Will be fine. I'll watch over Juana and the wee bairn while you sleep, and see to Mother, too. Go have a nap, that's an order," he insisted, wishing he could smooth the tendrils of dark red hair away from her forehead.

Renz would be gone tomorrow, like it or not, he decided. Having the man in the house was horrible for everyone, and it could not be tolerated any longer. He couldn't keep a proper eye on the ranch and on the weasel in his house at the same time, and he was just fortunate he had such a reliable foreman as Hector to take up the slack while he stayed on guard in his home. Yes, tomorrow the man would be going—whether he liked it or not.

The next day, however, things came to a head without his intervention. He and Maude were sitting in the dining room having dinner at noon the next day when Juana came stamping into the room, carrying Hannah, her eyes ablaze with fury.

"He's leaving, that *malvado*, that…that…" Words failed her, and she went off into a torrent of Spanish, stamping her feet. Jonas thought it likely she was maligning Renz's parentage.

Maude jumped up and took Hannah into her arms. "What happened, Juana? Why are you so angry? He didn't hurt you, did he?"

"That one?" Juana looked scornful. "As if he could! No, *mi amiga*, what he *did* do was laughable, however—he asked me again to marry him!"

"What?"

"*Sí*, he asked me to marry him, the fool. He thought I was just panting to be a gringo's wife—as if he or *anyone* could measure up to my poor Tomás! He said if we wed, then all would be well and that there could be no objection to his taking Hannah if he had a wife who could care for her and feed her."

"Never mind that he doesn't have more than a boardinghouse room to call his own," Maude murmured, amazed at the man's effrontery.

"He couldn't believe I refused to consider marrying him," Juana said. "He said I was foolish…and a few things worse than foolish."

Jonas jumped to his feet. "I'll just go make sure Mr. Renz is having no trouble getting his possessions packed up and ready to go," he said. If it became necessary for his fist to connect with Renz's face in order to assist his departure, that would be an added bonus.

Half an hour later, after he had seen Renz gallop down the lane that led to the road, Jonas reentered the house, thinking about the man's final words to him—"Thank you, and please tell the ladies that I thank them for giving me this precious time with my baby girl. Of course, it only served to show me that I could not possibly do as well as Miss Juana and Miss Maude are doing to raise her. If Miss Juana reconsiders my offer, she has but to leave word at the boardinghouse."

Glib words. He'd no doubt used such glib words to tempt Hannah's mother to trust him with her love. The man was a scoundrel. Jonas wanted to burn the sheets Renz had slept on in order to cleanse his house of any minute trace of the man.

Please God, don't let our Hannah grow up with any of her father's despicable traits, he prayed. *But surely if he and Maude brought her up with love and care and taught her well...*

He stopped on the threshold, threw back his head, and laughed. Not only had he just prayed—a thing he had barely done in years—but he'd thought of himself and Maude as a couple who'd raise Hannah as proper parents should.

What a dreamer he was. He'd barely begun to properly court the lovely woman who lived under his roof, and already he was thinking of raising Hannah with her. He was certainly getting ahead of himself.

"That's it, he's gone, then," Coira hissed as she stood at the window of her bedroom, leaning on her cane and on Maude's arm, and watching Renz ride off. "Good riddance, I say."

Maude had been more than a little surprised when Coira had been so eager to see the last of the man that she'd insisted on getting out of her bed to see him leave, and now, standing next to Jonas's mother at the bedroom window, she watched the cloud of dust that Renz's horse raised growing more and more distant.

"Yes, I hope we've seen the last of him," she murmured. "Though I told Jonas to tell him he was welcome to visit anytime he wanted to see his daughter." She froze when she realized she'd referred to Jonas by his first name, and waited for his mother's stinging rebuke for her familiarity.

But no rebuke came. Instead, the woman started back toward her bed. "Och, but that fair wore me out. You're a good lass, Maude, that ye are. Ye showed yerself to be a good Christian woman in the way ye treated the man."

"Thank you," she murmured. "I just tried to remember that it can't be easy for him, having a child and knowing he can't properly raise her."

"Though I'd have beat him with my cane if the bounder had tried to take wee Hannah."

Maude had to smile at Coira's repeated threat.

Just then, they heard the sound of the door opening at the front of the house, and a moment later, a hearty male laugh wafted up the stairs to them. It was Jonas, she knew.

Coira smiled. "Maude, I believe you're a good influence on the both of us, Jonas and me. I've not heard my son laugh for many a year."

Too touched to speak for a moment, Maude waited until she could talk without her voice shaking. "Thank you. And how was your visit with Reverend Gil the other day when he and the sheriff called? I meant to ask you, and then I forgot, what with keeping an eye on our 'visitor' and all."

Coira winced as she sat down on the bed, then shifted so Maude could help her lift her bony legs onto the mattress. But the smile she turned on Maude was beatific.

"He says there's a hope of heaven even for an evil woman like me, can you believe it? Even after I told him everything. 'Tis a marvel, truly. But I don't mind sayin' he's given me a lot to think about."

"Of course I believe it, Mrs. MacLaren. And if you'd ever like to talk about it some more, I'm always willing."

"Perhaps we'll do that one day soon," Coira said. "But just now, why don't ye go below and find my son? After hearing that laugh, I have a feeling he'll be wanting to see you."

Her announcement left Maude feeling giddy with anticipation as she left the room, and had her stopping in her room to check in the mirror that her hair was not askew and pinching her cheeks to make sure her face was full of fresh color.

She found him sitting at the bottom of the stairs, whistling a tune. At the sound of her footsteps, he looked up.

"Ah, there ye are," he said as if he'd been waiting for her appearance.

"I thought you'd be hard at work with the horse you've been gentling, now that Renz is gone," she said.

"Aye, I would be, but after a chat with Senora Morales I realized we have another problem."

"*Another* problem?" *Was the housekeeper threatening to leave again?*

"Aye, for she reminded me that Thanksgiving comes in two days and we're woefully unprepared, thanks to the distraction of our recent visitor."

"We are?" she asked, confused because Jonas didn't

look very distressed, though his lip had curled as he'd said "visitor."

"We are, though she assures me the pumpkins are ready to be made into pies. Hector and a couple of the hands are going out in the morning to try and bag a turkey or two, but that leaves us without cranberries and a number of other ingredients that I'm told are essential for a proper American feast, aye?" His golden-hazel eyes danced as he informed her of these things.

"And what can I do to assist you in this matter?" she said, not at all sure where this was leading.

"I was hoping you'd agree to accompany me on a jaunt into town to purchase some supplies in the morning. I'm not sure I'd get the right things, otherwise. We'd have to leave early and wouldn't be able to stay long, with Thanksgiving being the next day, unfortunately, and I'm planning to rent a fresh team of horses at the livery to bring us home, but I imagine we'd have time for a decent meal at your friend's café before we head back to the ranch. Are ye game for it, lass? And do you think the mercantile would have what we need?"

She could hardly believe her ears. Jonas MacLaren was asking to spend an entire day with her, and was willing to go into town and purchase food for a special American feast when he could have deemed whatever they had on hand to be sufficient. She wanted to pinch herself to prove she wasn't dreaming.

Evidently he took her goggling as hesitation, for then he said, "Now don't be worrying about who's to take care of Hannah and my mother. Juana's already agreed to double duty watching over both."

"Yes! And yes!" she cried joyously, amazed that

Juana had been able to keep from blurting out the news to her. Then she remembered their recent unwelcome visitor. "But what about Renz? You don't think—"

He'd been grinning at her joyous acceptance, but now he sobered. "No, I don't think that craven poltroon would dare to come back and go near little Hannah. Don't even think about it. Thanks to the preacher's strategy, that mollycoddle got a thorough lesson about why he's not prepared to be a father. He knows now that it's not all a matter of a holding a cooing, adoring cherub and looking forward to the day she calls him Papa. But just to set your mind at ease, Hector will spend as much time in the ranch house as he can, and I'm sure he thinks he's got the best end of the deal, getting to be inside with bonny Juana all day instead of getting his hands dirty."

Now Maude was grinning, too. "It will be such fun." Already she could imagine seeing the familiar buildings of Simpson Creek and getting to spend time with Ella at her friend's café. She'd call on Mrs. Meyer and assure the woman that she was happy at the ranch, and perhaps she'd see other friends while they were in town, too.

With any luck, some friends might be available to come to the café and eat with them, too. She'd get to hear about the wedding and, while she was in the mercantile, hear all the local news and gossip from Mrs. Patterson—that woman was the source of all information in Simpson Creek, even more so than the newspaper. She hoped Mrs. Patterson would still have some dried cranberries by the time they got there!

It would be a wonderful day, but she understood why their visit to town couldn't be long—Senora Morales would be up all night cooking as it was. She'd have to offer to help, once Hannah had gone to sleep.

Perhaps since Jonas had been willing to go back to town once, though, he might agree to a next time, when they could stay longer? But she must not think that way, she told herself—she was being greedy.

"Plan to wear something warm, if the day's anything like this one," Jonas was saying. He reached out and cupped her cheek with his hand for a brief moment.

"'Tis good to see you happy, lass," he said, the warm look in his eyes making her feel good inside. His touch made her feel all tingly and her heartbeat quickened.

"And now I'd better get outside and do a bit of honest ranch work myself today, since I won't be here tomorrow," he said. "I'll see ye at supper, Maude."

"Ah, Senor MacLaren is courting you now for sure," Juana said that night, when she and Maude were finally alone together in their room and Hannah was asleep in the little cradle beside the bed. "How exciting!"

"Now, we mustn't read too much into a trip into town," Maude cautioned, though she knew that her own anticipation of the day to come would render sleep difficult, if not impossible, tonight. "It's probably just a simple matter of a man wanting to make sure he gets all the right ingredients at the mercantile so we aren't eating oatcakes and haggis for Thanksgiving!"

Juana groaned in mock horror, and the two women shared a giggle. "The MacLarens couldn't be so cruel,"

Juana insisted. "But really, why would a Scotsman care about making sure he has a proper American Thanksgiving? I'm sure he's doing all of this for you. I know what I saw in his eyes as he gazed at you across the table tonight."

Maude was sure, too, despite the skepticism she'd felt obligated to voice. There had been such an intent look in those golden eyes when he'd cupped her cheek—not like an eagle spotting his prey, but like an eagle spotting his aerie after a long, wearying flight away from the nest. He'd looked like a man nearing home.

Chapter Sixteen

The day dawned crisp and cold, and there was frost on the grass when they set out, but dressed in her heaviest clothes, draped in a buffalo-hide robe and sitting by Jonas, Maude was warm enough to be comfortable and content, and the miles sped by as they headed toward Simpson Creek. The world seemed full of possibilities today, including the possibility that she could convince Jonas to end his constant isolation out at Five Mile Hill Ranch and purchase a Sunday house in town.

It would be so lovely to have a place to stay when coming in to attend church services. There was still the matter of him not yet sharing her faith, but if he cared about her, surely he would see that it was important? If his mother, of all people, was beginning to realize her need of faith, surely he would, too, before long?

Jonas seemed in a merry mood, whistling a tune from time to time as the team trotted along. He seemed to shed a heavy weight as the buckboard neared Simpson Creek, and Maude realized it wasn't often he left his responsibilities to the ranch and those who depended on him behind, even for a day.

"Penny for your thoughts," he said at one point, when they stopped to water the horses at a little creek that ran past the road.

"I was just thinking of the cloth I hope to buy at the mercantile," she told him.

"Making a new dress for yourself, are you?"

"No, I have clothes enough. I was thinking of making some more things for Hannah. She's growing like the proverbial weed, you know—"

"Aye, that she is," he said with a fond smile. "The wee bairn's not so wee anymore. The next thing we know she'll be walking, I reckon."

She chuckled. "That'll be awhile yet, but soon none of her clothes are going to fit her if I don't get busy and make some more."

"Your hands are always busy," he murmured, and there was a glow of approval in his eyes that sent warmth flooding through her.

"Perhaps the mercantile would have some little toy we could get for her," he said. "I know she has quite a selection, what with all the carved animals and pull toys Hector fashions for her, but perhaps there'd be something she doesn't have. Perhaps a wee dolly?"

His thought of buying Hannah a toy, and his frequent use of "we," especially in relation to the baby, made Maude feel good. It was becoming hard to remember the imperious, cynical, off-putting manner Jonas had displayed when she had first met him at the barbecue.

He'd be a good father to little Hannah...if he could just see his need of the Lord to guide him...

To her relief, Mrs. Patterson did have bags of dried cranberries in stock. "Shipped all the way from Massachusetts," she informed Maude proudly. "Wouldn't it be nice if you could just wade out into the bog where they grow and gather them for yourself?"

"I don't know," Maude said, picturing the cold, squishy mud she'd have to walk upon in a bog. "They don't have cottonmouth snakes up north, do they?"

"Land sakes, I don't know," Mrs. Patterson answered with a shudder. "Are y'all going to be in town for a while, or do you have to head back directly? Kate will be sorry she missed you," she said, referring to the niece who lived with her and helped mind the store. "Did you know she and Gabe got married, and are living over on Travis Street near the Bishops?"

"No I didn't—please give her my congratulations," Maude murmured. "Unfortunately we can't stay long today—we have to get the supplies back to the ranch in time to prepare everything for tomorrow's Thanksgiving meal. But we'll be having dinner at Ella's café after we finish here. If you see any of the Spinsters' Club members, please let them know they can find me there, if they have a minute to stop by and catch up. I was hoping to spot some of them on the street, but I didn't. Oh, may I see that bolt of cloth with the blue flowers?" she added, pointing to it behind the counter. It would be perfect for Hannah's clothes. Soon the cloth joined the growing pile of their purchases on the counter.

A few minutes later, their purchases loaded onto the wagon bed, they descended from the buckboard once again at Ella's café.

Ella came running out to greet them. "I thought I saw you drive past coming into town!" Maude's friend cried, sweeping Maude into a hug. "I was hoping you'd stop in."

"Yes, we had to go to the mercantile first—for a few things for Thanksgiving tomorrow," she explained. "It's not too late to have a bite to eat here, is it?"

"Of course not. Though the cowboys from the Sawyer ranch were just here—you're lucky that locust horde left anything behind," Ella said ruefully. "Come on inside. Nate's here having his own dinner, and I know he'll be glad to see you—and make your acquaintance, Mr. MacLaren," she said, smiling up at Jonas.

Marriage seemed to agree with Ella, Maude thought, admiring the easy, confident way Ella led them into her establishment and saw them seated, then brought over her new husband to meet Jonas. She envied the loving way Nate Bohannan, who'd arrived in Simpson Creek earlier this year as part of a medicine show, draped his arm around Ella's shoulder as he and Jonas talked.

Having put in their orders for today's special of chicken and dumplings and black-eyed peas, with peach pie for dessert, Maude followed Ella over to the kitchen area while Ella got busy at the stove.

"Business is good?" Maude asked, seeing that most of the tables were occupied with folks finishing up their dinners.

"Indeed it is. I sure miss having your help here as I did when we first opened the place," Ella admitted. "And I miss you at church, and the Spinsters' Club meetings…though I'm guessing you'd be graduating from the Spinsters soon, if the look in yon Scotsman's eye is anything to go by," she said with a laugh, nodding toward where Jonas sat. "Am I right?"

"Maybe…" Maude admitted with a smile, feeling the color rise into her cheeks once again. "Though it's too soon to say for sure. There's a lot of things that need to be settled…"

"All right, then, I won't tease you about it," Ella said, darting another look at Jonas, who was still deep in conversation with her husband. "It'll work out, in time. Remember how reluctant you were to go out there and take the job? Aren't you glad you went ahead and did it? And little Hannah? How's that little sweetie doing? I imagine she's grown so much I wouldn't recognize her," Ella said.

Maude detailed how big Hannah was getting, then went on to tell her friend about Renz's visit.

Ella lost her glad smile. "That scalawag," Ella growled. "Mrs. Meyer told me he'd been back to stay a few nights at the boardinghouse, full of himself as always. I was afraid she'd feel obligated to tell him where his daughter was, but had hoped he'd have the sense to leave well enough alone. It's a good thing you were able to show him how ill-equipped he was to take care of her."

"He's not still at the boardinghouse, is he?" Maude had no wish for Renz to know that she and Jonas weren't at the ranch house right now.

Ella blew out a breath. "No, Mrs. Meyer said he took off again—apparently right after he was out to see Hannah—leaving no word of where he was going. Same old Felix—he'll never change."

Maude sighed, feeling her tension at the mention of Hannah's father ease a bit with the knowledge that he was gone from Simpson Creek. The man was like a tumbleweed, always blowing wherever the wind sent him. *Why couldn't April Mae have made a wiser choice of a father for Hannah?*

But she shouldn't think that way, she told herself. If April Mae truly *had* made a wiser choice, Maude wouldn't have little Hannah now. And if it weren't for Hannah, she'd never have agreed to take the job at Five Mile Hill Ranch, and what a shame that would have been.

She went back to sit with Jonas just as Nate was rising. "I need to get back to the shop," he said.

"Your carpentry business is going well, too?" she asked, recalling how Nate had revealed himself as a skilled carpenter and craftsman when he'd first come to town. His fine work was on display all over Ella's café, for he had made the tables, chairs, shelves and counter himself.

"I've been busier than a barefoot boy on a red ant hill," he informed her with a wink. "Good to see you, Miss Maude. Jonas here was just tellin' me how you've changed life out at Five Mile Hill Ranch for the better."

"Oh, he was, was he?" The idea that Jonas had been praising her to Ella's husband made her stand taller and feel like she could accomplish almost anything.

"He sure enough was. Like I was telling Jonas, we hope you'll come back to town when you can stay longer. Don't be a stranger."

She thought about asking Nate if he'd heard of any houses coming available in town that they could rent for a Sunday house, but she thought she'd better not. She didn't want to try to push Jonas into a commitment he might not yet be ready to assume, especially in front of someone else.

Nate left then, and Ella soon brought their meal.

"Don't tell Senora Morales I said this, but 'tis good to eat someone else's cooking for a change," Jonas said, after finishing off his chicken and dumplings.

Maude had to agree. The housekeeper-cook's meals were spicy and flavorful, but relied heavily on chili peppers.

"Are ye having a good time today, Maude?" he asked her then. "Is the outing everything you'd hoped for? It's been good to spend some time with you away from all our other responsibilities. I'm sorry you didn't get to see more of your friends."

"It's all right," she said. "There'll be other times." She savored the idea that he cared about whether she was enjoying the day. She was loath to start the journey back, though she missed Hannah. "We've gotten everything we came for, so I suppose we'd better get on the road so Senora Morales has time to turn the ingredients we bought into a feast."

He sighed. "I suppose you're right."

They made their farewells and made their way back outside to the wagon. It had gotten colder while they dined, but that would give her an excuse to sit closer to him on the buckboard seat and share his warmth. He helped her climb back up to the driver's seat and arranged the buffalo hide blanket around her.

"I wish 'twas summer, so it wouldn't be dark so soon. We could have had a picnic at the creek, just the two of us. And when we'd eaten our food, I'd find a way to steal a kiss or two."

The casually uttered words made her gaze fly up to lock with his. Her pulse quickened.

"Is that too bold? Ye know I love you, Maude," he said. "There just hasn't been an easy way to show you, out at the ranch, with everybody there..." He clucked to the horses, and they headed slowly out onto the road that led east out of Simpson Creek toward the ranch.

"No, it's not too bold," she said, wondering if she dared be a little bold, too. Everything was not settled between them—his rocky relationship with God was still an issue, as was the possibility of his mother's disapproval. But she could at least let him know that she looked forward to a future for them, too. "In fact, I'm hoping you won't wait until next summer," she said, and raised her face to his in a clear invitation. If he kissed her now, he wouldn't be stealing it.

Apparently he didn't want to resist the invitation, for he did kiss her, the descent of his lips gentle and warm, his arm going around her to hold her close as if it was the most natural thing in the world. It was a moment she wished could go on forever.

"Maude..." he breathed. "Is it possible you've come to love me, too?"

She nodded shakily, her breath coming fast. "I think I began to love you the day of the barbecue," she admitted, gazing up at him, and then he was kissing her again, letting the horses choose their own pace, for they knew the way home.

"I don't know how ye could have," he said. "I was rather full of myself that day, as I recall."

She chuckled. "I can't argue with that," she said, remembering his disparaging remarks about men coming to the party to meet prospective brides. "Insufferable as you were, though, you were the handsomest man there," she added with a wink.

He roared with laughter and swept her up in a tight hug. "You're a daft lass, do ye ken? But you were the most beautiful one there, too, with your fiery red hair that looks as if it would burn my hand." As if to demonstrate that it didn't, he caressed the side of her head with one hand, while keeping hold of the reins with the other. After the team tried to stop and wade into the grass at the side of the road, though, he said, "I suppose I'd better pay attention to what I'm doing, or we'll still be far from home when night falls." But though he occupied both hands with the reins, driving the team didn't stop him from gazing at her.

"I want to marry you, my darling Maude, and be a father to little Hannah as well as your husband," he said. "I'll do whatever it takes to make you happy, I promise. I'll find a way to court you at the ranch and make you feel as treasured as you are to me."

He loved her, and he knew that she loved him. He wanted to marry her...

Suddenly, what she had longed for was happening so fast, and yet there was still the problem of his lack of belief.

If she agreed to marry him now, with their positions so opposite in the matter of faith, this would never change. He would never work to build his faith if she did not push him now.

"I love you, too, Jonas, and I want to marry you. And I love living at Five Mile Hill Ranch. But—" she held up a hand when it seemed as he might pull her close and kiss her again "—I feel so isolated there, never coming into town, never attending church."

The town of Simpson Creek pretty much ended at the creek it was named for and gave way to ranch land, except for a few scattered cottages near the road, but they were passing a row of small houses now, and to her delight, one of them boasted a for sale or rent sign in front of it.

"See that little house there? Why couldn't we rent it, Jonas, or find one in Simpson Creek about that size to stay overnight in so we could attend church? I'd understand that we couldn't attend every week… But it would come in handy when we came to town for supplies, also." *And if he was going to church with her, he'd sense the need of a relationship with the Lord. And then he'd sense the forgiveness God had for what he'd done in the past, and learn to forgive himself.*

He sighed and did not immediately answer. For the space of a few heartbeats, she thought she'd gone too far and ruined the moment. But she felt it was important to speak of the things that mattered to her now, while Jonas was in this yielding mood.

"Ye still want your Sunday house," he said.

Slowly, she nodded, keeping her eyes on him, holding her breath.

"Give me some time, sweetheart, to do some looking around the town. We're heading into winter, and even in Texas the weather may affect whether we're able to travel back and forth to town frequently, so the arrangements may have to wait a bit till spring. But I won't forget—you believe me, Maude, don't you?"

Sweetheart. He'd called her sweetheart.

His sudden fear that she would think he was making promises he wouldn't keep touched her heart, and she was quick to reassure him. "I know if you say you'll do something, Jonas, you will."

He gave her an appreciative smile. "That's my lass. I'll never lie to you."

It was a long journey back to Five Mile Hill Ranch, but absorbed in each other, it seemed as if they reached the gates of the ranch all too soon. They shared a rueful glance, knowing they'd have to leave this private bubble of happiness that surrounded the buckboard and resume their duties as companion and mother, son and rancher. But they'd find ways to be together, just the two of them, even at the ranch house—Maude knew this now.

She was not prepared, however, for the abrupt way the bubble burst. As soon as the buckboard pulled up in front of the house, Senora Morales threw open the door and ran shrieking up to the wagon, startling the horses and causing one of them to try to rear in the traces. It took a few moments for Jonas to regain mastery of the animals and calm them enough for either of them to make sense of what she was shouting—

"Senor MacLaren! You must save the *niña*—little Hannah! He's taken her, and Juana! And Hector is shot!"

Chapter Seventeen

Everything seemed to happen at once then—Maude launched herself out of the buckboard to the ground, demanding details from the housekeeper, nearly startling the horses yet again. One of the vaqueros appeared and Jonas turned the wagon and horses over to him and joined Maude by the housekeeper.

Senora Morales was near-hysterical herself, but with Maude clutching her and demanding to know what had happened, Jonas could see she was making an effort to collect herself.

"*Sì*, he came an hour or so after you left, that evil hombre! It was as if he knew you'd gone, Senor MacLaren, for he came straight into the house. Hector tried to stop him from going up the stairs, but that awful man shot him."

"How bad is the injury?" Jonas asked grimly, bracing himself for the news that his foreman might be dead.

The housekeeper shuddered. "Not too bad, senor, but messy—I think it will take long to heal. The shot was in the shoulder. But he will survive. After the shot, he could no longer block the staircase, and Hannah's father went up to the nursery, his gun still drawn. He said he would shoot anyone else who tried to stop him, that he just wanted his child. And he said Juana must go with him to feed the baby..."

"Jonas! You have to go after him!" Maude cried, grabbing his arm. "He should go to jail for what he did to Hector, and we can't allow him to take Hannah and Juana—"

"Of course we can't. We *won't*," he said, smoothing her hair, and then spoke to the vaquero holding the horses. "Take the team, unhitch them and give them feed. Senora Morales, go to the bunkhouse and summon as many of the hands as possible to form a posse. We'll ride as soon as I see Hector. And have one of them ride to town to notify the sheriff—and the doctor."

"But you can't possibly ride after him now, you've just come all the way from Simpson Creek," said another voice, and Jonas looked up to see his mother at the doorway. "And it's almost dark."

Coira MacLaren leaned heavily on her cane. One eye was bruised and swollen shut, and Jonas spotted a scrape along her left cheek and another on the right. The hot blood coursing through his veins turned to ice.

"Mother, what happened to you?" he shouted, and went to her side.

The old woman leaned against him, tears coursing down her pale, wrinkled cheeks. He put an arm around her to steady her.

"I told that caitiff he'd take Hannah and Juana over my d-dead body, and went after him with my cane," his mother said. "He…yanked the cane out of my hand and knocked me down." Her gaze dropped to the cane she leaned on, as if it had failed her. "He raised the cane and would have killed me, I think, if Juana hadn't gone after him. She fought him like a wildcat until he subdued her and tied her up. He said if she gave him any more trouble he'd kill me."

"He'll die for this," Jonas snarled, even as his heart despaired at the thought of the baby and Juana in the hands of that scoundrel, out there in the cold dark.

"Maude, I have to see how Hector is," he said. "Can you—"

He was about to ask her to help his mother back into the house, but Maude was already there, placing a trembling arm across Coira's back and under her to steady the old woman, though tears streamed down her own face.

His foreman had been placed in one of the upstairs bedrooms, and one of the housemaids was sitting by his bedside. He was sitting up, and a blood-splotched bandage covered his left shoulder. Bruises covered his temples and face.

At the sight of Jonas, he groaned and closed his eyes. "I am sorry I failed you, Senor MacLaren," he said. "I would rather have died than let that *malvado* take the baby—and my Juana."

"I know," Jonas said. "Don't be hard on yourself, amigo. You tried to prevent him, I can see that," he said, pointing to his foreman's bandaged shoulder. "We'll get them back safely, don't you worry," he added, wishing he could believe his own words.

When he went back downstairs, he saw that riders were assembling in front of the house and that Maude had succeeded in getting his mother inside and to a chair.

"I'll take her upstairs," he said, scooping the frail old woman up into his arms. "Come with me, please, Maude."

His mother groaned as he carried her up the stairs and again as he set her down as gently as he could on her bed.

"Maude, I'm going to ride out as soon as all my men are ready to go," he said.

"I want to go with you," she protested. "Hannah will be frightened. She'll—"

Need her mother, he knew she wanted to say.

"I know you want to come, sweetheart, but there's no one with medical skills here but you, and to be honest, if you went, you'd only slow the posse down," he told her, keeping his voice soft and understanding as he told her the hard truth. "I need you to stay here and take care of my mother and Hector. If there's any laudanum left among my mother's medicines, Hector should probably be given it," he said.

"But—"

"*Please*, sweetheart," he said, kissing the top of her head. "I need to know you're safe, at least. And don't you worry about Hannah. I'll get her back and Renz will rue the day—"

She sighed. "All right, I'll stay," she said, accepting the necessity. "But you mustn't kill him, Jonas," she cried. "Promise me you won't. Leave vengeance to the law and the Lord."

He wouldn't make a promise he had no intention of keeping.

"We're ready, Senor MacLaren!" one of the vaqueros shouted up the stairwell. He suspected they had known before he reached the ranch that they would be riding as soon as he returned home and heard the news. Hector had told him that as soon as the housekeeper had sounded the alarm, they'd ridden around the vicinity of the ranch in all directions, attempting to catch Renz before he got too far away, but they'd failed to find any trace of Renz or his captives.

"I have to go, sweetheart," he told Maude, holding her close for a moment. "Say a prayer for us."

"I will," she promised, "the entire time you're gone." A silver tear streaked down her cheek. "Go with God, Jonas."

"I'll bring her back, Maude. With God's help, I'll bring back our child."

He saw a spark gleam in her tear-drenched eyes at his words, and he realized what he had said. Hannah *was* their child, he realized. She had wrapped herself around his heart with her babyish coos and sweet smiles, not long after she had come with Maude to stay at Five Mile Hill Ranch. *He was going to be her father and raise her, together with Maude, please God.* And if God willed it so, not all the Felix Renzes in the world could prevent it.

Renz and his captives had gotten a big head start while he and Maude had enjoyed their blissful day away from the ranch, Jonas realized with regret. If only he'd listened to his gut, which had insisted that Renz had given in much too easily when he left the ranch, pretending to be discouraged by the demands of taking care of an infant and apparently content with securing permission to come back to visit. Now the madman apparently thought he'd solved all his problems by forcing Juana to go with them.

But Felix Renz hadn't reckoned with Jonas MacLaren, he thought.

He mounted a fresh horse held for him by one of the vaqueros. Two or three of them held blazing torches.

"Thank you for assembling so quickly," he said. "Did anyone see what direction they rode off in?"

But no one had, for they had been about their duties when Renz had stormed into the ranch house. They hadn't known of the kidnapping till the housekeeper had come screeching into the bunkhouse while they gathered for the noon meal.

"I figure Renz will have forced Juana to tell him where we went, so he won't have headed west toward Simpson Creek for fear of encountering us," he said, and prayed he was right. "So split up, a couple of you go north, a couple south, a couple west. I'll be going east. I think the fellow might make for Lampasas and hole up there, at least overnight. If any of you meet up with Renz, be extremely careful—remember, he's got a gun that he's clearly willing to use. Not to mention, he's got a woman and a baby with him and I don't think the scoundrel would scruple to use Juana as a shield."

"Oh, I don't think it's likely that sidewinder'd head

for Lampasas," opined one of his few Anglo cowboys, a grizzled veteran named Abner Calloway. "He'd have the Colorado to cross."

The thought of the fool trying to swim a horse across the chill waters of the muddy Colorado sent ice water skimming through Jonas's veins, especially when the he thought of the risk to Juana and Hannah. "But there's a bridge," he said, remembering it from trips into the town for supplies that couldn't be had in Simpson Creek.

Calloway shook his head. "Not after t'other night's storm, there isn't. It washed out, I heard tell. Till they get it repaired, there's only the old ferry."

It was a sudden ray of hope—a thin one. They might not have found the ferry. But what if they had, and they'd used it? *What if they'd used the ferry?*

"The way I remember it, old man Wainwright operates that," another cowhand said, "and he sure don't like operatin' it at night."

Until they reached the ferry, they couldn't know if Renz and his captives had used it. All they could do was keep going toward the river.

Upstairs, after dosing Hector with laudanum, Maude watched them ride out, then returned to the distraught, weeping woman in the bed.

"I failed them, Maude," Coira cried. "I failed your baby and Juana. That villain took my cane from me, the cane I was going to beat his brains in with, 'cause I'm just a useless, helpless old woman."

"Hush now," Maude said, smoothing back a damp

tendril of faded ginger hair from the woman's forehead. "Jonas will get them back. We have to believe that." She considered using some laudanum to sedate the woman, but they didn't have a very large supply and Hector might need it more for his pain.

"But they left hours ago! How will my son even know where to look, out there in the dark? If Jonas does find him, he'll kill him, and he'll have another death on his conscience. And there's nothing we can do here but wait..." She wailed as she said the last words.

"I disagree."

Coira's eyes flew open at the two calm words. "What can *we* do?" she cried, smacking the mattress with a clenched fist.

"We have a very powerful weapon at our disposal," Maude said, forcing herself to be calm, to say the words she could only half believe in her current state of fear and shock. "We can pray."

"Pray?" The words were a lash of scorn. "*I* used to pray, girl. I prayed that my husband would stop beating me and his son, but he didn't. 'Twasn't until Jonas and I took matters into our own hands that the beatings ended."

What could she say to that? Maude wondered. She hadn't been there, years ago in Scotland...*Dear Lord, she was so out of her depth here! If only Reverend Gil was here—he'd know what to say...*

But he wasn't here, and wasn't likely to be anytime soon, and now was when Jonas needed their support in prayer. It was the only thing they could do to help him.

"God says when two or three are gathered in His

name," she began carefully, "He's right there with us, and when we who believe agree on something in prayer, and ask Him for something within His will, He will grant it," Maude told her, infusing every bit of steadiness and faith that she could muster into her words. *How could a loving God refuse to grant her the return of her baby?*

Yet tragedies happened every day. After all, Hannah had lost her mother to death just a couple of days after she was born.

Coira stared up at her, her filmy old eyes hopeless. "How can I ask the Lord for anything? I'm a murderess. I'm not good enough to ask God for another breath."

"None of us are good enough," Maude said. "Not one. Yet God has promised to hear us. He heard the thief on the cross next to Jesus, we read in the Bible, and took him to Heaven with Him, even though the man had done wrong all his life. Let's believe that He will help us, Mrs. MacLaren," Maude said, taking the old woman's gnarled, shaking hand in hers. She bent her head. "Father God, we come to You in desperate need of Your help..."

It was like looking for the proverbial needle in the haystack—with the added challenge of darkness. Where would one demented man—for Renz had to be demented to do what he had done—run with a woman and child in the middle of November? There were no better men than the three men who rode with him, and they would follow him wherever he led, he knew that—but how were they going to find the group when Renz had several hours' head start? If only he hadn't been thinking of himself and his selfish need to spend time with Maude, away from the ranch…

But regrets would only slow him down, and he couldn't afford that. And he couldn't regret kissing Maude and letting her know he loved her, and learning that she felt the same way.

What would they do if he couldn't find Hannah and Juana for her? He was afraid the sorrow could destroy her.

Dear God, he prayed. *Please help me find them! Not for my sake, for I don't deserve anything good from You, but for Maude's sake.* Maude was likely praying now, even as she nursed Hector and watched over his mother.

Then he remembered the words from the Bible, read so long ago— *And I say unto you, Ask, and it shall be given you; seek, and ye shall find; knock , and it shall be opened unto you...*

Were those words meant for *him*? Why would the Lord bother to speak to *him*, when he had attacked his father with murder in his heart?

But he wasn't going to find them without all-powerful help. He *had* to believe God was willing to help him, even if it was more for Maude's, Juana's and the child's sake than for his.

Lord, I'm sorry for the awful things I did so many years ago. If You'll just forgive me, and enable me to find Hannah and Juana, I'll do whatever You ask of me the rest of my life. I'll go back to Scotland if You wish it and pay the price for our crime, if You'll just save Hannah and Juana for Maude.

He hadn't expected the peace that washed over him then. There was no guarantee, no heavenly voice promising the ones they sought would be found safely. It was peace in spite of circumstances.

"We'll cross the Colorado when we come to it, then ride east until we hit Lampasas. Once we're there, we'll rest the horses and ourselves after we check the hotel there and every place that scoundrel could possibly hole up with a woman and child," he called to the others.

But would Renz, with his perpetual lack of funds, choose a hotel, or would he try to find a cruder, but free, shelter? Would he even choose to spend the night out in the open, in a field somewhere? He thanked God that it rarely got down to freezing in this part of Texas, for Juana's and Hannah's sake, but it was still too cold at night for anyone but a thoughtless madman to have a baby outside overnight.

"But keep a sharp eye out for campfires—we'll check any we see. Watch for places they could use for shelter, too—overhanging rocks, abandoned cabins. How far are we from the Colorado do ye reckon, Calloway?"

"'Bout another mile or two, I'd say."

"The ferryman better be willing to take us across, or we'll operate the ferry for ourselves," he growled. Not for the first time, Jonas felt the doubts creep over him—that he'd chosen the right route, and that he'd find Hannah and Juana safe. But he still felt that sense of peace inside him at the thought of heading this way. He'd have to trust it—there was no other option.

He hadn't known of the bridge over the Colorado washing out, and if he hadn't known, there was an excellent chance Renz wouldn't, either.

They rode on, and Jonas kept peering ahead, hoping the fitful half moon would reveal the river ahead of them soon. He ordered the men to silence, remembering the warning that the ferry's owner didn't like making a crossing at night. There was a chance that Renz might still be on this side of the Colorado, and if so, he didn't want to alert the man. Though even a fool like Renz would hear the pounding of approaching horses' hooves if he was careful enough to listen.

And then, there it was ahead of them, a silver ribbon of water. When the horses paused, he could hear its gurgling song.

"That there's the ferryman's shack," Calloway called softly, pointing at a hulking mass on the bank that Jonas had missed on his first quick visual survey of the area.

"I believe I'll pay him a call and find out if he's seen our quarry," Jonas remarked. "Wait here, and be ready for anything."

"If he has, he probably sent 'em away and told 'em not to bother him till morning," someone said. "That ol' man don't like gettin' outa his bed at night for anything, as I recall. Be careful, boss."

"There's horses tied up, yonder," said another, and following the direction of the man's pointing, Jonas saw two horses tied up beneath the trees. He thought he recognized at least one of them as Five Mile Hill Ranch stock by a white patch on the beast's near hip.

They were here. He'd guessed right. *Thank You, Lord. Now please, keep us all safe as we rescue Hannah and Juana.*

Jonas reined his mount out ahead of the others and started toward the hut, aware of a prickling in his spine and a heightening of his senses. He hoped the ferryman wasn't a trigger-happy sort with late-night callers.

Dismounting near the door, he tied his horse to a low-hanging tree branch and walked forward, making no effort to mask his steps. An honest man wouldn't—but he kept a hand on the gun at his hip, too.

The shack appeared even cruder once he was close enough to knock. It looked as though river mud had been used to cover the cracks between the boards. It emitted a stench of stale grease and unwashed human. Not even a muskrat would deign to live there, he thought. The window at the side was a mere hole cut into the wood without so much as newspaper tacked over it to keep out the bugs in the summer or block the cold of the coming winter.

He heard a faint rustling inside, as if someone was getting off of a mattress made of dried corn husks.

He knocked. "Mr. Wainwright!" he called. "Sorry to be bothering you so late, but I need to talk to you. I'll make it worth your while."

Nothing.

He knocked again, harder. "Mr. Wainwright! I need to talk to you. It's urgent!"

"Come back in the mornin'," a querulous voice called back. "No one needs to be crossin' at this indecent hour." There seemed to be a strained quality to the man's voice. *Was there a gun to his back, warning him he'd better succeed in sending Jonas away?*

Suddenly he heard the high, clear wail of a baby, and then it was muffled, as if someone was trying frantically to quiet the child.

"Felix Renz, I know you're in there!" Jonas called. "Come out, if you want to go on living!" He let all the fury he felt show in his voice.

Suddenly a rifle barrel poked out of the makeshift window. "I think I have the advantage here, if you care about the girl and the baby," Renz called back. "Ride away."

He heard the ferryman's voice call out, "I don't want no trouble here…and he's got a lotta firepower, mister. Best do as he says."

"Send the woman and the child out, and we'll leave, and my men, too," Jonas called. "You can't win here otherwise, man, you have to know that. You're outgunned by far. I've a dozen riders with me, and you can't stay holed up in there forever. Let Hannah and Juana go, and we all ride away and forget about this." He didn't have a dozen riders, of course, and he hoped he would be forgiven the lie, but the half moon had gone behind some clouds, so he hoped Renz wouldn't be able to see that he had only three other men.

He had no intention of letting the man go, of course. He was going to make Felix Renz sorry he was ever born, as soon as Juana and the child were safe, and remove the threat Felix Renz represented forever.

"Go away, MacLaren. My daughter belongs with me, and I've got the woman to take care of her. I'm going to marry her, all right and decent, and we'll be a family."

He heard a cry of female indignation. "I told you I will *never* marry you, hombre *estúpido*!" he heard Juana mutter, followed by the sound of a sharp slap and a woman's whimper of pain.

Jonas's temper flashed, and he fought the desire to charge the hut, gun blazing, and force his way in, but he made himself remain still, knowing Juana and Hannah might well be the casualties of a gun battle in that tiny enclosed space.

A Bible passage he had heard once resonated in his mind for a moment. *Blessed are the merciful, for they shall obtain mercy.*

Mercy—for that man? We can talk about mercy once I see Hannah and Juana safe, Lord.

Yet he couldn't shake the words from his head—*Blessed are the merciful, for they shall obtain mercy.* Wasn't he, Jonas, guilty of a crime for which he craved mercy?

"Send them out, and no harm will come to you, Renz," he said again. "Not from me, and not from my men. We'll ride away, as I said. But we're not leaving till you do."

Jonas knew his men had heard the words exchanged between himself and Renz. They had to be thinking he'd lost his mind to be agreeing to let Renz go if he released his captives. He prayed he could trust them not to open fire if Renz showed himself—if only for the safety of his hostages.

The moments ticked on endlessly. Hannah had begun

a fretful crying, the way she did when she was over-tired or disturbed during sleep.

"Renz," he said. "It's getting late. Your daughter needs to be safe in her bed, back at the ranch. You don't want any harm to come to her," he asserted, and prayed that was true. "You have to let her go now—her and Juana."

Through the window, he heard a rustling in the shack and the sound of whispered voices. Then suddenly the door opened and Juana was there, gliding away from the hut. He couldn't be sure if she was alone, or...*Yes! She was carrying the child!*

"Over here, Juana," he called, his heart overflowing with thankfulness, but he kept a wary eye on the door. "You're doing the right thing, Renz. As soon as we can get them mounted, we'll ride away."

In seconds she had reached them, and he put his arm around the shaking, slender woman and the child. He heard the child's whimpering subside to a small cry of recognition. *"Thank You, God,"* he murmured. "You're safe, Juana, little Hannah. Thanks be to God." Then slowly, still keeping his eye on the shack, he began to back them away from the riverbank and toward the horses.

Not another sound came from the ferryman's shack.

Chapter Eighteen

To their credit, not one of his men asked him to explain why he had left without making Renz pay for what he'd done—not that they could have gotten a word in edgewise for the first mile or two, for he was far too busy reassuring Juana that Hector would make a full recovery from his wound. He knew Hector was fond of the young widow, but he had not realized how mutual their affection was.

It was the middle of the night before they covered the distance back to Five Mile Hill Ranch, but as soon as the horsemen pulled up in the yard, Maude flew out of the house and reached them as he assisted a weary Juana and sleeping Hannah from their horse.

"Jonas! You found them! They're safe! Oh, thank You, God, thank You!" she cried. In the course of embracing Juana and Hannah, the baby naturally woke up, and her excitement at seeing Maude added to the clamor of voices in front of the house. Juana lost little time in handing the baby off to Maude, then ran into the house and upstairs to check on Hector.

Jonas's mother was there, too, assisted downstairs by the housekeeper, and her lined face was the happiest he'd ever seen it.

"'Tis proud of you and thankful I am, my son," Coira said, her brogue as thick as if she'd never left Scotland. "So you made the caitiff pay for scaring us all to death?"

He saw Maude go still, and knew Renz's fate had been very much on her mind, too.

He shook his head. "I left him in the ferryman's hut, Mother, safe and sound, little as he deserved it. Oh, I was mightily tempted to put a bullet or two through his worthless hide, but someone had already convinced me that was the Lord's job."

He felt Maude's arms go around him then. "*Thank you*, Jonas," she said fervently.

"God be praised," breathed Coira. "I'm thankful for your soul's sake you had sense enough to listen to the lass. Thank you, Maude."

"Yes, thank you, Maude," he said, smiling down at the woman he still held tight in his embrace. "Mother, I made my peace with the Lord, and He helped us, thanks to Maude."

"'Twas a good day when you set foot in our house, Maude Harkey," Coira said, cupping Maude's cheek with a gnarled hand and kissing her forehead before turning back to her son. "Jonas, the sheriff arrived a bit ago, and let me know he'd already sent telegraph messages to all the nearby towns to hold Renz if he shows his face there."

"I hope they catch him soon," Jonas said. "*I* promised not to make him pay, but if the law takes him without my help, that's a whole different story." He chuckled grimly.

"Indeed it is," Coira agreed. "Son, I hope you're smart enough not to let *this* one get away," she said, nodding at Maude.

"Of course I won't let her get away, if she'll have me," he said with a grin at Maude that warmed her as if she'd suddenly been transported to noontime in July. "But we're all so tired, I think for now I'll send her and Juana and the bairn to bed, speak to the sheriff, then get some sleep."

By mutual agreement Thanksgiving dinner was postponed until Friday since neither Senora Morales nor anyone else had had time in the uproar to prepare it. But Thanksgiving would be celebrated all the same, even if it was delayed. After all, they had so very much to be thankful for.

Sheriff Bishop left at noon the next day after hearing Jonas's account of the events of the day before.

"I'll send my deputy out to talk to the ferryman to see if he knows which way the sidewinder went, but I doubt we'll see Felix Renz in these parts anymore," he said. "He'll know better than to show his face in Simpson Creek after what he's done. If he's at all smart, he'll head to Mexico. I'll charge him with kidnapping and assault if I ever see him again, since *I* didn't make any deals with him. He was fortunate that it was you and not me out there by the river last night."

"We appreciate your coming out, Sheriff," Jonas,

standing next to Maude, said at the door. "Our apologies to your good wife for keeping you from your Thanksgiving dinner."

"Prissy would be the first to tell you that she understands that my duty comes first," Bishop said. A smile lit his solemn face as he spoke of her. "A lawman couldn't ask for a better wife."

No sooner had he departed than Dr. Walker arrived, and Maude took him upstairs to see Hector. He pronounced himself very satisfied with the foreman's condition, for Hector had no fever or any other signs of infection because of Maude's and Juana's excellent care, and because the bullet hadn't remained inside him, but had exited out his back. The doctor left another bottle of laudanum in case the foreman needed it, but Hector was already declining to take it—clearly because he'd much rather savor the presence of Juana, who rarely left his bedside except to see to Hannah's feeding.

Dr. Walker also checked on Coira while he was there, and professed to be amazed at how well she was healing, despite the scattered bruises that had turned a garish purple overnight.

"It'd take more than a runt like Felix Renz to keep me down," Coira boasted. "Thanks to the willow bark tea and the dear girl who brews it for me," she added, nodding at Maude.

Hannah herself seemed almost totally unaffected by her wild ride across the countryside, other than being reluctant to let either Juana or Maude out of her sight.

Though he had ranch duties to catch up on, Jonas

seemed to crave Maude's presence as well, and spent as much time with her as he could. He didn't mention again what he'd said before to his mother, in front of her— *Of course I won't let her get away, if she'll have me.*

Had that been a proposal, or not? Maude wondered. *Had she been expected to reply to it, there and then? Did he think her amazed silence was a refusal?* Maude didn't know, but she sensed it was better to wait and see if he mentioned it again.

The household spent Thursday quietly as they recovered from the day before, but Friday morning Maude and Juana joined Senora Morales in the kitchen to help with the final Thanksgiving dinner preparations.

Senora Morales already had things well in hand, of course; the turkey was roasting in the oven and the delicious smell of the roasting poultry and the cranberry bread she'd baked filled the room. She set both women to peeling potatoes.

"What are you wearing tonight?" Juana asked Maude. "I imagine you'll dress up for dinner, since it is Thanksgiving, no?"

"I hadn't thought about it…" Maude was surprised at the question. Her Tejana friend didn't usually concern herself overmuch with clothing, since she still wore mourning, though she always looked nice. "I don't know…do you have any suggestions?" There seemed to be a suppressed excitement about Juana today, as if she knew something Maude didn't.

"What about the dark blue dress with the gold trim and velvet collar and cuffs?"

Maude stared at her friend. "You don't think it's too formal?" She had only brought the dress with her since she'd had to take all her belongings from the boardinghouse.

Juana shook her head. "Not at all—it's Thanksgiving. I think we should be festive—especially after what we've been through. But I will not be sitting with you and the MacLarens—Hector is allowed to eat a little solid food, starting today, and I think I will keep him company."

"He'll think you look beautiful." Maude said, realizing things must be getting serious between her friend and the ranch foreman. She hoped they'd both have time for all this primping once they were done with preparations for the feast.

When it came time to sit down to their belated Thanksgiving dinner, Maude was glad her friend had urged her to dress up. When Maude entered the dining room, she saw that Coira wore a skirt of MacLaren plaid with a white blouse and a matching plaid sash across her chest that fastened with an elaborate gold pin at her hip.

Her eyes didn't linger long on the elderly Scottish woman, though. Who could look at anyone else with Jonas MacLaren in the room? He'd also donned formal Highland dress for the occasion—a knee-length kilt of the MacLaren tartan topped by a short black velvet jacket and a snowy white shirt with a fall of lace at the neckline, as well as a fur pouch, that Maude had learned was called a sporran, that dangled in front of the kilt by silver chains. He wore knee-length stockings and black silver-buckled shoes. When he rose and bowed to her, she could see that a sash of MacLaren plaid draped down his back from a jeweled pin at his left shoulder. He looked even more splendid than he had that time she had daydreamed of him waltzing with her at the mayor's mansion.

"Maude, you look lovely," he murmured, coming and kissing her hand as if they stood in a grand ballroom and not the dining room of a Texas ranch with his mother looking on.

"And you, Jonas, are a s-sight to behold," Maude stammered, when she could finally find her voice.

He smiled. "I hoped you might find full Highland dress acceptable at an American feast," he said. "The occasion seemed to call for something besides my denim trousers and dusty boots."

Acceptable? There wasn't a woman alive who wouldn't find the sight of him magnificent, she thought in a daze. "You might start an entirely new fashion among the men of Simpson Creek," she said, amused at the idea.

He chuckled. "I think not. Well, you've waited long enough for your Thanksgiving meal, and Senora Morales promises the bird is done to a turn. Come and sit down, sweetheart."

Sweetheart. Maude felt like a princess, floating in a dream as he seated her between himself and Coira. Jonas volunteered an eloquent blessing over the food, a fact that showed Maude just how far he had come on his spiritual journey. Hadn't it been mere days ago when he'd scorned the idea of God caring about His people?

The meal was delicious, for the cook had been wise enough to forego her usual selection of fiery Mexican peppers and herbs, and cook the turkey and trimmings the traditional American way. Maude rediscovered her appetite and did her best to do justice to the feast. When the pumpkin pie was served, though, she found she had no more room and declined it until later.

Jonas stood. "I think it's time to propose a toast."

Maude goggled as Jonas went down on one knee beside her.

"Miss Maude, you have shown yourself an exemplary and devout lady, who has reminded me that the Lord never stops loving us. You have helped me relearn the value of mercy and of a relationship with our Heavenly Father. I cannot imagine my world without you in it. I love you. I love your daughter, too. And I want to be a father to little Hannah. Would you do me the extreme honor, unworthy as I am, of becoming my wife?"

Maude felt the tears of joy coming then, and she nodded, murmuring, "Yes, Jonas, with all my heart. Nothing would make me happier."

He reached into his pocket and brought out a ring, which he held out to her.

"'Tis the MacLaren betrothal ring," he said, and held the sapphire up to the light so that the deep blue stone took fire from the candles and shone.

"It's *beautiful*," she breathed, and he placed it on her finger. It fit as if it had been made for her by a master jeweler.

"Welcome to the family," Coira said. "I'm so pleased you'll be a MacLaren. Thank you for making my Jonas happy again. I never thought I'd live to see the day. We have much to be thankful for, here at Five Mile Hill Ranch."

"I couldn't agree more," Maude said, her gaze locking on Jonas's equally joyous one.

"'Maude MacLaren' has a nice ring to it, doesn't it?" he said. "I'm hoping you'll be willing to take my name before too long. I'm not a patient man, you know."

Maude felt as if she was cascading down a rushing waterfall. "Yes, we'll have to discuss setting a date," she said. She thought about walking down the aisle to meet him at the altar at the Simpson Creek Church.

"Don't let him rush you, dearie," Coira said. "Take all the time you need to plan a proper wedding. Good things come to those who wait, as they say."

They made an early evening of it, all of them still tired from their recent ordeal. Jonas escorted her to her room, kissing her tenderly at the door and promising to see her on the morrow.

"Ah, *querida*, you are glowing," Juana said as Maude entered the room. "Was it a good dinner?"

In answer, Maude held out her hand, letting the lamplight reveal her ring-clad finger.

"*Querida!* You are engaged?" Juana exclaimed. "He asked you to marry him? When will it be?"

"We haven't set a date as yet. We'll discuss that tomorrow, perhaps."

Juana chuckled. "But this is wonderful! I have news as well, *mi amiga*. Hector asked me to marry him tonight, too. We will not wed for a while, out of respect for my Tomás, and so that we may get to know each other better first."

Maude seized the other girl in a fierce hug of delight. "I'm so happy for you! Oh, Juana, hasn't God been good to us?"

Juana nodded. "He has certainly given me a good, kind man. Hector understands that Mrs. MacLaren will still need my help, even if I am Hector's wife, and Hannah will still need me close for a while, so I must remain in the house, though it would be nice to have a cottage of our own. We are trusting that the Lord will show us a way."

"Perhaps the MacLarens would let the two of you have a room in the house, for the time being," Maude said. "Would you like me to speak to Jonas about it?"

Juana nodded. "But there is no hurry, Maude. Enjoy your happiness. Set your wedding date. *Mi amiga*, you will make the most beautiful bride!"

"As will you, dear friend. I never thought my day would come, after so many of my fellow Spinsters' Club friends have made their matches," Maude murmured. "But there was a purpose in the waiting, wasn't there? The Lord had picked the right man out for me—I just had to wait until the time was right for us to meet… Oh, my goodness, I will have to speak to Milly Brookfield about making me a wedding dress!" she exclaimed, picturing several trips for fittings to the ranch east of them. There was no more skilled dressmaker than Milly in all of Texas. And Maude needed to be a beautiful bride for the man she loved with all her heart.

* * *

The next morning Maude and Jonas had just found a few minutes to steal away to the parlor together to discuss wedding plans over coffee when Senora Morales came into the room to say that Jonas had a caller.

"Who can that be?" Jonas growled, clearly frustrated at the interruption.

"He says his name is Horace Wallace, and he's the postmaster in Simpson Creek."

"Horace Wallace is here?" Maude asked, picturing her friend Caroline Wallace Collier's kindly old father, who'd run the town's post office as long as anyone could remember.

"Show him in," Jonas said, his brow furrowed. Clearly, he didn't think this could be good news.

Maude rose when the old postmaster was shown into the parlor. "Mr. Wallace, good morning. I hope you had a pleasant Thanksgiving."

"Hello, Miss Maude. Yes, we did. Sheriff Bishop tells me there was a bit of a ruckus out here, but that everything's all right now."

"Yes, that's true," Jonas answered for her, with a touch of his old high-handedness. Maude could tell Jonas wanted Wallace to get to the point. "What brings you out this way, sir?"

"Got a letter for you and your mother, Mr. MacLaren," Wallace said. "I would've given it to you when y'all were in town the day before Thanksgiving, but it came just yesterday. I know you don't make it to town often, and I thought it might be important, so I thought it best to bring it out."

"How kind of you," Maude told him, touched that the postmaster would go to such trouble.

"Not at all," Wallace responded affably. "Can't remember ever getting a letter from Scotland."

Chapter Nineteen

"The Brookfields and Mrs. Masterson get the occasional letter from their family in England, of course," Wallace went on, "but we never got any letters from Scotland."

Maude turned to look at Jonas. His face had gone white as chalk. She ached for the sudden hunted look in those golden-hazel eyes.

"Scotland, ye say?" His voice was strained, as if there was an invisible rope tightening around his neck.

"Sure enough," Wallace said, bringing a folded piece of paper out of his breast pocket and holding it out to him.

Even from where she stood, a few feet away from her beloved, she could see the foreign stamps on it.

"What's all the noise and commotion?" a woman's querulous voice demanded, and Maude whirled around to see Coira, with Juana at her side, coming into the room. "I've never had so many folks traipsing in and out of our house in so few days. A body can't get a moment's peace."

"Sorry to disturb you, Mrs. MacLaren, but—" Mr. Wallace began, then hesitated as Jonas crossed the room to his mother in a few quick strides.

"Mr. Wallace," Jonas said, "I'd like to introduce you to my mother, Coira MacLaren. Mother, this is the postmaster, Mr. Wallace. He..." He took a deep breath, then showed her the letter. "He's brought a letter from Scotland."

He slid an arm around his mother—in case she fainted at the news, Maude guessed. *Dear heavens, what was in that letter? If only the postmaster would go, so they could open it and find out. But did they really want to know?*

Coira gasped and her eyes went wide at the information, but conscious of their audience, she did an admirable job of maintaining her composure. "You don't say," she murmured. "Well, that is certainly an unexpected happening, to be sure. Thank you, Mr. Wallace, for troubling to bring it to us."

The postmaster grinned as if oblivious to the sudden tension in the little parlor. "Pleased to meet you, ma'am, I surely am, but I'd best not linger," he announced. "It's a long way back to Simpson Creek."

"But ye must not go all that way back without so much as a bit of nourishment by way of thanks," Coira told him. Maude could only guess how much the effort cost her to be so convincingly gracious. "Senora Morales has some fresh-baked muffins in the kitchen, and I'm sure there's a pot of coffee on the stove to wash them down," she said, and Maude saw her catch the housekeeper's eye.

"Come with me, Senor Wallace," the housekeeper said, and shepherded him out of the parlor.

There was silence as Coira sank weakly into a chair, and Maude sent a quick prayer upward that whatever was in this letter would not be too shocking for an old woman, burdened with guilt, to bear. She wondered if there were any smelling salts in the house in case Coira collapsed, but thought it better not to announce her fear by asking.

Instead, she poured a glass of water from the pitcher on the nearby side table and took it to Jonas's mother.

"What...do ye suppose it means, Jonas?" Coira asked her son in a quavering voice. All at once she was just a shadow of the imperious matriarch she had been. She seemed to have shrunk several inches in the past few minutes and looked at least a decade older.

"I'm sure there's no telling unless we open the letter," Jonas said reasonably enough as he handed her the letter, but he knelt by the chair, keeping an arm protectively around his mother's trembling shoulders.

"'Tis James's handwriting...I'd know it anywhere, even after all these years." Her hand shook as she stared at the letter she held, as if it was a sleeping rattlesnake.

"That's impossible," Jonas said in a flat, cold voice. "The man's been dead for years. Here, let me see that," he said, taking back the letter carefully.

Maude went to them then, and laid a gentle hand on his shoulder in a gesture of support. She was rewarded with a quick look, immense gratitude lighting those golden, compelling eyes of his.

Jonas picked up a letter opener that happened to be sitting on the end table beside them and slit open the envelope, then handed it back to his mother.

Still shaking, she unfolded the letter and squinted at it. At last, she gave it back to her son.

"Please read it aloud, Jonas. I find these old eyes can't make out his script anymore." Or perhaps she couldn't read because her hands shook the paper too much.

"Mother, I told you, it can't be—" Jonas began, then stared at the letter. "Dear Coira and Jonas," he read…

> "Yes, I am alive. I know you will be astonished to be reading this letter, much as I am to finally be writing it. It has taken me many years, not only to recover physically to the point where I could write it, and to come to the point where I felt able to adequately portray what is in my heart, but also to locate you. It has taken much investigative work by my skilled agent to find where you had fled to after leaving Scotland.
>
> "Before you read any farther, I want to allay your fears by telling you I have forgiven you for what you did. In your place, I would doubtless have done similarly, and probably would have reached my breaking point many years sooner, my poor long-suffering wife and son. There are not words adequate to express my sorrow about how I have treated you. Only now that I have seen the light do I realize how evil I was to both of you, and how justified you were in hating me."

At this point, Coira whimpered and began to weep—quietly, but the tears poured down her pale old cheeks. Maude handed her a handkerchief from her pocket, and when she had wiped her eyes, Jonas began to read again.

> "I do not know why I survived the beating, but I know it was God's mercy to me, a sinner, so that I could learn of His love for me. And once I had fully taken that in—if 'tis even possible for us to comprehend the magnitude of it this side of Heaven—I knew I had to forgive you for what you had done in the extremity of your suffering. And I *do* forgive you—freely and wholeheartedly, and with the hope that you will one day be able to forgive *me*. I know that for me, it seemed like I had dropped a hundred-pound weight off my shoulders when I let myself forgive you, my dear wife and child. I would not have you carry such a weight of guilt."

Maude closed her eyes for a moment. Hadn't she already thought of the guilt they carried as a burden?

Jonas glanced up at her, but she motioned for him to read on.

> "Coira will remember, I am sure, that I am a few years her senior. I am writing this letter now, not knowing how many more years I will be given in this life, for my heart is no longer strong. I wish more than anything to see both of you again and tell you how sorry I am for having been such a cruel tyrant, rather than a loving husband and father. To receive your forgiveness would be a balm to my soul. I know that I do not

deserve it, but I hope to receive grace at your hands, as I have from the Lord. It is a great deal I am asking, to be sure."

At this point, Jonas's voice grew hoarse and thick, and Maude looked over and saw that he was struggling to hold back tears.

"Let it go, Jonas dear," she whispered. "It's all right to weep." He'd been holding these tears back for many years.

After a minute or so he cleared his throat and said, "There's just a little left to be read," and took up the letter again.

"Accordingly, I am setting sail just a week after posting this letter, and hope that it will reach you in advance of my coming. The steamer *Victoriana* is scheduled to depart from Southampton, England, on November 20 and reach Galveston on or about December 11 if all goes well.

"If God wills it, I will survive the voyage and plan to take a room in a hotel there and await your coming. If you prefer that we do not meet and choose not to come, I will understand. But how I pray you will find it in your hearts to forgive me and that we can have a joyous Christmastime reunion, and spend the remaining years of our lives together at your Hill Country Ranch—if you are agreeable. If you choose to forgive me, but prefer that we go on living separately, I will be at peace with that, too, and will return to breathe my last in our native Scotland.

"But I am hoping for that joyous reunion to become permanent. I would cherish the chance to see the ranch that my son has bought, and to learn what has happened to you both during the years I lost with you.

"God has promised to 'restore the years that the locust has eaten,' and I cling to that promise.

"Writing in hope and with great love,
James MacLaren"

By the time Jonas had finished reading the letter, Maude was wishing she had a second handkerchief in her pocket, but in the stunned silence that followed, she forced herself to stop crying and see how the recipients of the letter were reacting.

When she looked up, mother and son were staring at each other, thunderstruck.

Coira was first to find her voice. "But how…how could he have been alive when we left him? I was sure he wasn't breathing…"

Jonas shrugged. "I checked for a pulse, and was sure there wasn't one, but my fingers were shaking so badly I could have missed it. 'Tis amazing, that's for certain."

"Aye…" Coira said, her lower lip trembling. "Jonas, what if it's a trick? What if the constables are the ones who've been investigating, and wrote that letter, and when we appear, they'll clap us in irons and take us back to Britain to hang?"

"Why would they need subterfuge? Why wouldn't they just appear at the ranch? Anyway, you said it was his handwriting," Jonas said. "Weren't you sure, after all?"

She stared at it again. "Aye, it's James's handwriting," she said. "No one forms a *J* the way he does, or writes with as bold and slashing a style. I should know, for I tried to forge his hand once," she said, a trace of returning humor to her voice.

"What will you do?" Maude asked at last, when neither of them seemed able to say anything more. Would they choose to go on living as if James MacLaren were indeed dead? Or had the Lord come into their lives just in time for them to realize what grace really meant?

She saw Jonas look at his mother and realized that he was waiting for her to speak. She'd been James MacLaren's wife, after all—still was, come to think of it. But it seemed she wanted him to speak first—he was the MacLaren, after all—at least for the time being. He must cede that title back to his father now, Maude realized.

"I believe I am quoting Holy Writ when I say, this is the Lord's doing, and it is marvelous in our eyes," he said, his lips beginning to curve upward at last. Coira was beginning to smile, too.

"Then you'll go to Galveston and meet with your father?" Maude asked, hoping she had understood him correctly.

"*We* will go," Jonas corrected her. "You, me, Mother, Juana and wee Hannah, for aren't you about to be family, sweet Maude, you and Hannah? And if all proceeds well, and you wouldn't mind delaying the wedding till afterward, he could be present for it."

"Oh, Jonas…" His mother sighed and had gone quite misty-eyed.

Maude was feeling pretty warm and misty-eyed herself at the thought that Jonas wanted her to be present on such a momentous occasion as this proposed reunion. But she managed to rally and make a daring request.

"I won't mind waiting," Maude said, "but there's a condition—I want you to wear Highland dress at our wedding." Perhaps, she thought, if James MacLaren was the sort of man his letter made him seem, she might even ask him to give her away, since she had no father to do the honors. But perhaps she should wait and see how things went when the MacLarens reunited.

At that, Jonas roared with laughter. "So my sweet Texas bride is already making conditions about marrying me? Liked the look of your groom-to-be in a kilt, did you now?"

"'Twill be the wedding of the decade," Maude said sweetly, thinking of the sensation it would cause in Simpson Creek, especially among her fellow Spinsters' Club members. All the Spinsters who had married thus far had wed handsome men, but no one else's groom had been so spectacularly attired as Jonas would be, if he went along with her idea.

"Done, sweetheart, if you'll wear a MacLaren tartan sash across your dress."

"It seems only fair," Maude said, and raised her lips for a kiss.

Chapter Twenty

Galveston, Texas

James MacLaren was the last person to disembark from the *Victoriana*, and Maude sensed that Jonas and Coira had already begun to despair that he hadn't come after all, or perhaps had died on the voyage. But Maude kept watching and was rewarded by the sight of the elderly man making his way down the gangplank, leaning only a little on a silver-knobbed cane. He wore full Highland dress, right down to a jaunty hat in the MacLaren tartan over a still-thick thatch of silver hair. An ocean breeze threatened to carry it away, but the gnarled hand that reached out to clutch it to his head was quick.

"There he is, Mother. That's him, isn't it?" Jonas asked, gripping Maude's shoulder tighter now.

"Aye, and he's still wearing that Glengarry hat of his," Maude heard Coira say, her voice tremulous. "He had that same hat when we married."

He had the same eagle-eyed gaze as his son, and he used it now to sweep over the crowd gathered to welcome those who had sailed on the *Victoriana*.

"He looks like you, Senor MacLaren," Juana observed.

Maude held Hannah, who was staring enthralled at the huge steamer, pointing at it and uttering little baby cries of excitement, totally unaware of the drama about to unfold.

Jonas had not worn full Highland dress, but today he'd worn a sash of MacLaren plaid, as had his mother, and Maude saw the moment when James MacLaren caught sight of them and the gleam of joyous recognition in those golden hazel eyes. Having reached the end of the gangplank, he hastened toward them, and Maude had time enough to send a quick prayer Heavenward that all would go well.

"Coira, Jonas, is that you?" the old man asked, his Scottish brogue thick with emotion and held-back tears.

"Yes, Father, it's us," Jonas replied as Coira gave a little cry and threw open her arms as if the past years had never intervened.

Feeling close to tears herself, Maude watched as the old man embraced and kissed first his wife, then, after eyeing him up and down, his son, murmuring, "You've come, both of ye—I had not dared hope so much." Then, throwing one arm each around wife and son, he pulled both of them close again and let his tears flow.

It was several minutes before any of them could bring themselves to let go.

Maude could see the scar that began under James's hair on his right temple and creased his cheek, and a smaller, fainter one that streaked down his other temple, but otherwise there was no evidence of the terrible event that had happened so many years—certainly not in the love that gleamed from each of their eyes.

"And who's this, then?" James MacLaren asked, when he had caught his breath, nodding toward Maude. "The bonny lass with the red hair, and the wee bairn in her arms? Is the child yours, then? Is this your wife? And how about this other lady?" he said, indicating Juana.

"She's about to be my wife," Jonas said, pulling Maude close. "Father, I'd like you to meet my betrothed, Maude Harkey, the sweetest lass in Texas, and her adopted daughter, Hannah, who already seems like a daughter to me. Beyond her is Senora Juana Benavides, who takes care of Hannah."

"Your Maude looks like a feisty lass, with that red hair," the elder MacLaren said with a laugh, and grinned at Maude so engagingly that she couldn't help but grin back.

"Aye, that she is, but she's also a woman of faith, and the reason we're here today," Jonas told him, smiling proudly. "'Tis Maude who's been taking care of Mother and who got us to see our need of the Lord."

"Well, then, God bless ye, Maude," James MacLaren said, cupping Maude's cheek with a gnarled hand. "And your little lass, too." He chuckled as Hannah made a grab for his hat, and reached up and plopped it on her head, laughing more as the child giggled, not at all afraid of this interesting stranger.

The sea wind picked up then, blowing coldly through the crowd.

"Son, yer mother and I are no' so young as we used to be, and it's December, after all. Could we find a place that serves hot coffee and soup to warm our bones, and we'll begin to catch up on the years?"

"Our hotel isn't far, Father, and there's a restaurant next to it. I'll help you to our carriage, then see to having your baggage delivered to the hotel."

Within the hour, they were sipping hot broth and tea at a table in Chez Campeche, a restaurant whose name bore tribute to the headquarters of the infamous pirate Lafitte, who had once made Galveston his base of operations. James declined the waiter's offer of a glass of whiskey, saying later to his son, "'Tis a teetotaler I am now, son, and have been since that awful night back in Scotland," he murmured. "I find I'm a better man without the influence of spirits. I wish I'd gained that wisdom before the drink tore us apart." It was the only reference he ever made to that terrible time, but determined to lighten the moment, he added, "'Tis not as if America would have a good whiskey, anyway."

Jonas laughed. Then James changed the subject.

"Ye say ye two are about to marry?"

"Aye, Papa. We might have done so already, but once we heard of yer coming, we wanted to wait so ye could be there." Exposure to his father's thick brogue had strengthened Jonas's Scots accent, too.

"Did ye now? And isn't that a wonderful thing for an old reprobate like me to hear? 'Twas generous of ye two," he said, and impulsively reached for Maude's hand and kissed it.

She smiled shyly at him, knowing she would indeed ask him to walk her down the aisle when they had a private moment.

"So ye're a prominent rancher, son? 'Twas what my agent told me, the one who located ye," James asked his son.

Jonas grinned modestly. "Aye, well, I'm a relative newcomer to the area, having bought Five Mile Hill Ranch just earlier this year, but I'm the only one around there raising sheep as well as long-horned cattle. Fine Blackies and merino sheep they are, as good as any in the Highlands."

"That's wonderful, son. And how about ye, wife? Will the town be scandalized to find ye're a married woman after all this time?"

Coira chuckled. "We live at some distance from Simpson Creek, so the town and I have not exactly gotten familiar with one another. But I imagine it'll be a nine days' wonder. Small towns soon find something else to talk about."

Juana took her leave with Hannah at this point, for the baby had gotten fussy, needing her nap.

"Ye say Hannah is yer adopted daughter, Miss Harkey?" James inquired, obviously puzzled as to Juana's role.

Maude took this opportunity to explain how she had come to adopt Hannah, and how Juana had just lost her baby, which enabled her to feed Hannah. James listened to it all, his head cocked like a bird's as he took in the details.

"Well, isn't all this a wonder," he said with a sweeping gesture that included all of them and all that had happened, "the way God works to knit us all together again after we're foolish enough to tear everything apart?"

To which Jonas, his mother and Maude could only say in unison a hearty "Amen."

* * * * *

Dear Reader,

Thanks for buying this latest installment in my Brides of Simpson Creek series. I hope you have enjoyed it.

I once had a great-aunt named Maude, for whom my heroine is named. Maude in my story and Maude, my great-aunt, are nothing alike except for their red hair—which my aunt kept till the day she died, thanks to Lady Clairol—and their peppery spirit. One of my treasured memories is of my great-aunt teaching me how to fish for perch and bluegill on the Concho River in Texas, where it ran past the tiny town of Christoval. I lost my elderly Aunt Maude too soon in my life, but I hope this story does justice to the spirited lady she must have been when she was young.

Those who have read others of my Brides of Simpson Creek stories know that I like to mix characters from the British Isles with my Texans, as I have done here with my Scottish hero, Jonas MacLaren. I really have eaten haggis in Scotland, though it wasn't properly "piped to the table" in my experience, either. It's something everyone should try—once, at least! ☺

Blessings,
Laurie Kingery

P.S. You can reach me via my website at www.LaurieKingery.com, or via Facebook, or Twitter (@LaurieKingery).

Benjamin Hewitt stared. It wasn't possible.

The man struggling with his oxen couldn't be Mr. Bingham. He would never subject himself and his wife to the trials of this journey. Why, Mrs. Bingham would look mighty strange fluttering a lace hankie and expecting someone to serve her tea.

The man must have given the wrong command because the oxen jerked hard to the right. The rear wheel broke free. A flurry of smaller items fell out the back. A woman followed, shrieking.

"Mother, are you injured?" A young woman ran toward her mother. She sounded just like Abigail. At least as near as he could recall. He'd succeeded in putting that young woman from his mind many years ago.

She glanced about. "Father, are you safe?"

The sun glowed in her blond hair and he knew without seeing her face that it was Abigail. What was she doing here? She'd not find a fine, big house nor fancy dishes and certainly no servants on this trip.

The bitterness he'd once felt at being rejected because he couldn't provide those things had dissipated, leaving only regret and caution.

She helped her mother to her feet and dusted her skirts off. All the while, the woman—Mrs. Bingham, to be sure—complained, her voice grating with displeasure that made Ben's nerves twitch. He knew all too well that sound. Could recall in sharp detail when the woman had told him he was not a suitable suitor for her daughter. Abigail had agreed, had told him, in a harsh dismissive tone, she would no longer see him.

It all seemed so long ago. Six years to be exact. He'd been a different person back then. Thanks to Abigail, he'd learned not to trust everything a woman said. Nor believe how they acted.

But Binghams or not, a wheel needed to be put on. Ben joined the men hurrying to assist the family.

"Hello." He greeted Mr. Bingham and the man shook his hand. "Ladies." He tipped his hat to them.

"Hello, Ben." Abigail Bingham stood at her mother's side. No, not Bingham. She was Abigail Black now.

Hannah edged closer to her. "I don't like storms."

Mary slipped an arm around her daughter. "Don't worry. We'll be at Katie's house before the rain catches us."

It turned out she was wrong. Big raindrops began hitting her windshield. A strong gust of wind shook the buggy and blew dust across the road. The sky grew darker by the minute. She urged Tilly to a faster pace. She should have stayed home.

A red car flew past her with the driver laying on the horn. Tilly shied and nearly dragged the buggy into the fence along the side of the road. Mary managed to right her. "Foolish *Englischers*. We are over as far as we can get."

The rumble of thunder became a steady roar behind them. Tilly broke into a run. Hannah began screaming. Mary glanced back and her heart stopped. A tornado had dropped from the clouds and was bearing down on them. Dust and debris flew out from the wide base.

LIEXP0315

Dear God, help me save my baby. What do I do?

She saw an intersection up ahead.

Bracing her legs against the dash, she pulled back on the lines, trying to slow Tilly enough to make the corner without overturning. The mare seemed to sense the plan. She slowed and made the turn with the buggy tilting on two wheels. Mary grabbed Hannah and held on to her. Swerving wildly behind the horse, the buggy finally came back onto all four wheels. Before the mare could gather speed again, a man jumped into the road waving his arms. He grabbed Tilly's bridle and pulled her to a stop.

Shouting, he pointed toward an abandoned farmhouse. "There's a cellar on the south side."

Mary jumped out of the buggy and pulled Hannah into her arms. The man was already unhitching Tilly, so Mary ran toward the ramshackle structure. The wind threatened to pull her off her feet. The trees and even the grass were straining toward the approaching tornado. She reached the old cellar door, but couldn't lift it against the force of the wind. She was about to lie on the ground on top of Hannah when the man appeared at her side. Together, they were able to lift the door.

A second later, she was pushed down the steps into darkness.

LIEXP0315